From Tam Lin's haunted woods
to the Britain of Merlin the Arch-Mage
to the world at the Dawn of Time . . .

STEP THROUGH THE GATES OF FAERY
INTO
IMAGINARY
LANDS

IMAGINARY LANDS

conceived and edited by
ROBIN McKINLEY

Greenwillow Books, New York

Introduction copyright © 1986 by Robin McKinley
"Paper Dragons" copyright © 1985 by James P. Blaylock
"The Old Woman and the Storm" copyright © 1985 by Patricia A. McKillip
"The Big Rock Candy Mountain" copyright © 1985 by Robert Westall
"Flight" copyright © 1985 by Peter Dickinson
"Evian Steel" copyright © 1985 by Jane Yolen
"Stranger Blood" copyright © 1985 by P. C. Hodgell
"The Curse of Igamor" copyright © 1985 by Michael de Larrabeiti
"Tam Lin" copyright © 1985 by Joan D. Vinge
"The Stone Fey" copyright © 1985 by Robin McKinley

Printed in the United States of America   10 9 8 7 6 5 4 3 2 1

Library of Congress Cataloging-in-Publication Data
Main entry under title: Imaginary lands.
Contents: Paper dragons / James P. Blaylock—
The old woman and the storm / Patricia A. McKillip—
The big rock candy mountain / Robert Westall— [etc.]
1. Fantastic fiction, English.   2. Fantastic fiction, American.
[1. Fantasy.   2. Short stories]   I. McKinley, Robin.
PZ5.I322   1985   [Fic]   85-21867
ISBN 0-688-05213-4

CONTENTS

INTRODUCTION

The idea for *Imaginary Lands* is several years old. I was visiting New York City, long before I had any notion to try living there—at the time I was (I thought) contentedly established in the Boston area, and was in New York only to go to the museums and spend too much money in the old-book stores. I'd been dizzied and delighted, and rather overcome by the noise and the crowds, and was now on my way home again—weighed down with my usual inordinate amount of luggage. It doesn't matter if I'm only to be gone four days, as in this case; I take six months' supply of reading material everywhere. Anyone who needs further explication of this eccentricity can find it usefully set out in the first pages of W. Somerset Maugham's story "The Book-Bag."

So I had just dragged and heaved and bumbled my way onto the Staten Island ferry. Of course after four days in the city my suitcase was even heavier, although at least the Strand Book Store will ship your purchases home to you. I was hanging over the side of the boat and panting, and watching Manhattan grow larger; Terri Windling was leaning on the rail—with somewhat less than my enthusiasm for the view, since she made this journey twice a day—beside me. Terri was on her way to her office; she was an editor at Ace Books. I had been staying at her book-crowded apartment, adapting very well to Mark Arnold's cooking and less well to being gamboled on in the small hours of the morning by two Siamese cats. "How would you like to do an anthology for us?" she asked tentatively.

I swung round from my contemplation of the urban skyline, and said, "I'd *love* to."

"Oh," she said, a trifle startled at my eagerness. "You would?"

It took only the rest of the ferry ride to settle on an idea for *Imaginary Lands*: that the stories, while all would be fantasy, must have a particularly strong sense of location, of the imaginary land each was laid in. It seemed a likely sort of starting point for me as editor, because landscape is very important to me, both at my typewriter and outdoors wandering around staring at things.

This did not in effect turn out quite as I expected. My first story came from Peter Dickinson, who sent me a piece of the extraordinary history of the land he was writing a novel about. It had been heavily advertised in several previous letters from its author as not anything that I would want, till I began to fear that he would convince himself, and decline to send it to me: whereupon I sent him a note full of capital letters and exclamation points. The day it finally arrived there was actually something on TV that I wanted to watch. But I read through the evening, fascinated, on one end of the sofa while my housemates watched TV on the other end, because no mere flickering cathode-ray tube could compete with the Obi and the story of "Flight."

The imaginary land in Jim Blaylock's "Paper Dragons" might look very much like some of the California coastline if you didn't know any better; as, until you arrived there, you might think Jane Yolen's story took place on a real island in a real river in southwest England. (This is a terrible thing for a stern and righteous editor to say, but "Evian Steel" is, to me, only incidentally laid anywhere at all; its importance is in the new light it casts on the tragedy of Camelot.) Anyone who has read P. C. Hodgell's "Godstalk" will be glad of another story of that land and its haunted shadows; Pat McKillip raises her imaginary land around the reader with no more specificity than her delicate use of words like mountain and storm, stone and river. And yet you recognize the landscape as something you've always known, deep in mind and bone, although McKillip is the first person to have been clever enough to write it down in a story. Joan Vinge's story illuminates the old folk tale of Tam Lin, and an enchanted bit of Scotland appears to you by the mere whisper of the hero's name; although I suspect that the roses of old Scotland are a magical land all of themselves. Michael de Larrabeiti's story is another sort of folk tale, laid in a walled city closely surrounded by enchantment; and Robert Westall wants us all to believe that his Northwich *exists*. Ha.

So not many of the stories are quite what I thought I was asking for. And yet I know myself the way a story may begin, with the best and firmest intentions, steadily driving down one track—and may then at any moment leap the rails and go shooting off in another direction entirely. You probably don't have much choice in the matter; you either follow it or lose it. I had something of that problem myself; fortunately, after two novels and several short stories there, I am well enough acquainted with Damar that I was in no danger of losing myself beyond its borders; but the ending of "The Stone Fey" is little as I anticipated, except for Aerlich.

But if I was surprised, I was also tremendously pleased at the wide variety of stories the authors in this book sent me, having first said only "Yes, I think so" or "Well, I'd like to try" in answer to my hopeful query letters: Might they like to write a story about an imaginary land for an anthology? My only sorrow (besides the awful light editorship has shed on my usual state of disorganization) about the anthology is that time and space would not allow it to be twice its present length. Some of the authors I wrote to could not meet the deadline for one reason or another; some hadn't a fantasy story in mind that they felt like telling just then. A few of them suggested that if I ever do another anthology I should write to them again. I'm keeping it in mind.

Well, that day I began with an eventful ride on the Staten Island ferry, I trundled off into the Wall Street section of Manhattan (my heavy suitcase on wheels, periodically falling over at curbs), heading uptown; and I burst into the Greenwillow office to say to my editor, Susan Hirschman, "I'm going to do an anthology for Ace! Isn't it wonderful?"

"Yes, probably," she said peaceably. "What is it about? Can Greenwillow do it too?"

Here is the result.

— Robin McKinley

PAPER DRAGONS

by

JAMES P. BLAYLOCK

TRANGE THINGS are said to have happened in this world—some are said to be happening still—but half of them, if I'm any judge, are lies. There's no way to tell sometimes. The sky above the north coast has been flat gray for weeks—clouds thick overhead like carded wool not fifty feet above the ground, impaled on the treetops, on redwoods and alders and hemlocks. The air is heavy with mist that lies out over the harbor and the open ocean, drifting across the tip of the pier and breakwater now and again, both of them vanishing into the gray so that there's not a nickel's worth of difference between the sky and the sea. And when the tide drops, and the reefs running out toward the point appear through the fog, covered in the brown bladders and rubber leaves of kelp, the pink lace of algae, and the slippery sheets of sea lettuce and eel grass, it's a simple thing to imagine the dark bulk of the fish that lie in deepwater gardens and angle up toward the pale green of shallows to feed at dawn.

There's the possibility, of course, that winged things, their counterparts if you will, inhabit dens in the clouds, that in the valleys and caverns of the heavy, low skies live unguessed beasts. It occurs to me sometimes that if without warning a man could draw back that veil of cloud that obscures the heavens, snatch it back in an instant, he'd startle a world of oddities aloft in the skies: balloon things with hovering little wings like the fins of pufferfish, and spiny, leathery creatures, nothing but bones and teeth and with beaks half again as long as their ribby bodies.

There have been nights when I was certain I heard them, when the clouds hung in the treetops and foghorns moaned off the point and water dripped from the needles of hemlocks beyond the window onto the tin roof of Filby's garage. There were muffled shrieks and the airy flapping of distant wings. On one such night when I was out walking along the bluffs, the clouds parted for an instant and a spray of stars like a reeling carnival shone beyond, until, like a curtain slowly drawing shut, the clouds drifted up against each other and parted no more. I'm certain I glimpsed something—a shadow, the promise of a shadow—dimming the stars. It was the next morning that the business with the crabs began.

I awoke, late in the day, to the sound of Filby hammering at something in his garage—talons, I think it was, copper talons. Not that it makes much difference. It woke me up. I don't sleep until an hour or so before dawn. There's a certain bird, Lord knows what sort, that sings through the last hour of the night and shuts right up when the sun rises. Don't ask me why. Anyway, there was Filby smashing away some time before noon. I opened my left eye, and there atop the pillow was a blood-red hermit crab with eyes on stalks, giving me a look as if he were proud of himself, waving pincers like that. I leaped up. There was another, creeping into my shoe, and two more making away with my pocket watch, dragging it along on its fob toward the bedroom door.

The window was open and the screen was torn. The beasts were clambering up onto the woodpile and hoisting themselves in through the open window to rummage through my personal effects while I slept. I pitched them out, but that evening there were more—dozens of them, bent beneath the weight of seashells, dragging toward the house with an eye to my pocket watch.

It was a migration. Once every hundred years, Dr. Jensen tells me, every hermit crab in creation gets the wanderlust and hurries ashore. Jensen camped on the beach in the cove to study the things. They were all heading south like migratory birds. By the end of the week there was a tiresome lot of them afoot—millions of them to hear Jensen carry on—but they left my house alone. They dwindled as the next week wore out, and seemed to be straggling in from deeper water and were bigger and bigger: The size of a man's fist at first, then of his head, and then a giant, vast as a pig, chased Jensen into the lower branches of an oak. On Friday there were only two crabs, both of them bigger than cars. Jensen went home gibbering and drank himself into a stupor. He was there on Saturday, though; you've got to give him credit for that. But nothing appeared. He speculates that somewhere off the coast, in a deepwater chasm a hundred fathoms below the last faded colors, is a monumental beast, blind and gnarled from spectacular pressures and wearing a seashell overcoat, feeling his way toward shore.

At night sometimes I hear the random echoes of far-off clacking, just the misty and muted suggestion of it, and I brace myself and stare into the pages of an open book, firelight glinting off the cut crystal of my glass, countless noises out in the foggy night among which is the occasional clack clack clack of what might be Jensen's impossible crab, creeping up to cast a shadow in the front-porch lamplight, to demand my pocket watch. It was the night after the sighting of the pig-sized crabs that one got into Filby's garage—forced the door apparently—and made a hash out of his dragon. I know what you're thinking. I thought it was a lie too. But things have since fallen out that make me suppose otherwise. He did, apparently, know

Augustus Silver. Filby was an acolyte; Silver was his master. But the dragon business, they tell me, isn't merely a matter of mechanics. It's a matter of perspective. That was Filby's downfall.

There was a gypsy who came round in a cart last year. He couldn't speak, apparently. For a dollar he'd do the most amazing feats. He tore out his tongue, when he first arrived, and tossed it onto the road. Then he danced on it and shoved it back into his mouth, good as new. Then he pulled out his entrails—yards and yards of them like sausage out of a machine—then jammed them all back in and nipped shut the hole he'd torn in his abdomen. It made half the town sick, mind you, but they paid to see it. That's pretty much how I've always felt about dragons. I don't half believe in them, but I'd give a bit to see one fly, even if it were no more than a clever illusion.

But Filby's dragon, the one he was keeping for Silver, was a ruin. The crab—I suppose it was a crab—had shredded it, knocked the wadding out of it. It reminded me of one of those stuffed alligators that turns up in curiosity shops, all eaten to bits by bugs and looking sad and tired, with its tail bent sidewise and a clump of cotton stuffing shoved through a tear in its neck.

Filby was beside himself. It's not good for a grown man to carry on so. He picked up the shredded remnant of a dissected wing and flagellated himself with it. He scourged himself, called himself names. I didn't know him well at the time, and so watched the whole weird scene from my kitchen window: His garage door banging open and shut in the wind, Filby weeping and howling through the open door, storming back and forth, starting and stopping theatrically, the door slamming shut and slicing off the whole embarrassing business for thirty seconds or so and then sweeping open to betray a wailing Filby scrabbling among the debris on the garage floor—the remnants of what had once been a flesh-and-blood dragon, as it were, built by the ubiquitous Augustus Silver years before. Of course I had no idea at the time. Augustus *Silver,* after all. It almost justifies Filby's carrying on. And I've done a bit of carrying on myself since, although as I said, most of what prompted the whole business has begun to seem suspiciously like lies, and the whispers in the foggy night, the clacking and whirring and rush of wings, has begun to sound like thinly disguised laughter, growing fainter by the months and emanating from nowhere, from the clouds, from the wind and fog. Even the occasional letters from Silver himself have become suspect.

Filby is an eccentric. I could see that straightaway. How he finances his endeavors is beyond me. Little odd jobs, I don't doubt—repairs and such. He has the hands of an archetypal mechanic: spatulate fingers, grime under the nails, nicks and cuts and scrapes that he can't identify. He has only to touch a heap of parts, wave his hands over them, and the faint rhythmic stirrings of order and pattern seem to shudder through the crossmembers of his workbench. And here an enormous crab had gotten in, and in a single night had clipped apart a masterpiece, a wonder, a thing that couldn't be tacked back together. Even Silver would have pitched it out. The cat wouldn't want it.

Filby was morose for days, but I knew he'd come out of it. He'd be mooning around the house in a slump, poking at yesterday's newspapers, and a glint of light off a copper wire would catch his eye. The wire would suggest something. That's how it works. He not only has the irritating ability to coexist with mechanical refuse; it speaks to him, too, whispers possibilities.

He'd be hammering away some morning soon—damn all crabs—piecing together the ten thousand silver scales of a wing, assembling the jeweled bits of a faceted eye, peering through a glass at a spray of fine wire spun into a braid that would run up along the spinal column of a creature which, when released some misty night, might disappear within moments into the clouds and be gone. Or so Filby dreamed. And I'll admit it: I had complete faith in him, in the dragon that he dreamed of building.

In the early spring, such as it is, some few weeks after the hermit crab business, I was hoeing along out in the garden. Another frost was unlikely. My tomatoes had been in for a week, and an enormous green worm with spines had eaten the leaves off the plants. There was nothing left but stems, and they were smeared up with a sort of slime. Once when I was a child I was digging in the dirt a few days after a rain, and I unearthed a finger-sized worm with the face of a human being. I buried it. But this tomato worm had no such face. He was pleasant, in fact, with little piggy eyes and a smashed in sort of nose, as worm noses go. So I pitched him over the fence into Filby's yard. He'd climb back over—there was no doubting it. But he'd creep back from anywhere, from the moon. And since that was the case—if it was inevitable—then there seemed to be no reason to put him too far out of his way, if you follow me. But the plants were a wreck. I yanked them out by the roots and threw them into Filby's yard, too, which is up in weeds anyway, but Filby himself had wandered up to the fence like a grinning gargoyle, and the clump of a half-dozen gnawed vines flew into his face like a squid. That's not the sort of thing to bother Filby, though. He didn't mind. He had a letter from Silver mailed a month before from points south.

I was barely acquainted with the man's reputation then. I'd heard of him—who hasn't? And I could barely remember seeing photographs of a big, bearded man with wild hair and a look of passion in his eye, taken when Silver was involved in the mechano-vivisectionist's league in the days when they first learned the truth about the mutability of matter. He and three others at the university were responsible for the brief spate of unicorns, some few of which are said to roam the hills hereabouts, interesting mutants, certainly, but not the sort of wonder that would satisfy Augustus Silver. He appeared in the photograph to be the sort who would leap headlong into a cold pool at dawn and eat bulgar wheat and honey with a spoon.

And here was Filby, ridding himself of the remains of ravaged tomato plants, holding a letter in his hand, transported. A letter from the master! He'd been years in the tropics and had seen a thing or two. In the hills of the eastern jungles he'd sighted a dragon with what was quite apparently a bamboo ribcage. It flew with the xylophone clacking of windchimes, and had the head of an enormous lizard, the pronged tail of a devilfish, and clockwork wings built of silver and string and the skins of carp. It had given him certain ideas. The best dragons, he was sure, would come from the sea. He was setting sail for San Francisco. Things could be purchased in Chinatown—certain "necessaries," as he put it in his letter to Filby. There was mention of perpetual motion, of the building of an immortal creature knitted together from parts of a dozen beasts.

I was still waiting for the issuance of that last crab, and so was Jensen. He wrote a monograph, a paper of grave scientific accuracy in which he postulated the correlation between the dwindling number of the creatures and the enormity of their size. He camped on the cliffs above the sea with his son, Bumby, squinting through the fog, his eye screwed to the lens of a special telescope—one that saw things, as he put it, particularly clearly—and waiting for the first quivering claw of the behemoth to thrust up out of the gray swells, cascading water, draped with weeds, and the bearded face of the crab to follow, drawn along south by a sort of migratory magnet toward heaven alone knows what. Either the crab passed away down the coast hidden by mists, or Jensen was wrong—there hasn't been any last crab.

The letter from Augustus Silver gave Filby wings, as they say, and he flew into the construction of his dragon, sending off a letter east in which he enclosed forty dollars, his unpaid dues in the Dragon Society. The tomato worm, itself a wingless dragon, crept back into the garden four days later and had a go at a half-dozen fresh plants, nibbling lacy arabesques across the leaves. Flinging it back into Filby's yard would accomplish nothing. It was a worm of monumental determination. I put him into a jar—a big, gallon pickle jar, empty of pickles, of course—and I screwed onto it a lid with holes punched in. He lived happily in a little garden of leaves and dirt and sticks and polished stones, nibbling on the occasional tomato leaf.

I spent more and more time with Filby, watching, in those days after the arrival of the first letter, the mechanical bones and joints and organs of the dragon drawing together. Unlike his mentor, Filby had almost no knowledge of vivisection. He had an aversion to it, I believe, and as a consequence his creations were almost wholly mechanical—and almost wholly unlikely. But he had such an aura of certainty about him, such utter and uncompromising conviction that even the most unlikely project seemed inexplicably credible.

I remember one Saturday afternoon with particular clarity. The sun had shone for the first time in weeks. The grass hadn't been alive with slugs and snails the previous night—a sign, I supposed, that the weather was changing for the drier. But I was only half right. Saturday dawned clear. The sky was invisibly blue, dotted with the dark specks of what might have been sparrows or crows flying just above the treetops, or just as easily something else, something more vast—dragons, let's say, or the peculiar denizens of some very distant cloud world. Sunlight poured through the diamond panes of my bedroom window, and I swear I could hear the tomato plants and onions and snow peas in my garden unfurling, hastening skyward. But around noon great dark clouds roiled in over the Coast Range, their shadows creeping across the meadows and redwoods, picket fences, and chaparral. A spray of rain sailed on the freshening offshore breeze, and the sweet smell of ozone rose from the pavement of Filby's driveway, carrying on its first thin ghost an unidentifiable sort of promise and regret: the promise of wonders pending, regret for the bits and pieces of lost time that go trooping away like migratory hermit crabs, inexorably, irretrievably into the mists.

So it was a Saturday afternoon of rainbows and umbrellas, and Filby, still animated at the thought of Silver's approach, showed me some of his things. Filby's house was a marvel, given over entirely to his collections. Carven heads whittled of soapstone and ivory and ironwood populated the rooms, the strange souvenirs of distant travel. Aquaria bubbled away, thick with water plants and odd, mottled creatures: spotted eels and leaf fish, gobies buried to their noses in sand, flatfish with both eyes on the same side of their heads, and darting anableps that had the wonderful capacity to see above and below the surface of the water simultaneously and so, unlike the mundane fish that swam beneath, were inclined toward philosophy. I suggested as much to Filby, but I'm not certain he understood. Books and pipes and curios filled a half-dozen cases, and star charts hung on the walls. There were working drawings of some of Silver's earliest accomplishments, intricate swirling sketches covered over with what were to me utterly meaningless calculations and commentary.

On Monday another letter arrived from Silver. He'd gone along east on the promise of something very rare in the serpent line—an elephant trunk snake, he said, the lungs of which ran the length of its body. But he was coming to the west coast, that much was sure, to San Francisco. He'd be here in a week, a month, he couldn't be entirely sure. A message would come. Who could say when? We agreed that I would drive the five hours south on the coast road into the city to pick him up: I owned a car.

Filby was in a sweat to have his creature built before Silver's arrival. He wanted so badly to hear the master's approval, to see in Silver's eyes the brief electricity of surprise and excitement. And I wouldn't doubt for a moment that there was an element of envy involved. Filby, after all, had languished for years at the university in Silver's shadow, and now he was on the ragged edge of becoming a master himself.

So there in Filby's garage, tilted against a wall of roughcut fir studs and redwood shiplap, the shoulders, neck, and right wing of the beast sat in silent repose, its head a mass of faceted pastel crystals, piano wire, and bone clutched in the soft rubber grip of a bench vise. It was on Friday, the morning of the third letter, that Filby touched the bare ends of two microscopically thin copper rods, and the eyes of the dragon rotated on their axes, very slowly, blinking twice, surveying the cramped and dimly lit garage with an ancient, knowing look before the rods parted and life flickered out.

Filby was triumphant. He danced around the garage, shouting for joy, cutting little capers. But my suggestion that we take the afternoon off, perhaps drive up to Fort Bragg for lunch and a beer, was met with stolid refusal. Silver, it seemed, was on the horizon. I was to leave in the morning. I might, quite conceivably, have to spend a few nights waiting. One couldn't press Augustus Silver, of course. Filby himself would work on the dragon. It would be a night and day business, to be sure. I determined to take the tomato worm along for company, as it were, but the beast had dug himself into the dirt for a nap.

This business of my being an emissary of Filby struck me as dubious when I awoke on Saturday morning. I was a neighbor who had been ensnared in a web of peculiar enthusiasm. Here I was pulling on heavy socks and stumbling around the kitchen, tendrils of fog creeping in over the sill, the hemlocks ghostly beyond dripping panes, while Augustus Silver tossed on the dark Pacific swell somewhere off the Golden Gate, his hold full of dragon bones. What was I to say to him beyond, "Filby sent me." Or something more cryptic: "Greetings from Filby." Perhaps in these circles one merely winked or made a sign or wore a peculiar sort of cap with a foot-long visor and a pyramid-encased eye embroidered across the front. I felt like a fool, but I had promised Filby. His garage was alight at dawn, and I had been awakened once in the night by a shrill screech, cut off sharply and followed by Filby's cackling laughter and a short snatch of song.

I was to speak to an old Chinese named Wun Lo in a restaurant off Washington. Filby referred to him as "the connection." I was to introduce myself as a friend of Captain Augustus Silver and wait for orders. Orders—what in the devil sort of talk was that? In the dim glow of lamplight the preceding midnight such secret talk seemed sensible, even satisfactory; in the chilly dawn it was risible.

It was close to six hours into the city, winding along the tortuous road, bits and pieces of it having fallen into the sea on the back of winter rains. The fog rose out of rocky coves and clung to the hillsides, throwing a gray veil over dew-fed wildflowers and shore grasses. Silver fence pickets loomed out of the murk with here and there the skull of a cow or a goat impaled atop, and then the quick passing of a half-score of mailboxes on posts, rusted and canted over toward the cliffs along with twisted cypresses that seemed on the verge of flinging themselves into the sea.

Now and again, without the least notice, the fog would disappear in a twinkling, and a clear mile of highway would appear, weirdly sharp and crystalline in contrast to its previous muted state. Or an avenue into the sky would suddenly appear, the remote end of which was dipped in opalescent blue and which seemed as distant and unattainable as the end of a rainbow. Across one such avenue, springing into clarity for perhaps three seconds, flapped the ungainly bulk of what might have been a great bird, laboring as if against a stiff, tumultuous wind just above the low-lying fog. It might as easily have been something else, much higher. A dragon? One of Silver's creations that nested in the dense emerald fog forests of the Coast Range? It was impossible to tell, but it seemed, as I said, to be struggling—perhaps it was old—and a bit of something, a fragment of a wing, fell clear of it and spun dizzily into the sea.

Maybe what fell was just a stick being carried back to the nest of an ambitious heron. In an instant the fog closed, or rather the car sped out of the momentary clearing, and any opportunity to identify the beast, really to study it, was gone. For a moment I considered turning around, going back, but it was doubtful that I'd find that same bit of clarity, or that if I did, the creature would still be visible. So I drove on, rounding bends between redwood-covered hills that might have been clever paintings draped along the ghostly edge of Highway One, the hooks that secured them hidden just out of view in the mists above. Then almost without warning the damp asphalt issued out onto a broad highway and shortly thereafter onto the humming expanse of the Golden Gate Bridge.

Some few silent boats struggled against the tide below. Was one of them the ship of Augustus Silver, slanting in toward the Embarcadero? Probably not. They were fishing boats from the look of them, full of shrimp and squid and bug-eyed rock cod. I drove to the outskirts of Chinatown and parked, leaving the car and plunging into the crowd that swarmed down Grant and Jackson and into Portsmouth Square.

It was Chinese New Year. The streets were heavy with the smell of almond cookies and fog, barbecued duck and gunpowder, garlic and seaweed. Rockets burst overhead in showers of barely visible sparks, and one, teetering over onto the street as the fuse burned, sailed straightaway up Washington, whirling and glowing and fizzing into the wall of a curio shop, then dropping lifeless onto the sidewalk as if embarrassed at its own antics. The smoke and pop of firecrackers, the milling throng, and the nagging senselessness of my mission drove me along down Washington until I stumbled into the smoky open door of a narrow, three-story restaurant. Sam Wo it was called.

An assortment of white-garmented chefs chopped away at vegetables. Woks hissed. Preposterous bowls of white rice steamed on the counter. A fish head the size of a melon blinked at me out of a pan. And there, at a small table made of chromed steel and rubbed formica, sat my contact. It had to be him. Filby had been wonderfully accurate in his description. The man had a gray beard that wagged on the tabletop and a suit of similar color that was several sizes too large, and he spooned up clear broth in such a mechanical, purposeful manner that his eating was almost ceremonial. I approached him. There was nothing to do but brass it out. "I'm a friend of Captain Silver," I said, smiling and holding out a hand. He bowed, touched my hand with one limp finger, and rose. I followed him into the back of the restaurant.

It took only a scattering of moments for me to see quite clearly that my trip had been entirely in vain. Who could say where Augustus Silver was? Singapore? Ceylon? Bombay? He'd had certain herbs mailed east just two days earlier. I was struck at once with the foolishness of my position. What in the world was I doing in San Francisco? I had the uneasy feeling that the five chefs just outside the door were having a laugh at my expense, and that old Wun Lo, gazing out toward the street, was about to ask for money—a fiver, just until payday. I was a friend of Augustus Silver, wasn't I?

My worries were temporarily arrested by an old photograph that hung above a tile-faced hearth. It depicted a sort of weird shantytown somewhere on the north coast. There was a thin fog, just enough to veil the surrounding countryside, and the photograph had clearly been taken at dusk, for the long, deep shadows thrown by strange hovels slanted away landward into the trees. The tip of a lighthouse was just visible on the edge of the dark Pacific, and a scattering of small boats lay at anchor beneath. It was puzzling, to be sure—doubly so, because the lighthouse, the spit of land that swerved round toward it, the green bay amid cypress and eucalyptus was, I was certain, Point Reyes. But the shantytown, I was equally certain, didn't exist, couldn't exist.

The collection of hovels tumbled down to the edge of the bay, a long row of them that descended the hillside like a strange gothic stairway, and all of them, I swear it, were built in part of the ruins of dragons, of enormous winged reptiles—tin and copper, leather and bone. Some were stacked on end, tilted against each other like card houses. Some were perched atop oil drums or upended wooden pallets. Here was nothing but a broken wing throwing a sliver of shade; there was what appeared to be a tolerably complete creature, lacking, I suppose, whatever essential parts had once served to animate it. And standing alongside a cooking pot with a man who could quite possibly have been Wun Lo himself was Augustus Silver.

His beard was immense—the beard of a hill wanderer, of a prospector lately returned from years in unmapped goldfields, and that beard and broad-brimmed felt hat, his oriental coat and the sharp glint of arcane knowledge that shone from his eyes, the odd harpoon he held loosely in his right hand, the breadth of his shoulders—all those bits and pieces seemed almost to deify him, as if he were an incarnation of Neptune just out of the bay, or a wandering Odin who had stopped to drink flower-petal tea in a queer shantytown along the coast. The very look of him abolished my indecision. I left Wun Lo nodding in a chair, apparently having forgotten my presence.

Smoke hung in the air of the street. Thousands of sounds—a cacophony of voices, explosions, whirring pinwheels, oriental music—mingled into a strange sort of harmonious silence. Somewhere to the northwest lay a village built of the skins of dragons. If nothing else—if I discovered nothing of the arrival of Augustus Silver—I would at least have a look at the shantytown in the photograph. I pushed through the crowd down Washington, oblivious to the sparks and explosions. Then almost magically, like the Red Sea, the throng parted and a broad avenue of asphalt opened before me. Along either side of the suddenly clear street were grinning faces, frozen in anticipation. A vast cheering arose, a shouting, a banging on Chinese cymbals and tooting on reedy little horns. Rounding the corner and rushing along with the maniacal speed of an express train, careered the leering head of a paper dragon, lolling back and forth, a wild rainbow mane streaming behind it. The body of the thing was half a block long, and seemed to be built of a thousand layers of the thinnest sort of pastel-colored rice paper, sheets and sheets of it threatening to fly loose and dissolve in the fog. A dozen people crouched within, racing along the pavement, the whole lot of them yowling and chanting as the crowd closed behind and, in a wave, pressed along east toward Kearny, the tumult and color muting once again into silence.

The rest of the afternoon had an air of unreality to it, which, strangely, deepened my faith in Augustus Silver and his creations, even though all rational evidence seemed to point squarely in the opposite direction. I drove north out of the city, cutting off at San Rafael toward the coast, toward Point Reyes and Inverness, winding through the green hillsides as the sun traveled down the afternoon sky toward the sea. It was shortly before dark that I stopped for gasoline.

The swerve of shoreline before me was a close cousin of that in the photograph, and the collected bungalows on the hillside could have been the ghosts of the dragon shanties, if one squinted tightly enough to confuse the image through a foliage of eyelashes. Perhaps I've gotten that backward; I can't at all say anymore which of the two worlds had substance and which was the phantom.

A bank of fog had drifted shoreward. But for that, perhaps I could have made out the top of the lighthouse and completed the picture. As it was I could see only the gray veil of mist wisping in on a faint onshore breeze. At the gas station I inquired after a map. Surely, I thought, somewhere close by, perhaps within eyesight if it weren't for the fog, lay my village. The attendant, a tobacco-chewing lump of engine oil and blue paper towels, hadn't heard of it—the dragon village, that is. He glanced sideways at me. A map hung in the window. It cost nothing to look. So I wandered into a steel and glass cubicle, cold with rust and sea air, and studied the map. It told me little. It had been hung recently; the tape holding its corners hadn't yellowed or begun to peel. Through an open doorway to my right was the dim garage where a Chinese mechanic tinkered with the undercarriage of a car on a hoist.

I turned to leave just as the hovering fog swallowed the sun, casting the station into shadow. Over the dark Pacific swell the mists whirled in the seawind, a trailing wisp arching skyward in a rush, like surge-washed tidepool grasses or the waving tail of an enormous misty dragon, and for a scattering of seconds the last faint rays of the evening sun shone out of the tattered fog, illuminating the old gas pumps, the interior of the weathered office, the dark, tool-strewn garage.

The map in the window seemed to curl at the corners, the tape suddenly brown and dry. The white background tinted into shades of antique ivory and pale ocher, and what had been creases in the paper appeared, briefly, to be hitherto unseen roads winding out of the redwoods toward the sea.

It was the strange combination, I'm sure, of the evening, the dying sun, and the rising fog that for a moment made me unsure whether the mechanic was crouched in his overalls beneath some vast and finny automobile spawned of the peculiar architecture of the early sixties, or instead worked beneath the chrome and iron shell of a tilted dragon, frozen in flight above the greasy concrete floor, and framed by tiers of heater hoses and old dusty tires.

Then the sun was gone. Darkness fell within moments, and all was as it had been. I drove slowly north through the village. There was, of course, no shantytown built of castaway dragons. There were nothing but warehouses and weedy vacant lots and the weathered concrete and tin of an occasional industrial building. A tangle of small streets comprised of odd, tumbledown shacks, some few of them on stilts as if awaiting a flood of apocalyptic proportions. But the shacks were built of clapboard and asphalt shingles—there wasn't a hint of a dragon anywhere, not even the tip of a rusted wing in the jimsonweed and mustard.

I determined not to spend the night in a motel, although I was tempted to, on the off chance that the fog would dissipate and the watery coastal moonbeams would wash the coastline clean of whatever it was—a trick of sunlight or a trick of fog— that had confused me for an instant at the gas station. But as I say, the day had, for the most part, been unprofitable, and the thought of being twenty dollars out of pocket for a motel room was intolerable.

It was late—almost midnight—when I arrived home, exhausted. My tomato worm slept in his den. The light still burned in Filby's garage, so I wandered out and peeked through the door. Filby sat on a stool, his chin in his hands, staring at the dismantled head of his beast. I suddenly regretted having looked in; he'd demand news of Silver, and I'd have nothing to tell him. The news—or rather the lack of news— seemed to drain the lees of energy from him. He hadn't slept in two days. Jensen had been round hours earlier babbling about an amazingly high tide and of his suspicion that the last of the crabs might yet put in an appearance. Did Filby want to watch on the beach that night? No, Filby didn't. Filby wanted only to assemble his dragon. But there was something not quite right—some wire or another that had gotten crossed, or a gem that had been miscut—and the creature wouldn't respond. It was so much junk.

I commiserated with him. Lock the door against Jensen's crab, I said, and wait until dawn. It sounded overmuch like a platitude, but Filby, I think, was ready to grasp at any reason, no matter how shallow, to leave off his tinkering.

The two of us sat up until the sun rose, drifting in and out of maudlin reminiscences and debating the merits of a stroll down to the bluffs to see how Jensen was faring. The high tide, apparently, was accompanied by a monumental surf, for in the spaces of meditative silence I could just hear the rush and thunder of long breakers collapsing on the beach. It seemed unlikely to me that there would be giant crabs afoot.

The days that followed saw no break in the weather. It continued dripping and dismal. No new letters arrived from Augustus Silver. Filby's dragon seemed to be in a state of perpetual decline. The trouble that plagued it receded deeper into it with the passing days, as if it were mocking Filby, who groped along in its wake, clutching at it, certain in the morning that he had the problem securely by the tail, morose that same afternoon that it had once again slipped away. The creature was a perfect wonder of separated parts. I'd had no notion of its complexity. Hundreds of those parts, by week's end, were laid out neatly on the garage floor, one after another in the order they'd been dismantled. Concentric circles of them expanded like ripples on a pond, and by Tuesday of the following week masses of them had been swept into coffee cans that sat here and there on the bench and floor. Filby was declining, I could see that. That week he spent less time in the garage than he had been spending there in a single day during the previous weeks, and he slept instead long hours in the afternoon.

I still held out hope for a letter from Silver. He was, after all, out there somewhere. But I was plagued with the suspicion that such a letter might easily contribute to certain of Filby's illusions—or to my own—and so prolong what with each passing day promised to be the final deflation of those same illusions. Better no hope, I thought, than impossible hope, than ruined anticipation.

But late in the afternoon, when from my attic window I could see Jensen picking his way along the bluffs, carrying with him a wood and brass telescope, while the orange glow of a diffused sun radiated through the thinned fog over the sea, I wondered where Silver was, what strange seas he sailed, what rumored wonders were drawing him along jungle paths that very evening.

One day he'd come, I was sure of it. There would be patchy

fog illuminated by ivory moonlight. The sound of Eastern music, of Chinese banjos and copper gongs would echo over the darkness of the open ocean. The fog would swirl and part, revealing a universe of stars and planets and the aurora borealis dancing in transparent color like the thin rainbow light of paper lanterns hung in the windswept sky. Then the fog would close, and out of the phantom mists, heaving on the groundswell, his ship would sail into the mouth of the harbor, slowly, cutting the water like a ghost, strange sea creatures visible in the phosphorescent wake, one by one dropping away and returning to sea as if having accompanied the craft across ten thousand miles of shrouded ocean. We'd drink a beer, the three of us, in Filby's garage. We'd summon Jensen from his vigil.

But as I say, no letter came, and all anticipation was so much air. Filby's beast was reduced to parts—a plate of broken meats, as it were. The idea of it reminded me overmuch of the sad bony remains of a Thanksgiving turkey. There was nothing to be done. Filby wouldn't be placated. But the fog, finally, had lifted. The black oak in the yard was leafing out and the tomato plants were knee-high and luxuriant. My worm was still asleep, but I had hopes that the spring weather would revive him. I wasn't, however, doing a thing for Filby. He stared long hours at the salad of debris, and when in one ill-inspired moment I jokingly suggested he send to Detroit for a carburetor, he cast me such a savage look that I slipped out again and left him alone.

On Sunday afternoon a wind blew, slamming Filby's garage door until the noise grew tiresome. I peeked in, aghast. There was nothing in the heaped bits of scrap that suggested a dragon, save one dismantled wing, the silk and silver of which was covered with greasy hand prints. Two cats wandered out. I looked for some sign of Jensen's crab, hoping, in fact, that some such rational and concrete explanation could be summoned to explain the ruin. But Filby, alas, had quite simply gone to bits along with his dragon. He'd lost whatever strange inspiration it was that propelled him. His creation lay scattered, not two pieces connected. Wires and fuses were heaped amid unidentifiable crystals, and one twisted bit of elaborate machinery had quite clearly been danced upon and lay now cold and dead, half hidden beneath the bench. Delicate thisses and thats sat mired in a puddle of oil that scummed half the floor.

Filby wandered out, adrift, his hair frazzled. He'd received a last letter. There were hints in it of extensive travel, perhaps danger. Silver's visit to the west coast had been delayed again. Filby ran his hand backward through his hair, oblivious to the harrowed result the action effected. He had the look of a nineteenth-century Bedlam lunatic. He muttered something about having a sister in McKinleyville, and seemed almost illuminated when he added, apropos of nothing, that in his sister's town, deeper into the heart of the north coast, stood the tallest totem pole in the world. Two days later he was gone. I locked his garage door for him and made a vow to collect his mail with an eye toward a telling exotic postmark. But nothing so far has appeared. I've gotten into the habit of spending the evening on the beach with Jensen and his son, Bumby, both of whom still hold out hope for the issuance of the last crab. The spring sunsets are unimaginable. Bumby is as fond of them as I am, and can see comparable whorls of color and pattern in the spiral curve of a seashell or in the peculiar green depths of a tidepool.

In fact, when my tomato worm lurched up out of his burrow and unfurled an enormous gauzy pair of mottled brown wings, I took him along to the seaside so that Bumby could watch him set sail, as it were.

The afternoon was cloudless and the ocean sighed on the beach. Perhaps the calm, insisted Jensen, would appeal to the crab. But Bumby by then was indifferent to the fabled crab. He stared into the pickle jar at the half-dozen circles of bright orange dotting the abdomen of the giant sphinx moth that had once crept among my tomato plants in a clever disguise. It was both wonderful and terrible, and held a weird fascination for

Bumby, who tapped at the jar, making up and discarding names.

When I unscrewed the lid, the moth fluttered skyward some few feet and looped around in a crazy oval, Bumby charging along in its wake, then racing away in pursuit as the monster hastened south. The picture of it is as clear to me now as rainwater: Bumby running and jumping, kicking up glinting sprays of sand, outlined against the sheer rise of mossy cliffs, and the wonderful moth just out of reach overhead, luring Bumby along the afternoon beach. At last it was impossible to say just what the diminishing speck in the china-blue sky might be—a tiny, winged creature silhouetted briefly on the false horizon of our little cove, or some vast flying reptile swooping over the distant ocean where it fell away into the void, off the edge of the flat earth.

THE OLD WOMAN AND THE STORM

by

PATRICIA A. McKILLIP

THE SUN ROSE, as it did every day, making the birds squawk, painting the world. But this rising was different. Arram sensed it as he stepped out of his house. His bare sole felt a newness. His eyes filled with a memory of light. He stood still, watching the night melt away, and for just a moment, time enough for the first warmth to touch his face, he knew that this was also the First Sunrise, when the Long Night had ended and the world began to form. The sun had risen so. The earth was old-new underfoot. Dreams and memories stirred in a breeze through the trees. Arram went for a walk in the new world.

The Sun, the painter, got out her paintbrushes of light. She drenched a bird in red and yellow as it swooped by. She spattered purple among the berry bushes. She painted stones and reflections of stones in the river. Arram passed his favorite rock, where he himself had painted his First Name. The Name had come to him in a dream: the First Name which the being that breathed through his body and saw through his eyes had called itself. Now it had Arram's name and voice. Arram had made a gift of the Name to the rock. It slept so calmly in the water, massive and yellow, a dreaming giant. Other people had liked it also: many pictures, gestures of affection, patterned its weathered sides.

Arram filled his belt-skin with water and turned away from the river. The flat earth, the Sun's domain, spread before him in a thousand shades of brown. He faced the Sun, felt her pour hot dark color into his hair, his body. Far away, another stone, huge and rounded with age, smoldered in the morning with a glow like fire. It caught his eye, greeted him with the common greeting: the languageless, timeless memory of the First Morning. Arram walked toward it.

A lizard scurried away from his foot. A hawk circled above him, then hurtled down, a fist of brown plumage. It rose again with a snake in its talons. Minute red flowers swarmed across Arram's path. Animal bones slowly buried themselves in the earth. Tracks of a live animal came across the desert, crossed Arram's tracks, and went their own silent way. A cloud smudged the sky, and another. The Old Woman who hated the Sun was smoking. The distant rock moved slightly closer to Arram. It had changed color: the fire had melted into brass. Have I been to that rock before? Arram wondered. Or do I only remember it from another time? Thoughts rambled pleasantly in his head; the world constantly changed under his eye. Is this walk mine? Or am I remembering an earlier walk? He stopped for a swallow of water. The ground simmered around him, blurred with light. The air droned and buzzed with invisible singers. A shadow passed over him, and he looked up. The Old Woman was puffing clouds all over the sky.

Arram walked on. When he grew hungry he killed a lizard and roasted it. The soul of the lizard went on its own walk, searching for another container. The rock began to loom across the horizon, bigger than Arram had thought. It darkened; the clouds were draining the Sun of color. The air was motionless, moist-hot. If I remember the rock, I should remember reaching it, Arram thought. But I don't. So this must be my own walk.

There was a fragment of red cloth on a thorn. Someone else had come that way and gone. In the dim, steamy afternoon, the voice of the desert was a vibrant bass hum. The Sun managed a final angry shower of light. She burned the cloud-edges of silver, struck sweat from Arram's face, turned the great wall of rock orange. A shadow, black as night, fell across Arram's path and he stopped, as though he had caught himself from stepping into a rift. He glanced up.Then down and up again. Someone lost a shadow, he thought surprisedly. There was nothing, even in the sky, that it belonged to. As his eyes fell again to the earth, a wind came up tasting of dust and rain, and sent the shadow tumbling across the desert like a leaf.

Now that's strange, Arram thought.

He continued his walk. The rain fell, drenching, warm as a lover. He opened his mouth and drank; he walked through water as through air, for who could know how many times his soul might have been a fish? He had dwelled in water, under the earth. He had died again and again, and been reborn to the same earth. Now he was a man, with a head full of misty memories. Dreams of other lives. There was nothing in the world to fear; he had been, or he would be, every shape in the world. But still, when two boulders crashed and split over his head, and the sky flashed a frosty color that was no color, the man decided it was time to run.

He reached the lacework of caves in the rock just as eggs made out of ice began to fall out of the sky. One struck him, a hard blow on his shoulder that drove him to his knees. He crawled the rest of the way into the cave, sat against the wall in the dim light, rubbing his shoulder and wondering at the force of the storm. The rock above his head seeped into his awareness. It had been battered times past counting, nothing could destroy it. I would like to be a rock now, Arram thought. A puff of smoke made him cough. A stone-painting on the cave wall was no longer a painting. It was the Old Woman. She lifted her pipe, made lightning flash, and Arram saw her face.

He stopped breathing. She was the ugliest woman in the world, as well as the meanest, and he wasn't sure what to say to her. He wanted to move very quietly and take his chances with the ice-eggs. But he hesitated, and as he sat motionless, the Old Woman passed him her pipe.

He took a puff, not knowing what else to do, and passed it back to her. "So," she said in her croaky voice, "you want to be a rock. Go ahead. Walk outside. You won't be a man very long. You won't be anything recognizable." She laughed a reedy insect-laugh. Her hair was white as river-froth, her nose humped and battered like the rock they sat under. She was shriveled, light as a bundle of twigs. She was crazy with jealousy of the Sun, and she was dangerous. Her eyes were the color of lightning.

Arram sighed. He thought with longing of the butterflies along the river, of his love putting her hands on his bare skin. Who would have thought a walk in the morning would have led to death? "The storm will end," he said softly, and she answered, "I am the storm."

His eyes flicked at it. The sky was growing darker, the ice was still falling constantly as rain. His throat closed suddenly. He wondered how far it could spread. It could batter homes to the ground, it could kill children . . . .

"You're so angry," he breathed. "Why are you so angry?"

"You made me angry!"

"Me? What did I do?"

"I saw how you looked at the Sun this morning! She rose and touched your face and you followed her without a thought . . . ."

"No, that isn't the way it was! She—I—"

"How was it? You looked at her as if she had never risen before. I saw you."

He nodded, confused. "That's the way it was. She was—But I—I was only remembering, the way I must have seen her first. When I was a child. Or in another time. The world—"

"Could you ever look at me like that?"

He leaned back, sighing again. He was silent, drawing his name on the ground in the dust, feeling the air in his lungs, the blood beat in his fingertips. "All right," he said after awhile, his voice detached, faraway. "You can kill me now. But first stop the storm."

She only growled something and the thump of ice in the dark sounded louder. Many living things would be left looking for shapes that night. He gazed at her, bewildered.

"Then what do you want?"

"Well, look at me! I am rain! I am thunder, I am lightning, I am bitter, bitter winds—I never have choices! Make me another shape. One that will move you to look at me the way you look at the Sun." She waved her pipe again, and the lightning swam over Arram's amazed face. "Do that, and the storm will stop."

"I'm only a man," Arram protested. "I walk naked in the world. I kill lizards and paint rocks and then I die. I have no power."

"But you don't know what power you might have had. In another time." She snapped her fingers impatiently and thunder rolled. "Think! Remember."

Arram tried to think. But each time he tried, the thunder snarled and the lightning spat. He could only think of the quiet river with ice-eggs smashing into it, the forest bruised and broken by the storm. He couldn't remember a life of magic power. He didn't even know anyone who could remember. The Old Woman herself was the most powerful being he had ever seen. More powerful it seemed, even than the lovely Sun, who had fled from this storm. Maybe, he thought suddenly, the Old Woman is so strong, so angry, that she never sees the simple world. How can she? She throws fire at it, she rains on it. Maybe if I tell her what I see she'll believe that I will have to die to make the storm stop, because I can't help her.

So he said, "In my forest there are red flowers, so big they overflow two hands. They are very beautiful, with many petals reaching toward the sky." The Old Woman was beginning to look annoyed. Her white brows flew together and a boulder crashed down the cliff outside. Arram cleared his throat and continued hurriedly. "They weren't always flowers. Once they were all young women who had no lovers. They cried and pleaded for lovers, but all the young men had died in a battle, and no one knew what to do. One day the great black Hunting Beetle came to them and said, 'I'll be your lover. The only lover all of you will ever need.' And of course they laughed and threw stones at him, making him scurry into a hole so he wouldn't get squashed. That night he crawled back out and looked wistfully over all the arms and legs and breasts of the sleeping women, all of whom he loved at once. He wished for them, and wished, and they sobbed in their sleep for the young men who would never come. And his desire and their sorrow kindled a magic between them, for all things are connected and the earth takes care of its own. In the morning, where the young women had laid, grew the loveliest flowers in the world. The beetle had his wish. And so did the young women: for even today the Hunting Beetle roams over all the flowers in the forest, feeding on their honey and freeing their seeds to the wind."

He stopped, feeling a little confused. He had meant to tell the Old Woman a simple story, but this had a magic in it he had never noticed. She was watching him puzzledly, puffing brief puffs on her pipe. The terrible sound of the ice storm seemed to have lessened a little. The Old Woman said finally, "That's no use to me. I wish and I wish, and nothing ever listens to me. But tell me another one."

Arram drew breath soundlessly and decided to tell her about the rock in the river, which surely had to be the simplest thing in the world. "In the heart of the river beside my home there is a great rock. It is very old, old as the First Morning. It is very peaceful, so peaceful sometimes you can hear it dreaming."

"You can?"

"Yes. It is hard and massive, so hard the river itself scarcely wears away at it. Only one thing ever came close to cracking that rock, and that thing was light as a breath. A butterfly. You ask me," Arram said, though the Old Woman hadn't, "how such a light thing could—"

"Get on with it."

"It's a simple tale."

"It doesn't sound simple."

"It's just about an old rock in a river. Anyway, one day the rock decided it was tired of being a rock."

"How do you know?"

"How do I know? I don't know. Someone told me the story. Or else I heard the rock remembering. It was very young then, and many things were still new. Caterpillars were very new. One big purple caterpillar fell out of a tree onto a leaf floating on the river. The leaf carried it downriver, where it bumped against the rock and the caterpillar crawled off with relief, thinking it had found land. But it toiled up a barren mountain instead. The hairs on the caterpillar's body tickled the rock, waking it, and it wondered what strange little being was trudging up its side. After a time, the little being stopped trudging and started spinning, for its time for change was upon it. The rock went back to sleep. For a long time there was silence. A star shone, a leaf fell, a fish caught a fly. Then one morning, the shell that the caterpillar had spun around itself broke open. The rock felt feet lighter than bubbles walking about on the warm stone. Their dreaming merged, for the butterfly was half-asleep, and the rock half-awake. And the rock realized that the purple hairy being which had crawled up its side was now a fragile, gorgeous creature about to take to the air. And the rock was so moved, so amazed, that it strained with all its strength to break out of its own ponderous shell to freedom in the light. It strained so hard that it nearly cracked itself in two. But the butterfly, who felt its longing, stopped it. 'Rock,' it said gently, 'you can live, if you wish, until the Final Evening. You saved my life and sheltered me, so I will give you a gift. Since you can't fly, I will return here on my Final Evening and bring you dreams of all the things I have seen along the river, in the forest and desert, as I flew. And so will my children. You will not need to fly, and you will not need to die.' And so, even to this day, butterflies rest in the warm light on that rock and whisper to it their dreams."

Arram stopped. They were both silent, he and the Old Woman. She puffed her pipe and blew smoke out of the cave, and far away a forest fire started. "I don't know this world," she said slowly. "This is the world *She* knows. The Sun. The world I know is harsh, noisy, violent. Tell me a story with me in it instead of her. And make me beautiful."

Arram accepted another puff from her pipe. His ears hurt from the thunder, his voice ached from his storytelling. He couldn't remember whether it was day or night; he couldn't guess whether he would live or die. He supposed he would die, since there was no way in the world to make the Old Woman beautiful. So he decided, instead, in his last moments, to tell her about the one he loved most in the world.

"The woman I love is not very beautiful either," he said, seeing her face in his mind. "She is very thin, and her nose is long and crooked. When she was younger, the other children called her 'Crane' because she grew so tall and thin she stooped." He paused to swallow, no longer caring if the Old Woman was listening, for he wanted to spend those last moments with his love. "She thought no one in the world would ever love her. But I did. She was light, like a bird, and shy like a wild thing, and full of funny movements. When I told her I loved her, though, she didn't believe me. She thought I was making fun of her and she hit me. The second time I told her, she threw a pot at me. So I had a sore ear and a sore shin. I went down to the river and sat wondering what I was doing wrong." He heard an odd, creaky sound, but he was too engrossed in his memories to wonder at it. "I decided to bring her all the beautiful things I could find and pile them at her door. I brought her flowers. I brought her bright snake skins. I brought her feathers, colored leaves, sparkling stones. I fell on my head out of trees collecting speckled eggs for her; I roasted myself in the desert to find purple lizards for her. And you know what she did with all those treasures? She threw them, she walked on them, she gave them away—every single thing. Finally, one day, I brought her the fattest fish I had ever caught, all roasted and ready for her to eat—and she burst into tears. I didn't know what to do. I wanted to cry. I wanted to pull her hair. I wanted to shake her until her teeth rattled. I put my hands on her shoulders, and a madness came over me, and I kissed her so long we both ran out of breath and fell on the floor. And when I looked at her, she was smiling." He paused. "Like you are now." He laughed himself at the memory, and at the shining in the Old Woman's face. "Look at you. You look just like her. Look—" His breath caught. He stared out at the quiet sky, at the blazing colors that arched from one end of the world to the other. The Old Woman's smile. He stood up, watching it, marveling, his face a lover's face, until the smile melted like pipe smoke, and the Sun burned away the clouds.

He went back home. His tall, shy, crooked-nosed love saw him as she filled the water-skins, and came to meet him, smiling. He took the skins from her; she tucked her hand in his arm.

"Where have you been?"

"For a walk."

"What did you see?"

"A rock. A shadow. A rainbow."

THE BIG ROCK CANDY MOUNTAIN

by

ROBERT
WESTALL

". . . the soda water fountain,
where the lemonade springs and the bluebird sings
On the big rock candy mountain."
—AMERICAN FOLKSONG

IT SHOULD NEVER have happened. They ought to have sailed straight on to Paris, France, where Hiram could've climbed the Eiffel Tower, strolled along the Bois de Boulogne with an independent air, cadged too much *vin ordinaire* out of Father at lunch, and watched in pleasant afternoon tipsiness the artists in berets and striped shirts painting execrable views of Notre Dame.

Instead, RMS *Aquitania* developed boiler trouble at Southampton, England. The Cunard Steamship Company offered all passengers another ship for Cherbourg, or they could stay safely aboard till the boilers were repaired. But Father remembered Aunt Mame. She had married a kilted hairy-legged Scotsman, who had carried her off to a castle in Kirkcudbright so soused in Scotch mist that she'd never been heard of again, except for a card every Christmas. Father was seized, while drinking a prelunch gimlet, with an urgent desire to go visiting Aunt Mame. Why, Kirkcudbright was only three hundred miles . . . a mere bagatelle. New York to Washington. Drive up one day, visit with her the next, drive down again the third. And still sail for Cherbourg on the *Aquitania*.

Once Father had made up his mind, he had the kind of terrifying persistence that could sink the *Titanic* all over again. Father had become a millionaire by making crazy decisions at a rate that left other tycoons gasping.

In half an hour they were standing on the quayside inside a small fortress of their purely essential luggage, while Father beavered his way into hiring a car. It was drizzling gently, with slight fog. Mom said it was always foggy and raining in England: part of the quaintness they ought to be enjoying. Hiram looked back longingly at the four funnels of the *Aquitania* and the rows of lighted portholes behind which they'd be serving lunch.

It turned out the British did hire cars—for funerals and weddings, and conveying people from the ships to the hotels, and from the hotels back to the ships. And always driven by uniformed chauffeurs; and within the boundaries of Southampton only.

Father called the American Embassy collect from a phone booth, and exploded. Words like "John Jacob Astor" and "Stars and Stripes" came floating out . . . he was obviously talking to a Texan, because at one point he told him where he could stuff the Alamo. That, in Hiram's opinion, had definitely done it. Back to the *Aquitania* for lunch and deckquoits.

So he was all the more amazed when eventually a huge car rolled out of the fog with blazing headlights; and an English voice so strangulated it could only belong to a duke enquired, "Mr. Hiram Schumaker?"

"The same," said Father. "Hiram Schumaker III and IV, Mrs. Schumaker, and Sonja. Put it there!" He held out a friendly hand to the fog and headlights. In response, a car door slammed and a figure was standing rigidly before him in peaked cap and highly polished knee-boots. Somehow Father's hand just withered back to his side.

The car was also impressive, with a hood like a Greek temple. It was so silent, Hiram thought the engine had stopped till he touched it and found the car gently quivering. In a trice, the chauffeur, whose name was Manners, had them inside, tucked under plaid traveling rugs. Father wanted to sit in the front to show Manners the way to Kirkcudbright. But somehow Manners conveyed that was not *done* in England. You sat in the back and gave instructions through a brass speaking-tube.

"It's not *democratic*," exploded Father.

"I think Mr. Manners finds democracy offensive, dear," said Mom. "He expects us to be aristocratic. Don't *lounge*, Hiram. Take that gum out of your mouth, Sonja!" They all sat stiff as ramrods, staring at the equally stiff back of Mr. Manners through the glass screen.

It was the strangest car. Little tapestry curtains at all the windows, held back by gold cords; little silver flower vases screwed to the doors, with bouquets of fern and carnation. The seats were worn creaking leather; the rest was shining mahogany, like a sideboard. It smelt of champagne and wet dogs, tobacco and gunpowder. And the deplorable fact was that England would not keep *still*. It was all hills. If they were not going up, they were going down, which as anyone born in Chicago knows is a disgusting way to behave. Up and down they went, up and down, like that storm they'd met off the Grand Banks of Newfoundland.

"If you look out of the window, Hiram," said Mom, "you won't get sick."

Hiram, just in time, looked out and felt a little better. But England couldn't make up its mind what to be. First a village of black-and-white cottages, like a picture-postcard. Next minute, they were alone on a bleak moor, apart from a crowd of bored-looking sheep. Next, they were passing through a town as grim as Pittsburgh, with belching chimneys and white-faced people staring as blankly as the sheep had done. Then a golden cornfield, with a row of men moving in line with scythes cutting the corn, as if McCormack had never invented the combine-harvester.

All of which Mom found quaint, till Hiram could have screamed.

They had a late lunch at what appeared to be the Wizard of Oz's castle. Father asked Manners to join them, but he just quivered from head to foot, like a potential winner of the Kentucky Derby. The food was awful. Father said Manners wasn't being aristocratic; he just knew a better place to eat. Probably a place cabmen go.

Afterwards, Father, calling out the names on every signpost they passed and consulting the road-map which he'd borrowed from the first-class library of the *Aquitania,* began to fret because they were falling behind schedule. It was already four o'clock and they were only halfway to Kirkcudbright. The car was fast; at one point on the open road they touched a hundred. But so little of the road *was* open. It didn't just go up and down, it also went left and right, frequently at right angles. As if it was afraid to cross a garden, or even a field, but must tiptoe round the outside, like a poor relation.

"The only long straight bits were built by the Romans," said Mom, "so the Ancient Britons couldn't hide round corners."

"Reckon the Ancient Britons won," said Father, bitterly.

Then there was the traffic; little flat carts pulled by trotting ponies; open carts selling milk straight into jugs from the churn; roofed carts selling massed ranks of oranges, apples, and cauliflowers. Men with refrigerators on tricycles, selling ice creams under the legend *"Stop me and buy one!"* Through all this, the great car picked her way, as the *Aquitania* had picked her way through the tugboats of Southampton Water, gracefully but slowly.

And then the fog came back, making yellow haloes round the early gaslamps, which Mom found quaint. She even wound down her window a little (making sure that Mr. Manners wasn't watching) and sniffed it ecstatically, announcing it smelt like a real London pea-souper.

"We are not going to London," said Father ominously, nibbling the ends of his Teddy Roosevelt mustache. "We are going
to Kirk-cud-bright."

But it was not to be. The fog thickened, until each
streetlamp was a long-awaited event. The voice-tube burped
suddenly.

"I am endeavoring to reach the town of Northwich, sir.
There's a reasonable hostelry called the Angel where you can
spend the night."

"The North *Witch*? Does she cast evil spells or something?
Or does the Angel stop her?" Hiram realized Father was being
jokey—a bad sign; he'd been hilarious the night before the
Wall Street crash.

"A *wich*, sir, is a salt-well, that provides an endless supply of
brine, which the inhabitants boil off into salt to make an hon-
est living." Mr. Manners was at his British stiffest. But Dad
thought he was being jokey, too.

"Yeah, yeah," he said. "We gotta song like that—'The Big
Rock Candy Mountain'—lemonade springs and things like
that! Good joke!"

"I have no knowledge, sir, of the folk customs of the United
States of America. But we are approaching Northwich."

Hiram gaped. It seemed to him they were traveling up a narrow spit of land, between two endless lakes that faded on each
side into the mist.

> "'On one side stood the ocean, and on one
> Stood a great water, and the moon was full.'"

Mom often quoted the English poet, Alfred Lord Tennyson,
when under stress.

"Where the hell's the moon," snapped Father, very Teddy
Roosevelt. "I can't see the goddamn moon."

But Hiram wasn't listening. Something was looming out of
the right-hand lake, and it wasn't an arm clad in white samite,
either. It seemed to be a tall factory chimney. And at its base,

pitifully drowned, the peaks of a row of factory buildings. Then the topmost branches of a dead tree . . . .

"Hey, Mom, floods . . ."

"Not floods, sir, subsidence. This is a subsidence area. The rocks below are pure salt for several thousand feet. When they pump out brine, great underground caverns form, then collapse, and the ground . . . sinks. The Northwich prophet, Nixon, prophecied that one day Northwich will sink entirely under the sea . . . ."

"You mean, like, tonight?" gasped Mom.

"Unlikely, madam. The best authorities think the process will take another several thousand years . . . ."

Northwich *leaned.* The fine church tower leaned gently west. Down the hill, the tall houses leaned a lot more, against great sloping beams of timber, like cripples on crutches. Pairs of houses leaned together, holding each other upright like drunken men. Great cracks ran down the walls, stuffed with rags, mud plaster, anything to keep the draft out. Doors were set askew like a boxer's broken nose; windows slanted in opposite directions, like the eyebrows of an enraged dowager duchess. The narrow old road was a patchwork of filled-in holes, making the car leap like a bucking bronco.

"It's like the San Francisco earthquake, frozen halfway," said Father. He had been in a suburb of San Francisco as a boy, the day of the earthquake. He was very proud of the fact, and the family very tired of it. "How do the people stand it?"

But the people, far from merely standing it, were going about their business of selling fish and shaking hearthrugs quite cheerfully in their caps and shawls, as if nothing whatever was happening.

In the center of it all, under a great flaring iron triple streetlight, the car drew up.

"The Angel, sir! A fine old Georgian coaching-inn."

It was a fine old inn, with Doric columns and many-paned

windows, and rosy light coming welcomingly through most. The only fault was that, like the *Titanic,* it was sinking by the bows. The left-hand side was four feet below pavement level, and the right-hand side at least ten. Roughly dug steps led down to the noble front door.

Mom took a deep breath and said, "Quaint!"

Father said, "Is it safe? It doesn't have any lifeboats!" Being jokey again.

"Safer than going on, sir!" said Mr. Manners. And indeed the fog had thickened suddenly, billowing like clouds of steam, and reducing the triple streetlamp to three pale moons. They groped their way towards the hazy rosy light that was now the only sign of the Angel. Inside, as good a lobby of polished mahogany, paneled from floor to ceiling, as anyone could wish. And a jovial landlord replete with beaming smile and red waistcoat. A pageboy to carry the bags, a roaring log fire . . . .

Of course it all sloped downhill to the right. Or did the ceiling slope down to the left? Certainly the fine grandfather clock leaned left, like the leaning tower of Pisa, though it was still going, with a loud, slow, reassuring tick.

Father braced his legs, as he had in the storm off the Grand Banks, and asked for rooms and dinner. He tried to book an equally good room for Mr. Manners, but that worthy said he had friends in the town, and was already suited. From the set of his lips, his dislike of democracy had not been weakened by circumstances.

After dinner, Hiram settled in his bedroom with his well-thumbed copy of *Huckleberry Finn* and a battered brass candlestick whose flame stuck out nearly at forty-five degrees. He sat on a stool by a cheerful flickering coal fire, and listened to the tick of the clock. The clock was sitting on the mantelpiece, its dial telling the wrong time, and a pendulum swinging behind a glass door. But the pageboy had told him it wasn't *meant* for telling the time. It was for listening to.

"You listen to the old clock, sir, listen to its ticking. 'Cos if her do stop, or the ticking changes, you get on your dressing gown, and get downstairs quick!"

"Oh, why?" Hiram had asked, as insouciantly as possible.

"'Cos if her do stop, or change her tick, sir, it means this old inn's on the move again, down into the bowels of the earth."

"Pull the other leg," said Hiram sharply. "It's got bells on it!"

"Cross me 'eart, sir," said the pageboy. "That's why you'll find an old clock in every bedroom of this hotel, an' all telling a different time. Why only the other night, sir, me and me brothers were tucked up four to a bed at 'ome, and our ol' clock stopped on the mantelpiece, an' afore we could move there was a rumble like someone tipping bricks outside. And when we all got outside, where our neighbors Mr. and Mrs. Yarwood had lived, there was just a hole in the ground. Mother, father, five kids, a cat, an' a dog all vanished as if they'd never been. An' a canary. An' old Yarwood owed me Dad ten shillings—he'll have to dig deep to get it back now. Still, it saves the expense of buryin' 'em; they just got the vicar to stand in the 'ole and say a few words . . . . So listen to that old clock tick, sir. It's your best friend.

The trouble was, it was a *very* old clock. Every few minutes, when you were least expecting it, its old heart missed a beat. Hiram had gone belting downstairs five times already, only to find the grandfather in the lobby still ticking steadily, and a lot of men in cloth caps amiably drinking and playing shuffleboard.

But he had lost all desire to go to bed, let alone take his clothes off.

There was a tapping on the door, and Sonja came in.

"Can I sleep here? I don't like my room. I put my ball on the floor and it rolled uphill."

"'Spect it'll do it here," said Hiram. They tried it, and the thing not only rolled uphill, but this way and that, as if it had a life of its own.

"Let's get out of here," said Hiram. "We can go buy candy, and get some fresh air."

"Fresh *what?*" asked Sonja. She stuck her head out of the window and smelled the fog, which was strong on soot and had a singeing salty smell.

But they wrapped up well in their coats and scarves and went tiptoeing past Father and Mom, who were sitting with the cloth-capped men, buying them drinks in a democratic fashion and being told such fearsome stories about subsidence and salt and floods that they noticed nothing. Hiram heard Mom say "How quaint" three times, with her hand to her throat, then they plunged out into the fog. They turned the corner, and ran into a scene like something out of Hell. A low rough wooden shed, stained white in patches. A great furnace roared in the middle of it, lighting great flat pans billowing steam with a fearsome red light, and huge full-bosomed women, stripped near naked, were drawing long rakes across the pans, drawing up great mounds of glistening wet white crystals. They ran on, before the women should notice.

The candy shop seemed pretty normal. Mirrors running right up to the ceiling, advertising Five Boys chocolate and Fry's Turkish Delight. The shopkeeper knew what a dollar was; but he said they'd have to eat and drink a dollar's worth of candy and what he called "hot sarsaparilla" on the spot, as he wouldn't give them any English change. Hiram thought the man a crook, but a pretty harmless and friendly and cheerful sort of crook, and he saw no reason why he shouldn't be as democratic as Father. So they sat down at a marble-topped table, and drank their hot red sticky glasses of sarsaparilla and tried all the kinds of candy bar they could see on display, one after the other, till their dollar was used up. It seemed to be going a terribly long way, and he only hoped that Sonja wouldn't end up making herself sick.

The man asked them if they had cowboys where they lived, and how much bother the Indians were, and if any of their family had ever been scalped . . . . Hiram thought he was kidding them along. *Nobody* could be that ignorant. Then it was their turn to ask questions.

Who was this Dixon the Prophet?

"Not Dixon, Nixon," said the man. "Oh, you don't want to worry about Nixon—he's been dead donkey's years—before Good Queen Bess's time. Bess's granddad was called Henry, and he had to fight for the throne of England wi' a King Richard, and they fought hundreds o' miles away. Old Nixon was ploughing a field at the time, an' he suddenly began having a vision about King Henry and King Richard, and he prophesied King Henry would win an' King Richard be killed. An' a week later, a messenger came to the town to say that was exactly what had happened. And when King Henry heard, he sent for Nixon and made him his court jester. But Old Nixon had a prophecy about himself—that he'd starve to death. It worried him so much, he took to sleeping in King Henry's pantry. An' when King Henry and all his court went away on holiday, they locked the pantry door not knowing poor Nixon was asleep inside, an' he *did* starve to death in the end, pore soul . . . ."

"Don't you know any stories with happy endings?" asked Hiram snappishly. "Everybody in this town has miserable stories."

"Aye," said the shopkeeper cheerfully. "Us Northwichers are a bit down in the dumps usually. It's on account of Roaring Meg."

"Roaring Who?" asked Sonja, her mouth agape.

"I expect she's the North Witch," said Hiram, bitterly.

"Lord love you, no. Roaring Meg's the great river o' brine that runs beneath this town, eating away the ground from under us. It was Roaring Meg that made those great lakes you'll have come across . . . . There's a story about that an' all. A pore milkman, wi' a horse an' cart was crossing that bit where them lakes are, when the earth collapsed . . . and neither him nor his horse nor cart were ever seen again. He's down there somewhere still. Bet his milk's gone sour by this time."

"I don't believe any of this," said Hiram, pointing to another bar of Five Boys chocolate, with his mouth still full of the last.

"Oh, don't you?" said the man. "Well just come here an' listen." He opened a door, and switched on a light, and Hiram saw a flight of steps leading downwards. Hiram thought of men who enticed children away and murdered them. On the other hand, it seemed pointless to stuff the children full of chocolate and hot sarsaparilla first. So they went. Into the cellar. Where the man opened another door, on another downward flight of steps, and said, "Listen!"

And they listened, into the dank-smelling dark. And heard a rushing like a mighty underground river.

"That's Roaring Meg, doing her evil work," said the man.

But Sonja was staring round, big-eyed, with her thumb in her mouth. She took it out and said, "This is a funny room!"

And it was. It didn't look like a cellar at all, but like a grand sitting room, with a great marble fireplace and large windows . . . but the only things they could see out of the windows were great balks of timber, holding back the earth. And there was rosy wallpaper hanging in damp strips off the wall.

"What *is* this?" asked Hiram.

"This, young sir, is the third story of a gentleman's house. My shop is the top story, the only one left above ground. But there are two more stories below us, and a cellar. All sunk into the earth over the years . . . ."

Hiram gave him a hard look. But he didn't look shifty, or giggle. "I've heard too many strange things for one night," said Hiram.

"Then I'll tell you another," said the man. "Then you can go home to bed, and sweet dreams—if you can. There's a place called Winsford, a bit south of here, where there's a salt mine, dry as a bone. And in that mine, when the Czar of Russia came to see it, they held a Grand Banquet for him, with the ceiling lit by chandeliers, and all the tablecloths snowy white, and all the silver forks and glasses gleaming. For it's always warm and dry down there—dry as a bone—the salt takes the moisture out of the air, and it's fifty-six degrees Fahrenheit, night and day, winter and summer . . . ."

"Hiram—I feel sick," announced Sonja.

"Tek her home, quick," said the man. "An' here's the rest of your chocolate bars to take with you."

Hiram thanked him, and somehow found his way back to the Angel. Sonja wasn't sick, and they got upstairs without Father and Mom even seeing them. Father was still being democratic, and even offering to sing "Big Rock Candy Mountain." He'd obviously had more of a skinful than usual, and in this town, Hiram didn't blame him.

Hiram went to bed, but not to sleep; he kept all his clothes on, even his tweed overcoat and cap; and his big, new-fashioned, rubber electric torch by his hand on the eiderdown. Everytime he closed his eyes, he became a slave to the ticking clock, which limped and stammered, playing with his nerves like a cat plays with a mouse.

"Damn Limey rubbish," he shouted, leaping off the bed and shaking it. But he hadn't even that consolation; it was an American clock, made by E. Ingraham of Bristol, Connecticut. He put it back on the mantelpiece, cravenly pleading with it to start ticking again. It obliged, and he closed his eyes. Must be near midnight.

A timid tapping. "Come in," he roared, much fiercer than he felt.

It was Sonja, also fully clad, eyes big as saucers, and clutching Hermione, the teddy bear she had long scorned, but kept on bringing on trips in a mood of pure forgetfulness.

"There's a man in my room," she said. "He keeps on tapping on the door and coming in."

"What *sort* of man? A waiter? A boot-boy?" Her greater terror made him feel bold, strong, and scornful.

"No . . . a funny man, all raggy with long hair and a beard. He doesn't say nothing . . . just makes grunting noises."

Hiram's courage cooled rapidly. *Anything* could happen in this place . . . not like Chicago. With people like Al Capone, at least you knew what they'd do to you. A ragged grunty man might do *anything.*

"Go get Father."

"Father's room's round the bend in the corridor, and that's where the grunty man keeps hiding . . . ."

Hiram listened; through the whole sagging dark mass of the Angel there was now silence.

"Stay here with me. Get under the eiderdown." Under the eiderdown, with Hermione between them, it felt a *little* better.

"He won't *dare* come in here," said Hiram, quite failing to convince himself. "You've been dreaming!"

As if to contradict him, there came a soft tapping. Sonja hurled her arms around Hiram's neck and buried her face in his chest like they did in the movies; the effect was of being strangled. The door swung open, revealing only empty darkness in the dim and dying glow of the fire.

"You didn't fasten it properly," he shouted to Sonja, in a strangled sort of way. "It always swings open, with the inn sloping." He had almost worked up enough courage to go across and shut it, when the creature entered.

It paralized Hiram. It came silent, barefoot, softly as an animal. Like an animal, it leaped onto the dresser, crouched, and stared at them. It had a straggly beard and a shock of wild uncombed hair. It sort of *capered,* never still.

Then it stared at them again. Its rags were parti-colored, green and brown, on arms and chest and legs . . . even in the firelight Hiram thought they were really red and yellow, under centuries of dirt.

They stared at it, and it stared back. Its eyes, too, were as big as saucers, with the white showing all around, like a madman's. And yet it made no attempt to attack them. Rather, it seemed as timid as a rabbit. Hiram waved a fist fiercely, and it

ran towards the door, whimpering. Then paused, and beckoned, urgently.

"It's . . . a sort of court jester," said Hiram.

"Maybe it's Dixon," suggested Sonja, who had allowed herself a furtive peep.

"Nixon," said Hiram; even near panic, he never missed a
chance to put Sonja down. "But they said he'd been dead donkey's years!"

"He doesn't *look* dead!" said Sonja. "Maybe that shopkeeper
was fooling us. Nixon! Nixon!" She called to the figure tentatively, as one might to a frightened cat. The figure responded
by waving its arms wildly, and nodding its head so much they
feared it might fall off. Then gestured them to follow him
again.

"Hey, if he's Nixon the Prophet, maybe he's telling us the
inn's going to fall down any minute!"

"Better warn Father. . . ." They followed the strange figure,
who was anxious, as a cat is, to keep some distance between
them. But at Father's door it pointed inside and shook its head
with equal vigor.

"No, he just wants us!"

"Mom says not to go with strange men!"

"Call that a *man*? More like a monkey. *I* say, let's see where
he goes. Maybe he wants to show us something."

They followed, down the dim stairs of the clock-ticking hall,
Hiram clutching his torch fiercely, as if it was a club. As they
turned on the landing, they saw Nixon vanish through a door
at the back.

They went through that door; Hiram shone his torch round,
with an authoritative flick. They were in the inn kitchen. Great
sides of bacon hung from hooks like pale corpses; there were
rows of cups, saucers, bowls, and things under white cloths for
breakfast.

"He must be hungry *again*," said Sonja. "Perhaps he's inviting us to a midnight feast . . . after all that chocolate I ate . . .
yuk!"

But of Nixon there was no sign, except another door darkly open beside the great fireplace. They investigated. "He's down there," said Sonja. "I can hear him snuffling and shuffling."

"Ugh, smells damp." But they descended stone steps, gone slimy, by the light of the torch. And came to another kitchen, just like the one above. Only with damp sleeking the stone floor-flags, and the windows bricked up. But it *was* a kitchen: same big sooty fireplace, huge table, and iron pots and hooks for cooking. Only they were red with rust.

"It's the kitchen they had before the kitchen upstairs," whispered Sonja, "only it sank into the ground . . . ."

They stared uneasily at another open door by another fireplace, at steps leading down again into the dark, from which the snuffling and shuffling sounds came up. They went down.

"*Another* kitchen," said Sonja. "Three kitchens below each other." But here the big table was of stone, and all the floor and all the walls were white stuff, like a powdery fur. Hiram picked off a bit on his fingertip, licked it. "Salt, pure salt. Oozing out of the walls."

Across the floor, to another gaping dark door, ran Nixon's bare black footprints.

"How *many* kitchens?" breathed Sonja.

But the next was the last, and the open door led them out into a cobbled street; or rather a cobbled tunnel, because above the poor broken walls and windows was not the night sky, but a glistening arch of slimy muddy rock.

"A whole street," breathed Hiram. "A whole *street* under the earth." His flicking torch beam picked out a wheelbarrow thrown on its side, with its load of white salt spilling out. There was an iron streetlamp, darkened forever; and a child's iron hoop, nearly rusted through. And a low dark creeping shape that made Sonja scream because she thought it was a rat, but it was only a poor leather shoe, thick with mold.

Hiram threw the great beam of his torch along the short street; it caught a little prancing figure, who nodded and beckoned enthusiastically.

They ran towards him, but he flipped down over a ledge; as they ran up they noticed a sound of rushing water.

The end of the street was a little quayside, where two small boats had been tied up. But now one had been cast off and was whirling the summoning, beckoning figure of Nixon into a low tunnel.

"Hey, hold on," said Hiram. "So far, we can climb back, but . . ." He shone the torch down; the stream ran strongly and so clear they could see the rocky bottom; but it was blue-blue, and little wisps of steam came off it.

"I guess this'll be Roaring Meg," said Hiram.

"Oh, c'mon," said Sonja, leaping down into the little rocking boat. "If Nixon can get back, so can we." She undid the chain that was holding it to the quay, and if Hiram hadn't jumped in, she'd have left him standing there.

There were no oars; the current simply swept them along. Hiram fretted; but Sonja sat there quite complacent, playing with the rusty chain. "I wonder if we'll find the milkman," she said thoughtfully.

Hiram swept his torch round and round in great arcs, trying to prove he was still master of the situation.

Now there were signs of human beings. Picks and shovels, coats hung on a wall, and caps hung above them.

"These must be the mines," whispered Sonja, "the abandoned mines."

"But why is everything crusted with ice?" whispered Hiram. "It's not even cold—it's quite warm, really." He couldn't even raise a shiver.

"Not ice, stupid—salt. Everything's encased in salt." And indeed, the great crystals, green and blue and yellow under the flashings of his torch, encased everything. The walls were walls of glass that reflected their little boat as they passed, so that they saw their own bodies and staring faces reflected, as if they too were encased inside the salt-ice, and lost forever.

Their boat stopped with a bump; they had run into the other

boat, which was tied up to the bank with a chain again, and empty.

"Do we follow?" whispered Sonja.

"We certainly do follow," said Hiram. He flicked the torch up to where Roaring Meg ran on. She plunged through a narrow hole, and beyond there was the sound like a waterfall.

"No choice," said Hiram.

They scrambled ashore. The tunnel went high, so high the torch couldn't find the roof. There were cold drafts coming from many directions, so they knew they were in a huge cavern.

"Where now?"

"Follow the road," said Hiram.

For there was a little country road. It even had fences and gates on either side, and tall long-dead plants growing on the verges. And they came upon a quaint old high signpost, saying "Wincham, 2 miles."

But everything was encased in salt-crystals.

"They use salt to preserve things," said Hiram, and shivered. "Salt will preserve anything."

"It's like a time sandwich in the earth . . . . I wonder if we'll find the milkman."

"He was going to Wincham when . . ."

Then, far ahead, the beam of the torch fell on a cart standing in the road, with a milk-churn in it. And something hunched-up beside the churn; and something else standing beyond the cart, that the torch couldn't reach . . . .

"Hiram, I'm scared."

"We gotta go on. There's no other way."

They went on tiptoe on the slippery salt-glazed road. They didn't mean to look up as they passed the cart but . . .

There he was, just sitting there looking at them, his cap pulled right down over his ears, and his overcoat collar and muffler pulled up to his nose, and everything, even his nose, covered with salt crystals. And the horse, still standing, was covered with salt crystals, too. They just stared and stared in horror.

"Cold, for the time of year," said the milkman in a friendly way, like he wanted to be friends. And the crystals on his cap and muffler tinkled as he spoke.

"You're alive," said Hiram, stupidly.

"Aye, alive. Wondrously preserved by the salt. An' the horse, too." As if in agreement, the horse shook itself, as horses do. It sounded like a great glass chandelier, clinking musically in the draft.

"Are you looking for Nixon?" asked the milkman. "He passed not long since. He passes quite often in his travels. Brings me a bite to eat, and a bit o' hay for the horse. Sometimes newspapers, though they're always the wrong date. Sometimes too early, sometimes too late, so I can never tell what year it is. Still, it stops us getting bored. I tell the horse all the news—not that he understands much, but he sometimes shakes his head over the state of things."

"How can you *bear* it?" asked Sonja. "Down here?"

"Ha'nt got much choice, little missus," said the milkman. "I suppose it's the state to which God called me that terrible day in 1892, when the earth gave way. I'm luckier than some down here. I'm alive and can walk about a bit, though it's getting more difficult as these salt-crystals get heavier. There're more people down here than ye might think, an' Nixon keeps us lively, wi' news o' what's happening up above. Then there're things like that feller all in black, wi' the gun . . . ."

"What fellow?"

"The one Nixon's following now. As I said, they came past not five minutes since, as far as I can tell the time in the dark. My pocket watch stopped years ago."

"Thank you, sir," said Hiram politely. "Which way did they go?"

"Through Wincham, towards Winsford."

"Is there nothing we can do for you?" asked Sonja.

"You wouldn't have a bit o' tobacco? No, you're too young. Don't worry about me, little missus. You get used to it, after a bit. But if you see Nixon, tell him I could do wi' a glim o' candle."

They sped on; the tunnel began to slope upwards, the air to get drier. "Winsford," said Hiram. "isn't that where the Czar of Russia . . . oh, my *God*—that man in black. He must be one of those Anarchists—the sort that throw bombs—he's going to try to assassinate the Czar. That's what Nixon's worried about. Hurry!"

They sped up the shallow slope. No more crystals now, just salt soft and white as snow underfoot, each separate grain winking in turn, in the light of the torch.

And then light was streaming down in front of them: the soft warm yellow light of candles. There was the tunnel mouth, and a great cave, with stalactites of salt dangling blue and green from the roof. But rich Turkey red carpets had been strewn on the floor, and there were tables laid with sparkling white cloths, and candelabras full of candles, and silverware shining, and many men, some sitting, some standing, all in somber black. All except a little group dressed in splendid blue and red with sashes and medals and golden stars on their chests.

"That's the Czar," said Sonja, "the one with the biggest beard."

And at that moment, from a side passage, stepped out a figure in a black cloak, with a broad-brimmed black hat, such as they had never dreamt of seeing outside a comic strip. And he raised a long pistol, aimed straight at the Czar's head . . . .

Nobody noticed, except Hiram and Sonja, and Nixon behind him, capering and frantic, but for some reason quite unable to *do* anything.

"Hiram—*deal* with him," shrieked Sonja. But Hiram was rooted to the spot, quite unable to move.

But something, maybe Sonja's high-pitched shriek, made a

man look up from the table. And in an instant, three other men had stood up, quite blocking the Czar from view. And the next second, the Anarchist was struggling in the hands of three huge police-constables in pointed helmets and tunics buttoned up tightly to their chins. Handcuffs clinked solidly, and he was led away.

Everyone sat back down at their tables, and, after a short pause, continued talking and eating. Even the Czar, though he did look a trifle pale and sweaty. Nobody noticed Hiram and Sonja; nobody seemed able even to *see* them. So they slipped out of the side tunnel, and walked around the Turkey red carpet quite freely, slipping between the hurrying waiters. Sonja even tried to count the medals on the Czar's chest as he ate, but there were too many to count, the way he kept moving his arms about. Sonja wanted to take a plate of pork chops off the side table for the milkman, and some cabbage for the horse, but Hiram thought better not. And from another tunnel mouth, a grimacing, approving, winking, eyebrow-lifting, capering Nixon was beckoning it was time to go.

It took a long time, but they made it, climbing up through the endless kitchens of the Angel. And so to bed, each in their own room, for who could fear poor dear, helpful Nixon now? They were quite sad to part from him; they waved and hoped one day to come and visit with him again . . . .

Hiram wakened late, even by his own watch, let alone that darned clock . . . well, at least the inn hadn't fallen into a hole during the night.

And then he remembered Nixon. God, what a *crazy* dream. All this crazy town! He drew back the curtains and stared out. The sky was that English gray like a workman's flannel shirt. You felt the clouds were resting on top of your head. The buildings still leaned, like cripples on crutches.

It *had* been a dream, hadn't it? But it had left a heavy mark on his mind. And a heavy mark on his body, too, like he'd been climbing and scrambling and burrowing and scraping all night . . . .

Better go and check up with Sonja; only he was reluctant, because she'd just laugh at him, and probably tell Father.

By the time he'd made up his mind, she wasn't in her room. She was downstairs already, breakfasting with Father.

They'd all come down late for breakfast, and sat late eating it. It wasn't just Sonja who looked worn out, thought Hiram. Mom and Father looked worn out, too. All that whiskey and democracy . . . The landlord kept on asking whether they'd like a little more bacon, or a little more toast or tea. (He didn't seem to have *heard* of coffee.) He didn't ask them whether they'd slept well either, which was very unusual for a landlord.

It was Manners who finally got them up from the table, clean-shaven and immaculate in his newly-pressed uniform and shining knee-boots, with a tartan traveling-rug over his arm, ready to tuck them in for the new day. "Your bags are packed and in the car, sir," he told Father, reprovingly. "We have a fair drive yet. And some interesting things to see. The Cumbrian Mountains, which are made entirely of green roofing-slate . . ."

"*Roofing-slate?*" gasped Mom, giving him an old-fashioned look.

"Best roofing-slate in Britain, madam. And we pass the graphite mine at Keswick, where they mine the stuff inside all the lead pencils in the world."

"A *pencil mine?*" uttered Mom direly, the blood of her Pilgrim Fathers churning menacingly in her veins.

"And Gretna Green, on the Scottish border, where the blacksmith has the power to marry anybody, young or old, without a license."

"Is he an *Episcopalian* blacksmith?"

"He will marry anybody ma'am, Catholic, Buddhist, or Seventh Day Adventist."

"*Are* we halfway to Kirk-cud-bright, Manners?" asked Father nervously.

"A little over halfway, sir," said Manners, reassuringly.

"*Dear!*" said Mom to Father. "You have us halfway through a *madhouse* . . . pencil mines, Buddhist blacksmiths, indeed! I never met your Aunt Mame . . . and what feelings of kinship I have for her are wearing pretty thin. When do we reach the Big Rock Candy Mountain, Manners, and the lemonade springs?"

"I have no idea of what you are speaking, madam!" said Manners, keeping his face deadly straight.

"*Dear!*" said Mom. "It may be cowardly, but I hear Cherbourg and Paris, France calling. My cousin Elmer was there last spring, and he said *everything* was perfectly normal. Except the public conveniences, and at least they don't flush lead pencils or lemonade."

Father rose to the occasion like a man; he flicked back a lock of hair, twitched his mustache, looked his most Teddy Roosevelt, and announced, "Next year, we do Great Britain, but *good*—a whole month. Drive us back to Southampton, Manners. I want to be back aboard the *Aquitania* in time for dinner."

"Sir," said Manners, without expression.

As they got into the car, Mom said, "Hiram—your shoes are *soaking*."

Hiram hesitantly began to tell what had happened with Nixon the Prophet, but he soon faltered under his mother's eye and trailed off.

"Hiram," said Mom. "How can you bring yourself to tell such whoppers. You *dreamed* it."

"Didn't. That's why my shoes are wet."

"Then why aren't Sonja's, since she's supposed to have been with you?" They all looked. Sonja's shoes were bone-dry.

"Such *stuff,*" said Mom, and settled down inside her tartan rug to watch out for the next horror that Great Britain might sling at her. "Too much chocolate you had, young man— *and* too much hot sarsaparilla. But that inn was enough to give anyone nightmares. I forgive you. Drive on, Manners."

But every now and then, Hiram kept glancing at his shoes. An odd thing was happening. As they dried, they were turning white. Great white patches grew across them. Tiny crystals glistened. He put his finger down, then licked it.

Salt.

He looked up, and caught his traitorous sister's eye. She grinned and opened her purse. Inside was one shoe, and that was turning white as well. He gaped.

"I changed my shoes," she mouthed silently, across Mom's incomprehending face.

"Why?" he mouthed back.

"Why upset them?" She pulled a face at Father and Mom. Father and Mom never saw; they had found something else quaint.

"So you were there all the time?"

She nodded with a conspiratorial grin, as the great car began to climb Salisbury Plain.

"If this is a *plain*," Father asked Manners, "why are we climbing?"

"I have no idea, sir," said Manners, keeping his neck very still. "We should have a sight of Stonehenge in a moment."

"Next year," said Father, "I'll sort out you British. We'll take a whole month, I *swear* it!"

Mom shuddered delicately, as the car swept on towards Southampton, the *Aquitania*, dinner, and sanity.

Author's Note

I made up Hiram and his family, Manners, and Hiram's dream. All the rest, about England and Northwich, is absolutely true. Even about the Czar of Russia, dining in

*state down the Winsford Salt Mine (though as far as I
know, no one tried to assassinate him). I know, because I
live here. But this was the Northwich of the 1890s to the
1930s; it's quieted down a lot since then.*

—*R. A. W.*

FLIGHT

by

PETER DICKINSON

*(Notes on the transactions
between the Empire of Obanah —
latterly the People's Obate of Obanah —
and the White Rock Tribe.)*

HE EMPIRE of Obanah is normally dated as having been founded at the Battle of Festulu when the First Ob, known as the World Elephant, overcame the army of the Nineteen Nations and thus finally subjugated the vast and varied tract of land between the Dead Lakes and the northern desert.* Details of the battle are familiar from *the Glory of the Elephant* and need not be repeated here.

Immediately after the battle the Ob symbolically asserted his authority by issuing his first Sublime Decree, to the effect that all his peoples might henceforth continue to practice their own religions and customs and use their ancient laws, with two additions. First, they must incorporate worship of the Ob as the ultimate truth of their faiths. Second, that they must pay taxes to the Ob according to no less than their capacity. His officials were instructed to carry out the Decree with tact, followed by firmness.

---

*No apology is made for including facts which are theoretically "known to every schoolboy." The ideological struggle of the last few decades has meant so much rewriting of history on both sides of the ocean that even the events of A.O.1 cannot be taken for granted. The present writer feels he can afford objectivity only because it seems unlikely that these words will be published.

The instruction was interpreted in this manner: The priests of each tribe were approached and the Decree and instruction were explained to them. They were then told that the question of taxes would be settled first, and the degree of firmness needed for that would be assumed also to apply when it came to the question of religion. A tribe which showed itself obstinate over taxes would be likely to be as obstinate over religion, and few priests would survive the ensuing application of firmness. The priests of the tribes which proved reasonable over tax matters would be allowed to decide in what manner Ob-worship should be incorporated in their rituals.

Two examples of how the system worked in practice will suffice. The prosperous trading tribes of the Mud River Basin already worshiped a God-king, whom they kept unseen for five years, and then had ritually drowned by priestesses who had been blinded at birth so that even they should not break the tabu while performing their sacred function. The longer the king took to die, the better would trade be in the next five-year cycle. Here an apparent problem was overcome by incorporating into the chant of the priestesses a few lines proclaiming that not even a God-king was an adequate substitute for the Ob, and the fact of his dying showed this to be so. In view of the level of taxes raised in the Mud River Basin, this was considered acceptable.

The farmers who cultivated the rich volcanic soil on the slopes of the then-dormant ranges of West Parue worshipped a twenty-four-breasted goddess with most of the ordinary fertility rituals in a somewhat exaggerated form, including the duty of each head of household to copulate publicly with the goddess at the full moon. Obvious difficulties arose, but the Parue economy was just as obviously capable of supporting a high tax burden. There seemed likely to be an impasse until an official asked how the farmers got the strength to perform their holy feat, and it was tentatively suggested that like so much else in farming it probably came from the sun. The Ob then allowed it to be known that he was already the Sun on Earth and when, if ever he died, it would be in order to become the Sun in Heaven. Honor was thus saved, religion confirmed, and finance put on a serious footing.

Inevitably certain tribes proved obstinate. The most tragic of these were the bean-eating people of an island in Kala Lake called Tenu-Tenu. They had the misfortune not to believe in any God at all, maintaining that life was purposeless, that there was no after-life, and the only sensible course was to pass the time agreeably. For the Tenui this chiefly meant perfecting the techniques of the nose-flute, on which they performed with a skill never since approached. One might think there was no problem in such a people adopting some undemonstrative form of Ob-worship. The Ob himself appreciated music and maintained a band of nose-flautists. But the Tenui were convinced that the smallest departure from their faith in the pointlessness of life would impair the purity of their music. In view of their intransigence and the general indigence of bean-eaters, the Ob confirmed the dictates of his Decree and the Tenui ceased to exist. The order was carried out, even to the court musicians.

These, and hundreds of other dealings with the tribes, are detailed in the long and seldom-read central section of *The Glory*. It may be thought that a work which existed only in the oral tradition for eight hundred years must be of little historical value, but this is not the case. When the World Elephant ordered the composition of *The Glory*, his main object was not self-aggrandizement but the creation of a permanent record of the administrative details of his empire, especially those concerning taxation. Every means was used to make the verse both memorable and difficult to alter. Systems of patterning were invented so that any change would show up in a lack of symmetry with lines and items elsewhere. It is also possible to see when any section is missing.

One such section concerns this paper. It is the only one of which it is possible to say with certainty was missing from the very beginning. The poets left the oral equivalent of a blank in their great work, expecting to fill it in when the Ob had finally brought to heel the one recalcitrant tribe in all his dominions, usually referred to as the White Rock Tribe.*

He never did, and nor did any of his successors.

The first chapter of the story is found in the document wrongly known as *The Secret Glory*. This was composed on orders from the Ob and contains details of his reign which he did not choose to be publicly known. While it remained in the oral tradition, it was chanted only once in the reign of each Ob, the night after his return from the funeral ceremonies of the Obo.**

With the invention of writing, one manuscript was made to be read once to each succeeding Ob. It has to this day never been published, but Professor Duninga, while in power during the brief interregnum before the inauguration of the People's Obate, insisted on inspecting it. He was convinced of its authenticity, and told the present writer that it contains interesting facts about the rise of the World Elephant to supreme power, including details of the deaths of his nine elder brothers. This account of the meeting between the World Elephant and the White Rock Tribe derives from conversations with the late professor during his exile.

In the ninth year of his reign the World Elephant was on tour

---

*The name by which they called themselves is unknown.
**Old Obango had unusually few true verbs, but nouns had temporal suffixes (*cf* ex-wife, emeritus professor). Ob was an archaic word for elephant. When the 12th Ob died in the manner which will be described, he became the Obo, or was-elephant; when the 13th died he took over that title and the 12th became the Obolo, or exceedingly-was-elephant. The Algabio, or State Council, which confirmed the succession of the 15th Ob, chose as part of its duties on that blood-soaked occasion the sobriquet by which the 12th would henceforth be referred to, the Idiot. The gap between death and choice of sobriquet accounts for the fact that many Obi are known by names they would not have chosen for themselves.

in the Pargalate of Quassa, bordering the desert in the far northeast of his dominions. On his way he received homage and worship both from his own officials, including the Pargal, and the tribes he ruled through them. He listened to intertribal disputes and other complaints and settled them according to his conceptions of justice and mercy. At one such session a wizened little aboriginal wormed his way between the legs of officials and began to screech in an incomprehensible language. The officials tried to hustle him away, but the Ob, discerning from their demeanor that they were not simply embarrassed by the savage's lack of court manners, insisted on an interpreter being found.

It turned out a simple-seeming case. The man belonged to a tribe of baboon-eaters. Being too old to snare food for himself he depended on his son, who had recently been killed by men of a neighboring tribe dropping stones on the young man's head.

"In that case," said the Ob, "let the chief of this other tribe stand before us and say his say."

The officials shuffled. By Sublime Decree all parties to any intertribal dispute must be available to stand before the Ob and receive his mercy or justice. Again the Ob discerned that here was more than a matter of his officials' shame at their incompetence or terror of the Decree.

"What is the name of this tribe?" he asked.

The officials did not know, though hitherto they had conducted the tour with exemplary attention to such details.

"Where do they live?" asked the Ob, in what *The Secret Glory* describes as his dangerous small voice.

Nobody knew even that until the old man was asked and pointed northeast.

"Perhaps there is good hawking in that direction," said the Ob. "Let preparations be made."

So, after two-and-a-half-days' riding through scrub and then desert, the World Elephant set eyes for the first and last time upon White Cliff, a broad pillar of limestone rising from the plain for several hundred feet, with almost vertical sides. It was the only feature of its kind between horizon and horizon. As they rode nearer, the old baboon-eater who had been their guide tried to refuse to go on.

"Have him bound and carried," said the Ob. "Those are big vultures."

"Eagles, perhaps, your brightness," said a courtier.

The Ob reined in to study the black shapes that spiraled in the updraught round the pillar, sharp against the blue of sky or the white of stone.

"Neither," he said. "My Lord Pargal, why did you not tell me you had birds of such size in your territory?"

Since the court hearing, the Pargal of Quassa must have felt that his limbs were hanging very loose in their sockets. Even the Mailed Fist families, the nucleus of the army with which the Ob had won his empire, were not immune from the penalties of breaking a Sublime Decree.

"I have never seen them, your brightness," he stammered.

A little later, when four of the creatures came swooping towards the riders, the old baboon-eater shrieked with fear. The Ob told his retinue to halt and rode forward with the Pargal at his side.

"Those are not birds, my lord," he said.

The creatures swooped extremely fast, black triangles against the glare of the noon sky. It was only in the last few seconds of their flight that the Ob was able to make out that each was in fact an enormous kite which carried a naked man in a harness fastened to its struts. A round object the size of two clenched fists dangled from the mouth of each man. The Ob raised an arm in salute. Two kites swooped directly over him, the kite-riders opening their mouths to drop their loads. One grazed the Pargal's knee. The other smashed into the neck of the Ob's mare and broke it.

The Pargal leaped down, seized the dazed Ob by the shoulder and in spite of his majestic weight heaved him onto his own saddle, slashing his glove across the horse's haunches to send it galloping out of danger. He himself ran back, zigzagging and covering his head with his shield. The two kite-riders who had dropped their loads were already gliding towards the cliff but the others had circled for a second strike. Both missed the Pargal, but narrowly. He found the Ob sitting placidly among his retinue, watching the cliff.

The Ob spoke as follows.

"The Lord Pargal of Quassa owes us many lives. For the breaking of our Sublime Decree arms and legs were destined to quit their sockets. We have been led unwarned into peril of our life. Hands have been laid on our divine person. Most heinously we have been kept in ignorance of a people that has not welcomed our rule, paid our taxes, worshiped our brightness. How many sons and brothers and cousins should die for these crimes? A thousand? Ten thousand? Let someone else count. In return we owe the Pargal a horse. Hear then our decree. The Pargal is deposed from his Pargalate of Quassa. We create this White Rock and the desert for a hundred thousand paces around it a separate Pargalate, the White Rock Pargalate. Of this the deposed Pargal of Quassa shall be Pargal, with the additional title of Watcher of the Rock. He and his sons hereafter. And if any set foot outside the boundaries of their Pargalate before I or one of my sons set foot on the summit of White Rock, all those lives shall be at once forfeit. The Decree is Sublime."

The Pargal* kissed the earth and began to grovel for the customary nine hours. Meanwhile the Ob and his retinue rode a circuit round White Rock, testing the kite-riders' range by

---

*The meagerness of their province's resources meant that the Pargali of White Rock were unable to keep up the state due to that title, and were thus normally referred to by their secondary title as Watchers. The custom continued even after their sudden access of wealth in the 29th Obate.

keeping a series of scouts between themselves and the cliff. Two courtiers had the honor to die thus protecting their sovereign, three had broken bones, and some horses were lost.

The Ob studied the nature of the cliff. It was all nearly vertical, but wherever there was a hint of a slope terraces had been built. Groups of stone huts clung to the cliff like the combs of wild bees. On ledges too small to terrace grazed dark brown sheep herded by children, who swooped from cranny to cranny on their own small kites, like house-martins. All the while the Ob rode, kite-riders came swooping out, starting from a height well above the cliff-top, slanting toward their target, dropping their missiles (round stones carried in cradles of thongs) whether they reached it or not, and gliding back toward the cliff. They knew their range to within a few paces and would be almost at ground level before the updraft caught them and they could spiral again for height. The updraft seemed constant, though not equal on all sides of the pillar. Nowhere was there any sign of a place where the lower parts of the cliff could be climbed.

The Ob said nothing all this while, and nothing when he rode away that evening, leaving the Watcher to begin his duties when his nine hours' groveling was over. Only one further comment by him on the White Rock problem is recorded.*

Such was the first contact between the Empire and the White Rock Tribe. The reader must not think that because this paper is concerned with such contacts they were in any way central to the history of Obanah. Apart from two or three episodes they were to the highest degree marginal. To take a century at random, the sixth was a period of grand events, ranging from the revolt of Asku and the consequent Year of Three Obi to the

---

*Few Obi can have paid much attention to the details of this document, as by tradition the chanting accompanied the ritual in which the new Ob demonstrated his right to six selected wives of his predecessor.

discovery of the continent of Kastu by Admiral Nang and the disastrous currency collapse that followed the importation of fleetloads of cheap ivory. We have written records for the sixth century, besides the two epics of Sridan Sridan. Neither in the dry official documents nor in the apparently world-embracing vision of the literary genius is there one mention of White Rock. Many Obi must have lived out their reigns and not given the problem a moment's thought, hearing the name mentioned only once, during the ritual chanting of *The Secret Glory*.

And yet, despite immense lapses, the problem can be said to have nagged. The last words of the World Elephant provide a metaphor for this continuous if subliminal irritation. During his forty-eight-year reign he was entirely occupied with other matters, but as he lay dying, surrounded by his Algai, he was heard to sigh. The Algangha was then a certain Chinak Chinuka, renowned for the subtlety of his counsel. He made a sign to silence the chanter who was relating the list of the conquests of the World Elephant.

"What ails the brightness?" asked Chinak.

"We have not conquered all," whispered the dying Ob.

"Between the Dead Lakes and the Desert ten thousand tribes quail before the brightness," said Chinak.

"But not the White Rock Tribe," said the Ob.

"Hear my poor counsel," said Chinak. "By Sublime Decree all tribes in the Empire pay tribute to the Ob and worship his brightness, or they cease to exist. A Sublime Decree is all-powerful. It follows that a tribe that does not so worship and pay tribute does not exist."

The Ob lay silent. Then he was seen to smile.

"In the next hour," he said, "we propose to return to heaven and become the sun. We shall no doubt be in need of subtle counsel. Let the Algangha Chinak Chinuka precede us. The Decree is Sublime."

The Chinak Doctrine, despite inauspicious beginnings, may be said to have prevailed during the reigns of the next ten Obi, during which no information is recorded concerning the White Rock Tribe. The one possible exception is a ballad known as "The Wild Bird." Professor Duninga left notes among his papers arguing that this dealt with an incident concerning White rock, though the few other scholars who have studied it have usually done so only in order to demonstrate how its boring and repetitive obscurities prove the decline in the poetic art since the composition of *The Glory*. Professor Duninga's reading of the event behind the ballad is as follows:

In a freak desert storm a child of the White Rock Tribe was blown from the cliffs on his kite and captured by termite-gatherers, who took him to their overlord, the Watcher. The Watcher gave orders that the child should be tamed and educated. For a long while he fought his captors with the blank frenzy of a bird, but at length he forgot his wildness, accepted his fate, and learnt Obango. He then told the Watcher that his accident had befallen him because he had been given his first kite on the eve of his fifth birthday, on which day, by custom, he was to have made his first solo flight and ceased to be a baby. Because of the coming storm the ceremony was postponed, but in his disappointment he had stolen out and tried to fly alone and thus been swept beyond help. The Watcher then asked if he could build himself a new kite and he replied that he thought he could. The wreckage of his old one was there for a model, and he had only watched his father build and repair kites, but had flown with him to learn the skill. At any rate he succeeded well enough in his task. He was then ornamented with silver bracelets and leg-rings, taught messages of peace and taken by night to the foot of the rock. From a safe distance the Watcher saw the kite catch the dawn updraft and spiral upwards beside the cliff to land by some huts. Some hours later four kites came gliding out. Seeing that the men bore in their teeth what seemed to be the usual missiles the Watcher kept beyond their known range. They dropped their burdens perfunctorily and swung back towards their eyrie. Riding forward the Watcher saw that the answer to his messages consisted of two forearms and two lower legs, still wearing their silver rings and bracelets.*

With the death of the 12th Ob, the Idiot, we are on surer ground. The evidence comes partly from the Annals (transcribed three centuries after the event from the oral record) and partly from a more extensive boast-ballad composed in honor of the important Mailed Fist family of Shohu-Ga.

Though there can be no doubt that the 12th Ob came from the true lineage of the World Elephant, he was a sport, displaying features uncharacteristic of his race. He seems to have been an idealist and dreamer. He shocked his contemporaries by his practice of monogamy, and it is plausible to suppose that owing to this aberration he was actually listening when *The Secret Glory* was chanted to him. At any rate on his first tour of the Northeast he insisted on visiting the Pargalate of White Rock, normally omitted from the itinerary on account of its remoteness and poverty, besides its being a standing insult to the ruler, a blotch on the brightness of the Ob.

The Watcher received his sovereign with gratification, and was able to explain the difficulties of carrying out military operations against a natural fortress when the supposedly taxable populace of the Pargalate consisted of a few baboon-eaters and termite-gatherers. The Ob listened, and then gravely suggested that against an obstacle impervious to assault by force the greater and more beautiful power of love should be tried.

Next morning, against vehement advice, he left his retinue

---

*The reader should remember that the ballad is very obscure and Professor Duninga's reading of it both speculative and controversial. Other scholars believe that it refers to a different incident involving some other tribe.

beyond the limits of flight and went forward alone, unarmed, wearing his ceremonial sun-robe and gold-plumed headdress. When the kite-riders swooped out towards him he raised both arms in greeting and walked on. To the relief of his courtiers and the astonishment of the Watcher, the kite-riders made no attempt to harm him, but swirled out in increasing numbers from the cliff and escorted him as he strode on. Only when the retinue rode in to join their lord were they driven off with showers of boulders.

The Ob reached the foot of the cliff. Ropes were let down and he was hauled to the lowest group of huts. From there, sometimes carried shoulder high, sometimes swung from point to point on rope cradles, he was seen to climb through increasing antlike swarms of the White Rock people toward the summit of the cliff. With deep emotion his followers saw him stand at last on that precipitous brink. They waved and cheered. The White Rock folk also appeared highly excited, though they soon withdrew reverently clear of his brightness. He himself did not move and gave no sign. He was still standing there when the kite-riders left him, sudden as a flight of flock-birds, gliding down to their homes. The sunset glinted off his robe and headdress. Then came the rapid desert dusk and he could be seen no more.

It was possible, the retinue told themselves, that the Ob, who had his own methods of worship, had chosen this majestic spot for a solitary vigil. They maintained the thesis with lessening conviction next day, and next night. On the third morning they discerned by the sag of his body that he was held upright by being bound to some kind of post. Also his attendants were now vultures.

The Shohu-Ga boast-ballad, already referred to, does not deal directly with these events. It describes the confirmation ceremony of the 15th Ob, one part of which was the choice of a sobriquet for the 12th Ob, a matter over which there turned out to be unusual controversy. The representatives of the Dalalithi family argued that the Sublime Decree of the World Elephant was now satisfied, in that one of his descendants had stood on the summit of White Rock and its people had worshiped him according to their custom. Dalalithi therefore proposed the sobriquet of the Saint, because by his self-sacrifice the 12th Ob had redeemed his race from lasting dishonor. An unstated corollary of this argument was that the Pargal of White Rock, the Watcher, who though poor came from a bloodline that tended to breed very beautiful men and women and was for this reason related to Dalalithi through several marriages, would now be free to leave his barren Pargalate, resume his ancestral lands and honors, and at last pay a number of remitted dowries.

The representative of Shohu-Ga moved a counter-resolution, that the 12th Ob should henceforth be known as the Idiot, for reasons the speaker considered too obvious to be worth stating. One of these reasons was no doubt that Shohu-Ga now held the Pargalate of Quassa. Numbers on either side of the motion were roughly equal, but Shohu-Ga and their allies had smuggled more swords into the Algabio. The outcome is, of course, history.

No real attempt seems to have been made to avenge the death of the Idiot. In his brief reign he had offended powerful interests, in particular his brother the 13th Ob, by failing to leave the six wives necessary to complete the ritual inaugurating the next reign. To heap insult on insult, the Idiot's single wife hanged herself rather than participate in the ceremony. For this and other reasons White Rock was left with none but the Watcher to watch it for five more reigns. Then the terrible interregnum, usually referred to as the Qualabba, swept the Empire.

Because the Qualabba is claimed by the People's Obate as a precursor of their own revolution, no event in Obango history has been subject to so much rewriting and reinterpretation on both sides of the Great Ocean. For this reason a brief and objective account will be given here. The Qualabba was in essence a religious crusade of peculiar ferocity. It began with the eruption of Mount Parue and the chain of sister-volcanoes in the southwest. This great natural disaster smothered farmlands over a wide area with a deep layer of barren ash, but its effects were not merely local. There were unprecedented rains and floods elsewhere, as well as several earthquakes. Such upheavals are bound to occur in a great and varied empire, but this time they were compounded by the arrival on the scene of a prophet—a prophet who, despite the strangeness and fervor of his beliefs, turned out to be a military and administrative genius.

This man, whose name was Agbag, seems genuinely to have foreseen the Parue eruptions and to have warned his fellow farmers against them in explicit terms. He had already gathered a small band of followers, and naturally the fulfillment of his prophecy added immensely to his prestige, and the widespread ruin, misery, and discontent resulting from the eruptions provided him with a horde of fresh recruits. Ploughshares were beaten into swords and the Qualabba began.

The details of Agbag's creed were straightforward. He had been shown in a dream that the world was a great yam, whose destiny was to be eaten by the Celestial Hog. But the yam was infested with maggots in the shape of humans. Not until the yam was cleansed of the maggots would the Celestial Hog consent to eat it and thus inaugurate the true, spiritual life of the universe. Therefore it was the duty of all believers to further this process. Their only excuse for not beginning with themselves was that this would leave the world still infested by unbelievers. The unbelievers had to be slaughtered first, and then the beautified Army of the Hog could unite in a glorious mass suicide.

The Empire was ripe for such a movement. The Algabio was split into feuding factions and had virtually ceased to function since the bloodletting at the confirmation of the 15th Ob, and had been replaced by inefficient, corrupt, and frivolous coteries of court favorites. Recent Obs had taken little interest in the duties of government, being preoccupied with a doctrine of Ob-worship started under the 13th Ob, the Fruitful, in an endeavor to compensate for the deficiencies of the 12th. Under this doctrine the prime ritual function of the Ob was to beget at least one son upon a woman from every distinct tribe in the Empire. The woman, once pregnant, was sent back to her tribe to bring forth the Sun-begotten among her own people. Had modern statistical techniques been available it would have been possible to demonstrate that the Obi had, in the Parue proverb, bought more fields than their oxen could plough.

But even allowing for social breakdown in the provinces and collapse of government at the center it must have been hard for contemporaries not to feel that the Qualabba was somehow divinely ordained and directed. Every decision Agbag made, until the closing stages of his campaign, must have seemed inspired. His first move took him not towards the apparently easy cattle-plains of eastern Parue, but south into the red hill country into which the great range degenerates. Here he converted isolated tribes of metal-workers, sweeping their smith-priests into his army to provide weapons. Moving on south-westward into the rain forests—a direction no serious military analyst would have contemplated—he erupted onto the banks of the Ulu River at the exact season at which the Ului held the remarkable firework oracle by which they had long maintained dominance over the network of lesser tribes surrounding them.

It is typical of Agbag's intuitive genius, his eclectic but synthetic approach to the problem of slaughtering all mankind, that he should have at once ordered his converted smith-priests to cooperate with those of the Ului in producing new weapons. Many of both died ("were cleansed" in the jargon of the Qualabba) during what would now be called the crash program of experimentation, but when four months later Agbag faced at Dalikiliki, the first serious army sent south by the Ob to suppress his revolt, he did so with nine cannons. After their brief bombardment the wild charge of the fanatics was enough to overwhelm an army ten times the size of Agbag's.

Only after Dalikiliki does Agbag seem to have grasped the scale of the problem his vision had set him. Hitherto his method had been the crude one of slaughtering everybody but those capable of bearing weapons and willing to be converted, but confronted with the mass of the Empire he perceived that he would need an administrative structure with which to command and control its obliteration. In two years, out of nothing, he contrived the most efficient and least corruptible bureaucracy Obanah was ever to know. In order to control it, direct his armies, and supervise the elaborate supply system needed to maintain those armies in the field, Agbag expanded and adapted the old crop notation system of Parue into the form of writing which is fundamentally that we still use today. He chose generals and officials without regard for lineage, tribe, or wealth, but solely for the combination of ability with fanaticism.*

But however remarkable the total edifice, it was all built with a single purpose, that every human within the borders of the Empire (to Agbag every human in the known world) should submit one way or another to the Qualabba, and then the final cleansing would begin.

Like the World Elephant, he succeeded in his aim, with the exception of a single tribe.

The Qualabba came late to White Rock, but it would be untrue to say that its energies were spent. It was still at the

---

*E.g., the leper-general Zaaxa, who was so wasted with his disease that his arms and legs were stumps and he had to be strapped into his saddle and led to the battlefield. His campaigns are still thought relevant in the military academies of both Obanah and Kastu.

height of its power. The first reports sent back to Agbag evidently did not make the nature of the problem clear. He gave orders that the rock must be stormed and its people converted or massacred, then turned his mind to larger campaigns. Only six years later, when these were successfully completed, did the Prophet set eyes on White Rock. It must not be thought that the local leaders of the Qualabba had pursued their campaign with the same ineffectualness that the original Watcher had shown in response to the orders of the World Elephant. Far from it. What seems to have caught Agbag's attention was the disproportionate expenditure of resources, mainly in the shape of human lives, which this remote and minor campaign had cost the Qualabba. So he came to see for himself.

For once the fervor of Agbag's inner vision blinded him to outer realities. Perhaps it was difficult, even for a soldier of genius, to grasp the idea that a small and primitive tribe was accidentally equipped to resist the armies that had conquered an empire. Be that as it may, his vision told him that here was the final obstacle to his crusade. He publicly pronounced that the Qualabba would end at White Rock. When that had fallen all Obanah would have fallen and the great and longed-for self-slaughter would begin. The summit of the rock was the destined place for the death of the last man on Earth, the prophet himself. All the armies of the Qualabba were summoned to fulfill this destiny.

As with many a great soldier before and since, the nature of Agbag's genius had changed. The dash and audacity of his early campaigns had given way to skill in maneuvering enormous masses of men and material. Efficiency had replaced intuition, force daring. So now skill, efficiency, and force were deployed. The photographs of Kastuan spy-planes show clearly the three most astonishing relics of the siege, the vast and uncompleted ramp, the pit from which were dug the materials to build it, and the sixty kilometers of paved causeway along which were dragged the supplies to feed and equip the army of

laborers and soldiers. At the height of the effort Professor Duninga claimed that the actual besiegers may have numbered
just under two hundred thousand men. Let it be remembered
that the nearest river is 140 kilometers away and that the scattered waterholes in the desert can mostly be drunk dry by a
train of ten camels. These figures may suggest the cost in human energy needed to sustain an army that size on so inac-
cessible a front. The whole strength of the Qualabba was
sucked into the final effort, so that elsewhere in the Empire
the first faint stirrings of recovery were able to begin.

The effort was not enough. As the photographs show, the
ramp stopped short about eighty meters from its destination.
Agbag's plan foundered upon the laws of mass and gravitation.
When the work began, five hundred meters out across the desert, he was able to protect his laborers from the stone-dropping
tactics of the kite-riders by working at night and building shel-
ters which moved forward as the ramp progressed. But the
closer the work moved to the cliff, the greater the weight of
missile a kite could carry, and could drop, what's more, from a
greater height. No material available to Agbag would withstand
the impact of a stone weighing twenty kilograms and dropped
from a hundred meters. The effectiveness of the kite-riders'
bombing may still seem improbable, but there are innumerable
records, first in the old annals of the hereditary Watchers, then
in the library of White Rock University, and latest of all in the
reports of the White Rock Observation Project, of the custom
of the kite-riders (whether as ritual or game is not known) of
choosing targets on the plain below and dropping stones on
them with great accuracy. Another measure of their primitive
skill is the recorded fact that when Agbag restricted work on
the ramp to the hours of darkness, even on moonless nights
the kite-riders were able to prevent its advance by bombing the
target, as it were, by memory. Though there is probably little or
no updraft from the cliff by night, the ramp by now was close
enough for a kite-rider to leap from the cliff summit, glide
down until he was over the slope up which the laborers toiled

with their loads, and glide back to some perch well above the level of the plain. Any structure erected to protect the slope was destroyed at leisure by daytime bombing.

The ramp was only the main prong of the assault. Continual attempts were made by scaling parties with ladders and grappling irons, and occasional footholds were gained during the nights, but could never be sustained by day. Where one of the lower clusters of huts was captured, no advance could be made from it because of the lack of communication between cluster and cluster, except by flight.

By now Agbag's army had muskets, but the state of the art was too primitive for accurate aim at a flying man, where one came within range. Agbag ordered the construction of mortars, the largest of which had a caliber just over a meter and was known as Dongalongu, or the Voice of the Hog. The trajectory of the missiles hurled by these weapons was high enough to attack the huts of the kite-riders, but only when they were fired from within range of counterattack by the kite-riders. Agbag could afford the loss of innumerable ordinary soldiers, but not of the skilled artillerymen of the Ului.

Another normal technique of siege, starvation, did not apply. In fact the besiegers were in worse condition than the besieged.* Several attempts at tunneling were made, starting

---

*The mystery of the White Rock water supply was not solved until the spy-plane photographs, already referred to, were available for study. They show that the upper surface of the great pillar is saucer-shaped, the outer slopes being covered by terraces, but the main basin being bare rock pocked with several hundred pits, manmade or man-enlarged. There is no rainy season in the desert, only rare and violent thunderstorms, but the tremendous updraft from the rock interrupts the flow of air that carries these rainclouds. The resulting downpours, though still not frequent, must have been sufficient to keep the water-pits supplied through dry spells. For instance, no rain is believed to have fallen on the rock during the Great Drought of A.O.1087-9, but the White Rock Observation Project, of which Professor Duninga was then Director, could detect no alteration in the behavior of the inhabitants. Some surfaces of the cliff display signs of water erosion, but the aerial photographs

with a nighttime push to hack far enough into the cliff to be under its protection by daybreak, but as soon as the entrances to these tunnels were apparent it became possible for the kite-riders to block them with boulders tumbled from the cliff top and by the same means to prevent attempts to shift the blockage. A tunnel begun from further out, approaching the cliff below the desert surface, was still uncompleted after several cave-ins when the Qualabba came to its abrupt end.

Catastrophe theory might explain the suddenness of the event. At one moment, despite immense losses, the siege was being maintained at full pressure, and the next it had melted away. The whole crusade had been powered by the infallibility of Agbag's vision. He had announced that the Qualabba would end when White Rock fell and could not go back from that. His word was as unquestionable as the Sublime Decree of an Ob. But his armies, as they toiled and died, must have steadily discovered the reality of the problem he had set them. Each setback, each failure, was a seed of doubt, and at last one of these seeds germinated.

Agbag was inspecting the Dongalongu. He was dissatisfied with its effect at extreme range and insisted on its being dragged towards the cliff, telling the gunners they were under the protection of the Celestial Hog. At first it seemed as if he spoke the truth, for the gun was hauled towards the cliff and set up without interference, but while the loading process was underway a flight of kite-riders swooped out towards it. The Dongalongu presented a large target with its train of oxen and their drivers and other laborers and attendants, but in the first rock-shower the four men who died were all Ului gunners.

---

show that the gullies cut into the rim by these overflows have been painstakingly blocked. Limestone is porous, so it is thought that the pits must have been lined with some impermeable material, but enough moisture seeps through elsewhere to sustain the vegetation on the ledges used for grazing livestock. More elaborate systems of irrigation must have been used for the larger terracings, but how these worked is not known.

The Ului are a famously unexcitable people, greeting even the explosion of a firework factory with a shrug and a proverb. The remaining gunners muttered for a moment in Ulu, then seized the prophet, stuffed him into the mouth of the Dong-alongu, and fired the touchhole. His guards, apparently, watched without interfering. So, as Agbag had prophesied, the Qualabba ended with his own dead body on the summit of White Rock.

The tide of the crusade retreated over an empire in chaos. Such tribes as remained struggled back into being, but of the 416 languages which are reported from before the slaughter, fewer than 200 have since been spoken. The bloodshed did not immediately cease. Regiments of fanatics roamed the land "cleansing all they met." Two such bodies met by accident at Qus-qus and without discussion embarked on a process of mutual slaughter so intensive that within an hour only three men out of four thousand were left alive. The revival of the Obate in such circumstances might well be considered a miracle, and was certainly regarded as such by orthodox believers for centuries to come. Stripped of supernatural trimmings this is what seems to have happened:

The priestesses of Mud River had been engaged on the cinquennial drowning of their God-king when the warriors of the Qualabba burst onto the scene and slaughtered everyone in sight. The one person not in sight was the God-king himself, being under water. A priestess had just inserted a reed in his mouth to revive him, so he was able to breathe. It took him time to realize that the ritual had gone amiss, and then to free himself from his bonds and emerge. By then the Qualabba had swept on. The drowning pool being set in dense scrub typical of the Mud River terrain, other members of the tribe had escaped slaughter. To them the return of their God-king—his successor being among those "cleansed"—must at first have seemed no more than a sign of hope, but as they continued to survive through occasional "after-cleansings" it became more than that. From the first the God-king's apparent death and resurrection were accepted as evidence of his divinity, without theological superstructure, but as the years of hiding went on a new mythology, adapted from the old, came into being. As has been mentioned, the Mud River priesthood had long ago accepted for political reasons the concept that their God-king was drowned for being an inadequate substitute for the Ob, but this had remained no more than peripheral to the ritual. Now it moved to the center. A God-king who had miraculously survived drowning must have done so as a sign that he was not an inadequate substitute. It followed that he must be the true Ob, and should be worshiped as such. It was even possible that the man was in a line of descent from the World Elephant, thanks to the activities of the 13th Ob and his successors in disseminating that line among the tribes. Among the orthodox such descent became dogma and genealogies were produced to support it.

Be that as it may, by the time a semblance of peace had settled on the old empire the legitimacy of the Mud River Ob was accepted over a wide area. This acceptance was partly due to the innate ability of the Mud River tribe to see opportunities for profitable trading, and thus to bring a standard of living above subsistence level to the areas with which they came in contact. Their recovery of the rest of the old empire was not achieved without military engagements, but the armies that fought for them were almost wholly composed of mercenaries. The Obi of the period after the Qualabba, known as the Middle Obate, ruled what was essentially a commercial empire. Though Mud River drains the furthest corner of the Empire from the desert where White Rock towers, the destiny of the kite-riders was deeply influenced by this fact, though they themselves can never have known it.

After the collapse of the Qualabba, White Rock was left alone. The termite-gatherers and baboon-eaters, who had survived the crusade by retreating yet further into the dry lands, returned to their old territory but kept well clear of the flight-limits. The heir of the hereditary Watcher had been sent with them for safety and now returned to take up his family's undemanding duties. Not until the reign of the 23rd Ob, the Golden, fourth of the Middle Obate, did a Watcher (who, it will be remembered, was forbidden by Sublime Decree to leave his Pargalate) pay homage to his sovereign. The Ob spent ten minutes just within the border, judged the place devoid both of threat to the Empire and of taxable resources, confirmed the Watcher in office, and left.

Four generations later rubies were discovered in the sacred gorge of the termite-gatherers. In fact both aboriginal tribes had long known of their existence—probably since before the time of the World Elephant—and had used them for ritual purposes.* It is possible that the Watchers had also known, at least since the sojourn of one of that line with the termite-gatherers during the Qualabba. For some generations they may have tried to protect their primitive subjects from the iron laws of commerce that now governed the Empire, but in the end those laws proved too strong. There were huge profits to be made, and the ethos of the times declared that to refuse to make them was not merely foolish and indolent, but actively sinful. One cannot but sympathize with the Watchers, looking across the frontiers of their Pargalate at the stupendous wealth of families who were not socially their superiors, but who were able to run their fiefs as prosperous trading concerns.

By this period Obangan economic theory had assimilated the lesson of the disastrous ivory inflation of the 27th Obate. There could be no question of allowing a Ruby Rush. By Sublime

---

*It now seems probable that both tribes were branches of a single culture. The rubies were used to send as peace-tokens between groups of both tribes, the messenger being a young girl who was then retained as a bride. This system, combined with the strict division of males into baboon-eaters and termite-gatherers, allowed a small and scattered population to minimize the dangers of interbreeding.

Decree the White Rock Pargalate was declared an aboriginal preserve with strictly controlled access. The borders were strongly policed and the activities of illicit ruby dealers suppressed with the very considerable degree of severity that has been a feature of the Obangan legal system since its inception. As cover for mining activities the University of White Rock was founded, its ostensible function being the study of the three desert tribes. It is a sad irony that by the time the soon immensely wealthy university began to take that part of its duties seriously, the termite-gatherers and baboon-eaters, deprived of their source of rubies in the sacred gorge and thus of their system of bride-exchange, were no longer there to be studied. But the total isolation of the White Rock tribe was now reinforced by a further ring of defences, and no serious attempt to intrude was made during the next two centuries.

There was one episode, however, which though hardly serious in itself, turned out to have enormous consequences. It has been mentioned as a peculiarity of the hereditary Watchers that their family tended to produce children of outstanding physical beauty. Since the discovery of the ruby seam, and the consequently more frequent visits of reigning Obi to that remote Pargalate, daughters of the house had been numbered among the royal wives with great regularity. The visit of the 33rd Ob, the Earthbound, for his installation as Chancellor of the University was not expected to produce any such result, as the monarch was known to cross with reluctance the threshold of the Queens' Palace. But his eye lit on the eldest son of the then Watcher and his passion was at once inflamed. "We came for rubies," he is said to have announced, "but we will take hence a jewel beyond jewels." Concealing his dismay the Watcher pointed out that by Sublime Decree his son was forbidden to cross the border of the Pargalate, under pain of dismemberment. (It was for this reason, no doubt, that he had risked his monarch setting eyes on the boy in the first place.) The Ob responded by countermanding the Decree. His accompanying Algai tried to argue that this was an unconstitutional maneuver, undermining for the whim of a moment the Sublimity of all other decrees. So shocked were they that they appear to have gone beyond the limits of prudence, and the Ob is said to have led the boy to his couch that night up a staircase composed of their headless bodies.*

The boy left the Pargalate next morning, the first male of his line to cross the border for over twenty generations. He seems to have been a lively and athletic lad and to have appreciated the opportunities presented by his royal lover's restless journeyings round his dominions. He was physically hardy, a daring horseman and sportsman, always eager for adventure.

Next spring the royal cortege was passing through the magnificent mountain scenery of North Parue and the boy saw the great pink buzzards soaring among their native cliffs. Their mode of flight reminded him of the kite-riders of White Rock, and he perceived that here were updrafts in which he might himself learn to fly. It will be remembered that the University of White Rock had been set up ostensibly to study the tribes of the desert, but by the time it started on the task only the White Rock tribe was left to study, and that at a distance precluding normal anthropological methods. The work was thus channeled into what could be done, and this included theoretical study of modes of flight. The absence of a similar outcrop in the desert and the travel restrictions imposed by the need to control ruby-smuggling had precluded practical experiments. The boy, it will also be remembered, was the child of generations of Watchers of the Rock. He would not casually have noticed the flight of the kite-riders. He would have studied it keenly and, that being his nature, yearned to emulate it.

The Ob refused his favorite nothing. The Professor of Aero-

---

*This anecdote must be treated with caution. It first occurs in pamphlets published by the Kastuan Independence Movement, as a typical example of the tyranny of the Obate.

dynamics was summoned from the University and ordered to convert theory to practice, which he soon did, at the cost of no more than a dozen lives. The Ob kept his lover chained to his person during these early experiments, but once the major problems were solved the boy was permitted to make the attempt himself. Soon he was reveling in the freedom of air, and the sport became popular in court circles. Refinements were quickly made in apparatus and technique and a considerable degree of skill was attained.

From the first, no doubt, the boy had had the idea of making contact with the White Rock people, but for some years the lack of a takeoff point—the Rock itself not being available—made this impossible. The difficulty was overcome by Otokoko's invention of the high-pressure steam winch.* Six years after their first meeting the Ob and his favorite returned to White Rock Pargalate. The royal cortege, always immense, now included a corps of laborers and the materials to construct a track, plus trolleys and a winch.

Presumably the young man had minimized the danger of the enterprise. Perhaps after long adulation he had come to believe that there was no peril from which his lover's power could not protect him. Or perhaps, weary of endless protection, he deliberately sought a danger beyond the reach of that power. One must remember that by the heredity of centuries he was, as it were, programmed to watch the Rock for the day when one of his family could make contact with the kite-riders.**

---

*The history of the early industrial revolution lies largely outside the scope of this paper, but there is no doubt that the rapid development of the big steam-engines of the mining magnates into much lighter high-pressure engines capable of hauling railway wagons and so of transforming communication within the Empire stems from Otokoko's invention. Hitherto he had only designed and built elaborate stage machinery for court spectacles, but seized the opportunity to ingratiate himself by enabling the royal favorite to ride his kite in areas devoid of natural takeoff points.

**It must not be thought that no other attempts had been made. Time and again the Watchers, and later the scholars of the University, had tried the

Be that as it may, the Ob seems to have watched without apprehension as the winch chugged and gathered power, the gears were engaged and the trolley rattled at increasing speed along the track until the gold and purple kite soared upward, the young man clinging to the cable and not releasing it until he was high enough to glide all the way to the Rock and catch the updraft from its surface. The kite-riders let him spiral halfway to the summit before, swooping out of huts and caves and down from the tower of air, they closed round him like starlings round an owl. He carried pistols and daggers. Several dark kites tumbled to earth before the mob broke up. Tatters of gold and purple cloth floated in the wind as some of the kite-riders swooped out toward the Watchers and dropped their bloody burdens on the sand.

Professor Duninga told the present writer that he had long ago abandoned the effort to explain to his Kastuan hosts the genuine power held by ancient authority over even the most educated Obangan intellect, and the ritualistic thought structures that have persisted through the revolution and still pervade the People's Obate, both rulers and ruled. The effects, both short-term and long, of the death of the royal favorite provide examples of this. What seems to have impressed contemporaries even more than the grief of the monarch, emphatically though this was manifested, was the dramatic vindication of the original Sublime Decree of the World Elephant, issued nearly seven hundred years earlier. The heir of the first Watcher had left the Pargalate, and as a direct result had been torn limb from limb.

---

obvious approaches, such as bringing lures of food or trinkets by night to the foot of the cliff. These were invariably smashed with dropped stones.
Professor Duninga speculated that the kite-riders had a tabu against human contact with the plain or anything emanating from it. This would account for the ferocity of their reaction when creatures of the plain attempted to approach them, especially by flying up. Their treatment of the 12th Ob remains unexplained.

The Ob himself felt this. It was his own countermanding of the Decree that had caused his lover's death. The blood was on his head. Always a man of extreme gestures he retired into a period of mourning which lasted until his death twenty years later, but before doing so issued a Sublime Decree forbidding all forms of flying and all theoretical studies of manned flight. Such prohibitions were not unusual, witness the well-known decree against the eating of parrots' eggs—also issued on the death of a royal favorite though this time from indigestion— which provided the spark setting off the Kastu revolt of A.O.812, the severity of whose repression was responsible for the Kastu War of Independence and thus for the political map of the world as we see it today.

There were from the first both economic and geographic reasons reinforcing the Decree, chiefly those involving the dynamic expansion of the rail system, but it would be a mistake to ignore psychological factors. To this day senior members of the People's Algabio do not like it to be publicly known that they have engaged in air travel, and the hysterical reaction of the Obangan press to any increase in the Kastuan Air Force bears witness to the strength of this ancient phobia, and to the massive continuity of Obangan thought processes.*

Perhaps but for the thirty-six-year leadership of Chairman Abafang this phobia might have been overcome. The child of Paruan farmers, his peasantlike suspicion of strangers deepened into paranoia over the decades, his rule becoming a ferocious autocracy paralleled only in the reigns of the most

---

*A characteristic of political discussion in the People's Obate is that it is entirely carried out in historical terms. The more contentious the issue, the further back in time is the historical parallel chosen for discussion. Indeed the affairs of White Rock, never mentioned as a contemporary phenomenon, surfaced recently in the official media with a detailed if tendentious account of the death of the 12th Ob, not out of any interest in the tragedy itself, but as a warning against a faction in the People's Algabio which was arguing for the making of peaceful overtures towards Kastu.

bloodthirsty of the ancient Obi. In the light of the effectiveness of Kastuan air power during the Continental War, another leader might have decided to sanction the development of an Obangan Air Force. Instead, resources were poured into the field of rocketry, firstly as a defense against aerial attack but later, with that uncontrollable expansiveness which seems to be inherent in military establishments, into all possible fields of warfare. With Chairman Abafang's backing the research establishment at Ulu was able to survive the ludicrous series of failures and disasters of their early years. These also had the effect of lulling the Kastuan military into a false security, resulting in a sudden reversal in the balance of striking power between the continents from which Kastu is still striving to recover. The "accidental" arrival of a transoceanic missile at the 1113 Diggipuk Air Show signaled the change. It is the imbalance that is so dangerous. If both sides possessed matched and equal strength, the prospect of a Second Continental War would be no more than a nightmare, instead of an imminent event. This is the most serious consequence of the apparently trivial tale of the death of one young man in a remote province nearly four centuries ago.

We have run ahead of ourselves, because other consequences flowed from the event. The one which chiefly concerns us is the deliberate isolation of the White Rock Pargalate by the downgrading of the University to a merely ritual status, without pupils or faculty. All revenue from the ruby mine was sequestered and remained so until the seam was exhausted some eighty years later. The Pargalate reverted to being the most backward province of the Empire, of no interest at all to central government.

So it remained through the upheavals of the Kastu War of Independence, the social transformation of the later industrial revolution, and the Continental War. Even the terrible eruption of the Civil War and the triumph of the People's Obate at first barely touched it, beyond Professor Duninga's decision during his brief period of power to set up the White Rock Observation Project, and his retirement there as Director after his fall. Later the remnants of the royal armies took refuge in the desert and with erratic support from Kastu began the long and futile campaign of resistance whose only result has been to deepen the suspicions of the leadership of the People's Obate of all Kastuan overtures, and at the same time, if subliminally and through the medium of innumerable "Resistance" films, to inculcate in the ordinary Kastuan a belief that any fight between the Obate and pro-Kastuan forces is going to end, against all the odds, with the good guys winning. (In none of these films, incidentally, does a natural feature remotely resembling White Rock occur, though much trouble is taken to film them in locations resembling the northeastern desert.)

Nine years ago the White Rock people ceased to exist, except as a problem for historians and anthropologists. The minds of the People's Algabio, though less twisted than that of Chairman Abafang in his later years, remain opaque to Kastuan observers. It was natural for them to choose the almost uninhabited desert as the site for the first atomic explosion tests, natural too to adapt Professor Duninga's Observation Project and the buildings of the ancient university as the research base for the project, but it is impossible to tell whether it was by accident or design that the first devices were detonated immediately upwind of the great limestone pillar. No attempt was made to reduce fallout; indeed Professor Duninga told the present writer that he had reason to believe that the devices were deliberately made as "dirty" as possible, with the object of studying the effect on a human population.

At a point in history when it seems inevitable that both Kastu and Obanah will shortly succumb to the "cleansing" so earnestly desired by the fanatics of the Qualabba, it may appear perverse to regret the vanishing of one small tribe, with nothing known about its language, customs, beliefs, or economic and social structure. We have lost a remarkable opportunity to study a community unchanged since our remote ancestors learned to make their first weapons by chipping one flint with another. It is possible that the files of the People's Algabio contain a few lifeless details—some study does seem to have been carried out. In his last conversation with the present writer Professor Duninga said that his cousin (who would, but for the upheavals of the present century, have become hereditary Watcher of the Rock) was among those sent, apparently without protective clothing, into the deserted huts and caves. The Professor's cousin was not a physicist or biologist but an ethnologist. Naturally, communications between Obanah and Kastu being what they are, no detailed report has been made available this side of the ocean, but occasional brief messages still sometimes reach the network of Obangans in exile. The agent who tricked the Professor into keeping his fatal appointment carried such a message as his credentials. It purported to come from the Professor's cousin, who had been interned immediately after the completion of the report on fallout effects at White Rock, but had later been released when he himself developed radiation-induced leukemia. As he lay dying he asked a friend to carry a message to the Professor. In his conversation with the present writer, just referred to, the Professor appeared highly excited by the news.* He had no doubt about its authenticity, despite two previous attempts on his life by agents of the People's Obate, and was expecting to learn more later

---

*It may be worth mentioning that the present writer first came to know Professor Duninga while gathering material for his own book, *The Last Lost Chance,* which argues that it was Professor Duninga's over-attention to peripheral matters, such as the affairs of White Rock, which led to the overthrow of his Liberal Alliance and thus to the eventual triumph of the People's Obate. The Professor, while disputing the thesis with characteristic courtesy, admitted a life-long if minor obsession. "My mother's brother was the last Watcher," he said. "I spent many school holidays at White Rock. My eyes have seen what the World Elephant also saw, the kite-riders circling in their citadel of air."

that evening. In view of what we now know of the untrust-worthiness of the messenger, his trust in the message may seem misplaced, though its very peculiarity to some extent authenticates it. It was, in the Professor's words, as follows: "Their main crop was beans, and there was a nose-flute in every dwelling."

EVIAN
STEEL

by

JANE
YOLEN

Ynis Evelonia, the Isle of Women, lies within the marshy tidal river Tamar that is itself but a ribbon stretched between the Mendip and the Quantock hills. The isle is scarcely remarked from the shore. It is as if Manannan MacLir himself had shaken his cloak between.

On most days there is an unsettling mist obscuring the irregular coast of the isle; and only in the full sun, when the light just rising illuminates a channel, can any passage across the glass-colored waters be seen. And so it is that women alone, who have been schooled in the hidden causeways across the fen, mother to daughter down through the years, can traverse the river in coracles that slip easily through the brackish flood.

By ones and twos they come and go in their light skin boats to commerce with the Daughters of Eve who stay in holy sistership on the isle, living out their chaste lives and making with their magicks the finest blades mankind has ever known.

The isle is dotted with trees, not the great Druidic oaks that line the roadways into Godney and Meare and tower over the mazed pathways up to the high Tor, but small womanish trees: alder and apple, willow and ash, leafy

*havens for the migratory birds. And the little isle fair
rings with birdsong and the clanging of hammer on anvil
and steel.*

*But men who come to buy swords at Ynis Evelonia are
never allowed farther inland than the wattle guesthouse
with its oratory of wicker wands winded and twisted
together under a rush roof. Only one man has ever slept
there and is—in fact—sleeping there still. But that is the
end of this story—which shall not be told—and the
beginning of yet another.*

LAINE STARED OUT across the grey waters as the
ferret-faced woman rowed them to the isle. Her
father sat unmoving next to her in the prow of the
little boat, his hands clasped together, his jaw
tight. His only admonition so far had been, "Be strong. The
daughter of a vavasour does not cry."

She had not cried, though surely life among the magic
women on Ynis Evelonia would be far different from life in the
draughty but familiar castle at Escalot. At home women were
cosseted but no one feared them as they feared the Daughters
of Eve, unless one had a sharp tongue like the ostler's wife or
Nanny Bess.

Elaine bent over the rim of the hide boat and tried to see her
reflection in the water, the fair skin and the black hair plaited
with such loving care by Nanny Bess that morning. But all she
could make out was a shadow boat skimming across the waves.
She popped one of her braids into her mouth, remembering
Nanny's repeated warning that some day the braid would grow
there: "And what knight would wed a girl with hair a-growin'
in 'er mouth, I asks ye?" Elaine could hear Nanny's voice, now
sharp as a blade, now quiet as a lullaby, whispering in her ear.
She sighed.

At the sound her father looked over at her. His eyes, the

faded blue of a late autumn sky, were pained and lines like runes ran across his brow.

Elaine let the braid drop from her mouth and smiled tentatively; she could not bear to disappoint him. At her small attempt at a smile he smiled back and patted her knee.

The wind spit river water into her face, as salty as tears, and Elaine hurriedly wiped her cheeks with the hem of her cape. By the time the boat rocked against the shore her face was dry.

The ferret-faced woman leaped over the side of the coracle and pulled it farther onto the sand so that Elaine and her father could debark without wading in the muddy tide. When they looked up, two women in grey robes had appeared to greet them.

"I am Mother Lisanor," said the tallest one to the vavasour. "You must be Bernard of Escalot."

He bowed his head, quickly removing his hat.

"And this," said the second woman, taking Elaine by the hand, "must be the Fair Elaine. Come child. You shall eat with me and share my bed this night. A warm body shall keep away any bad dreams."

"Madame . . ." the vavasour began.

"*Mother* Sonda," the woman interrupted him.

"Mother Sonda, may my daughter and I have a moment to say good-bye? She has never been away from home before." There was the slightest suggestion of a break in his voice.

"We have found, Sir Bernard, that it is best to part quickly. I *had* suggested in my letter to you that you leave Elaine on the Shapwick shore. This is an island of women. Men come here for commerce sake alone. Ynis Evelonia is Elaine's home now. But fear you not. We shall train her well." She gave a small tug on Elaine's hand and started up the hill and Elaine, all unprotesting, went with her.

Only once, at the top of the small rise, did Elaine turn back. Her father was still standing by the coracle, hat in hand, the sun setting behind him. He was haloed against the darkening sky. Elaine made a small noise, almost a whimper. Then she popped the braid in her mouth. Like a cork in a bottle, it stoppered the sound. Without a word more, she followed Mother Sonda toward the great stone house that nestled down in the valley in the very center of the isle.

The room in the smithy was lit only by the flickering of the fire as Mother Hesta pumped the bellows with her foot. A big woman, whose right arm was more muscular than her left, Hesta seemed comfortable with tools rather than with words. The air from the bellows blew up a sudden large flame that had a bright blue heart.

"See, there. *There.* When the flames be as long as an arrow and the heart of the arrowhead be blue, thrust the blade in," she said, speaking to the new apprentice.

Elaine shifted from one foot to another, rubbing the upper part of her right arm where the brand of Eve still itched. Then she twisted one of her braids up and into her mouth, sucking on the end while she watched but saying nothing.

"You'll see me do this again and again, girl," the forge mistress said. "But it be a year afore I let you try it on your own. For now, you must watch and listen and learn. Fire and water and air make Evian Steel, fire and water and air. They be three of the four majorities. And one last thing—though I'll not tell you that yet, for that be our dearest secret. But harken: what be made by the Daughters of Eve strikes true. All men know this and that be why they come here, crost the waters, for our blades. They come, hating it that they must, but knowing only at our forge on this holy isle can they buy this steel. It be the steel that cuts through evil, that strikes the heart of what it seeks."

The girl nodded and her attention blew upon the small fire of words.

"It matters not, child, that we make a short single edge, or what the old Romies called a *glady-us*. It matters not we make a long blade or a double edge. If it be Evian Steel, it strikes true." She brought the side of her hand down in a swift movement which made the girl blink twice, but otherwise she did not move, the braid still in her mouth.

Mother Hesta turned her back on the child and returned to work, the longest lecture done. Her muscles under the short-sleeve tunic bunched and flattened. Sweat ran over her arms like an exotic chain of water beads as she hammered steadily on the sword, flattening, shaping, beating out the swellings and bulges that only *her* eye could see, only her fingers could find. The right arm beat, the left arm, with its fine traceries of scars, held.

After a while, the girl's eyes began to blink with weariness and with the constant probings of the irritating smoke. She dropped the braid and it lay against her linen shirt limply, leaving a slight wet stain. She rubbed both eyes with her hands but she was careful not to complain.

Mother Hesta did not seem to notice, but she let the fire die down a bit and laid the partially finished sword on the stone firewall. Wiping her grimed hands on her leather apron, she turned to the girl.

"I'm fair famished, I am. Let's go out to garden where Mother Sonda's set us a meal."

She did not put her hand out to the girl as she was, herself, uncomfortable with such open displays. It was a time-worn joke on Evelonia that Hesta put all her love into pounding at the forge. But she was pleased when the girl trotted by her side without any noticeable hesitation or delay. "A slow apprentice is no apprentice." Mother Hesta often remarked.

When they stepped out of the shed, the day burst upon them with noisy celebration. Hesta, who spent almost the entire day everyday in her dark forge, was always pleased for a few moments of birds and the colorful assault of the green landscape drifting off into the marshy river beyond. But she was always just as happy to go back into the dark fire room where the tools slipped comfortably to hand and she could control the *whoosh-*

whoosh sigh of the bellows and the loud clangorous song of metal on metal.

A plain cloth was spread upon the grass and a variety of plates covered with napkins awaited them. A jug of watered wine—Hesta hated the feeling heavy wines made in her head when she was working over the hot fire—and two stoneware goblets completed the picture.

"Come," Mother Hesta said.

The word seemed to release the child and she skipped over to the cloth and squatted down, but she touched nothing on the plate until Hesta had lowered herself to the ground and picked up the first napkin. Then the girl took up a slice of apple and jammed it into her mouth.

Only then did Hesta remember that it was mid-afternoon and the child, who had arrived late the evening before and slept comforted in Mother Sonda's bed, had not eaten since rising. Still, it would not do to apologize. That would make discipline the harder. This particular girl, she knew, was the daughter of a vavasour, a man of some means in Escalot. She was not used to serving but to being served, so she must not be coddled now. Hesta was gentle in her chiding, but firm.

"The food'll not disappear, child," she said. "Slow and steady in these things. A buyer for the steel comes to guesthouse table and he be judging us and we he by what goes on there. A greedy man be a man who'll pay twice what a blade be worth. Discipline, discipline in all things."

The girl, trying to eat more slowly, began to choke.

Hesta poured the goblets halfway full and solemnly handed one to her. The child sipped down her wine and the choking fit ended suddenly. Hesta made no reference to the incident.

"When you be done, collect these plates and cups and take them to yon waterhouse. Mother Argente will meet you there and read you the first chapter of the *Book of Brightness*. Listen well. The ears be daughters of the memory."

"I can read, Mother Hesta," the girl said in a quiet little voice. It was not a boast but information.

"Can you? Then on the morrow you can read to me from the chapter on fire." She did not mention that she, herself a daughter of a landless vassal, had never learned to read. However one came to the *Book*—by eye or ear—did not matter a whit. Some were readers and some were read-tos; each valued in the Goddess' sight, as Argente had promised her many years ago when they had been girls. So she comforted herself still.

"Yes, Mother," the girl said. Her voice, though quiet, was unusually low and throaty for one her age. It was a voice that would wear well in the forge room. The last novice had had a whiny voice; she had not remained on the isle for long. But this girl, big-eyed, deep-voiced, with a face the shape of a heart under a waterfall of dark hair, was such a lovely little thing, she would probably be taken by the Mothers of Guesthouse, Sonda, Lisanor, and Katwyn, no matter how fair her forging. Sometimes, Hesta thought, the Goddess be hard.

As she watched the girl eating, then wiping her mouth on the linen square with an easy familiarity, Hesta remembered how mortifying it had been to have to be taught not to use her sleeve for that duty. Then she smiled because that memory recalled another, that of a large, rawboned, parentless ten-year-old girl she had been, plunging into the cold channel of the Tamar just moments ahead of the baron who had claimed her body as his property. He had had to let her go, exploding powerful curses at her back, for he could not himself swim. He had been certain that she would sink. But her body's desperate strength and her crazed determination had brought her safely across the brackish tide to the isle where, even in a boat, that powerful baron had not dared go, so fearful was he of the rumors of magic. And the girl, as much water in as without, had been picked up out of the rushes by the late forge mistress and laughingly called Moses after an old tale. And never gone back across the Tamar, not once these forty years.

In the middle of Hesta's musing, the girl stood up and began to clear away the dishes to the accompaniment of a trilling song sung by a modest little brown bird whose flute-like tunes came daily in spring from the apple bough. It seemed an omen. Hesta decided she would suggest it to Mother Sonda as the bird name for the vavasour's child—Thrush.

There were three other girls in the sleeping room when Elaine was left there. Two of the girls were smoothing their beds and one was sitting under a corbeled window, staring out.

Elaine had the braid in her mouth again. Her wide gray eyes took in everything. Five beds stood in a row along the wall with wooden chests for linen and other possessions at each bed-foot. A fine Eastern tapestry hung above the beds, its subject the Daughters of Eve. It depicted about thirty women at work on a large island surrounded by troubled waves. Against the opposite wall were five arched windows that looked out across the now placid Tamar. Beneath the windows stood two high-warp looms with rather primitive weavings begun on each.

One of the standing girls, a tall wraithy lass with hair the insubstantial color of mist, noticed that Elaine's eyes had taken in the looms.

"We have been learning to weave. It is something that Mother A learned from a traveler in Eastern lands. Not just the simple cloths the peasants make but the true *tapissiers* such as the one over our beds. *That* was a gift of an admirer, Mother A said."

Elaine had met Mother Argente the night before. She was a small white-haired woman with soft, plump cheeks and hands that disguised the steel beneath. Elaine wondered who could admire such a firm soul. That kind of firmness quite frightened her.

She spun around to set the whole room into a blur of brown wood and blue coverlets and the bright spots of tapestry wool hanging on the wall. She spun until she was dizzy and had to stop or collapse. The braid fell from her mouth and she stood hands at her side, silently staring.

"Do you have a name yet?" the mist-haired girl asked.

After a moment came the throaty reply. "Elaine."

"No, no, your bird name, she means." The other standing girl, plump and whey-faced, spoke in a twittering voice.

Mist-hair added, "We all receive bird names, new names, like novices in nunneries, until we decide whether to stay. That's because the Druids have their trees and tree alphabet for *their* magic, but we have our little birds who make their living off the trees. That's what Mother A says. It's all in the *Book*. After that, if we stay, we get to have Mother names and live on Holy Isle forever."

"Forever," whispered Elaine. She could not imagine it.

"Do you want to know *our* bird names?" asked whey-face.

Before Elaine could answer, the tall girl said, "I'm Gale—for nightingale—because I sing so well. And this is Marta for House Martin because she is our homebody, coming from Shapwick, across the flood. And over there—that . . ." she hesitated a moment, as much to draw a breath as to make a point, "that is Veree. That's because she's solitary like the Vireo, and a rare visitor to our isle. At least she's rare in her own eyes." She paused. "We used to have Brambling, but she got sick from the dampness and had to go home or die."

"I didn't like Bram," Marta said. "She was too common and she whined all the time. Mother Hesta couldn't bear her, and that's why she had to leave."

"It was her chest and the bloody cough."

"It was her whine."

"Was not."

"Was."

"Was not."

"Was!"

Veree stood and came over to Elaine who had put the braid back into her mouth during the girls' argument. "Don't let their squabblings fright you," she said gently. "They are chickens scratching over bits of feed. Rumor and gossip excite them."

The braid dropped from Elaine's mouth.

"You think because you're castle-born that you're better than we are," scolded Marta. "But all are the same on this holy isle."

Veree smiled. It was not an answer but a confirmation.

"We will see," hissed Gale. "There is still the forging."

"But she's *good* at forging," Marta murmured.

Gale pursed her mouth. "We will see."

Veree ignored them, putting a hand under Elaine's chin and lifting her face until they were staring at one another, grey eyes into violet ones. Elaine could not look away.

"You are quite quite beautiful," Veree pronounced at last, "and you take in everything with those big eyes. But like the magpie, you give nothing away. I expect they'll call you Maggie, but *I* shall call you Pie."

Beyond the fingers of light cast by the hearthfire was a darkness so thick it seemed palpable. On the edges of the darkness, as it crowded them together, sat the nine Mothers of Ynis Evelonia. In the middle of the half circle, in a chair with a firm back, sat Mother Argente smiling towards the flames, her fingers busy with needlework. She did not once look down to check the accuracy of her stitches but trusted her fingers to do their work.

"Young Maggie seems to be settling in quite nicely. No crying at night, no outlandish longings for home, no sighing or sniffles. We needn't have been so worried." Her comment did not name any specific worrier, but the Mothers who had voiced such fears to her in the privacy of their morning confessionals were chastised all the same.

Still chaffing over the rejection of her suggested name, Hesta sniffed. "She's too much like Veree—high strung, coddled. And she fair worships the ground Veree treads which, of course, Veree encourages."

"Now, now Hesta," Mother Sonda soothed. She made the same sounds to chickens agitated at laying time and buyers in the guesthouse, a response in tone rather than actual argument. It always worked. Hesta smoothed her skirts much like a preening bird and settled down.

Sonda rose to stack another log onto the embers and to re-light a taper on the candlestand. A moth fluttered towards the flame and on reaching it, burst with a sudden bright light. Sonda swept the ashes onto the floor where they disappeared into shadows and rushes. Then, turning, she spoke with a voice as sweetly welcoming as the scent of roses and verbena in the room.

"Mother A has asked me to read the lesson for this evening." She stepped to the lectern where the great leather-bound *Book of Brightness* lay open. Above it, from the sconce on the wall, another larger taper beamed down to light the page. Sonda ran her finger along the text, careful not to touch either the words or the brightly colored illuminations. Halfway, she stopped, looked up, and judging the stilled expectant audience, glanced down again and began to read.

The lesson was short, a paragraph and a parable about constancy. The longer reading had been done before the full company of women and girls at dinner. Those who could took turns with the readings. All others listened. Young Maggie, with her low, steady voice and ability to read phrases rather than merely piece together words, would some day make a fine reader. She would probably make a fine Mother, too. Time—and trial—would tell. That was the true magic on the isle: time and trial.

Sonda looked up from the text for a moment. Mother Argente always chose the evening's lesson. The mealtime reading was done from the *Book*'s beginning straight through to the end. In that way the entire *Book of Brightness* was heard at least once a year by everyone on the isle.

As usual, Sonda was in full agreement with Mother A's choice of the parable: on constancy. In the last few months the small community had been beset by inconstancy, as if there were a curse at work, a worm at the heart inching its way to the surface of the body. Four of the novices had left on one pretext or another, a large number in such a short time. One girl with the bloody flux whose parents had desired that she die at home. One girl beset by such lingering homesickness as to render her unteachable. One girl plainly too stupid to learn at all. And one girl summoned home to be married. Married! Merely a piece in her father's game, the game of royalty. Sonda had escaped that game on her own by fasting until her desperate father had given her permission to join the Daughters of Eve. But then, he had had seven other daughters to counter with. And if such losses of novices were not enough—girls were always coming and going—two of the fully vowed women had left as well, one to care for her aged and dying parents and take over the reigns of landholding until her brothers might return from war. And one, who had been on the isle for twenty years, had run off with a Cornish miller, a widower only recently bereaved; run off to become his fourth wife. Constancy indeed!

Sonda stood for a moment after the reading was over, her hands lingering on the edges of the *Book*. She loved the feel of it under her fingers, as if the text could impress itself on her by the feel of the parchment alone. She envied Mothers Morgan and Marie who could write and illumine the pages. They were at work on a new copy of the *Book* to be set permanently in the dining common so that this one, old and fragile and precious, would not have to be shifted daily.

Finally Sonda took her place again on a stool by Mother A's right hand.

Mother A shifted a moment and patted Sonda's knee. Then she looked to the right and left, taking in all eight women with her glance. "My sisters," she began, "tomorrow our beloved daughter Vireo will begin her steel."

Elaine awoke because someone was crying. She had been so near crying herself for a fortnight that the sound of the quiet weeping set her off, and before she could stop herself, she was snuffling and gulping, the kind of sobbing that Nanny Bess always called "bear grabbers."

She was making so much noise, she did not hear the other weeper stop and move onto her bed, but she felt the sudden warmth of the girl's body and the sturdy arms encircling her.

"Hush, hush little Pie," came a voice, and immediately after her hair was smoothed down.

Elaine looked up through tear-blurred eyes. There was no moon to be seen through the windows, no candles lit. The dark figure beside her was faceless, but she knew the voice.

"Oh Veree," she whispered, "I didn't *mean* to cry."

"Nor I, little one. You have been brave the long weeks here. I have seen that and admired it. And now, I fear that I have been the cause of your weeping."

"No, not you, Veree. Never you. It is just that I miss my father so much. And my brother Lavaine, who is the handsomest man in all the world."

Veree laughed and tousled the girl's hair. "Ah, there can be no *handsomest* man, Pie. All men be the same to the women who love and serve the bright goddess flame here."

"If I cannot still love my Lavaine, then I do not want to *be* here." She wiped at her eyes.

"You will get over such losses. I have." Veree sat back on the bed.

"Then why *were* you crying? It was that which woke me." Elaine would admit that much.

Veree shushed her fiercely and glanced around, but the other two girls slept on.

Elaine whispered, "You *were* weeping. By the window. Admit it."

"Yes, sweet Pie, I was crying. But not for the loss of father or brother. Nor yet for house and land. I cry about tomorrow and tomorrow's morrow, and especially the third day after when I must finish my steel." She rose and went towards the window.

Elaine saw the shadow of her passing betwixt dark and dark and shivered slightly. Then she got out of her bed and the shock of the cold stone beneath the rushes caused her to take quick, short steps over to Veree who sat by the open window.

Outside a strange moaning, part wind and part water, sighed from the Tamar. A night owl on the hunt cried, a soft ascending wheeze of sound.

Elaine put her hand out and touched Veree's shoulder, sturdy under the homespun shift. "But what are you afraid of? Do you fear being burned? Do you fear the blade? I had a maidservant once who turned white as hoarfrost when she had to look upon a knife, silly thing."

"I fear the hurting. I fear . . . the blood."

"What blood?"

In the dark Veree turned and Elaine could suddenly see two tiny points of light flashing out from the shadow eyes. "They have not told you yet about the blood?"

Elaine shook her head. Then realizing the motion might not be read in the blackness, she whispered, "No. Not yet."

Veree sighed, a sound so unlike her that Elaine swallowed with difficulty.

"Tell me. Please."

"I must not."

"But *they* will soon."

"Then let *them*."

"But I must know now so that I might comfort you, who have comforted me these weeks." Elaine took her hand away from Veree's shoulder and reached for a lock of her own hair, unbound from its night plait, and popped it into her mouth, a gesture she had all but forgotten the last days.

"Oh little Pie, you must not think I am a coward, but if I tell you when I should not . . . I would not have you think me false." Veree's voice was seeped in sadness.

"I never . . ."

"You will when I tell you."

"You are wonderful," Elaine said, proclaiming fealty. "You have been the one to take me in, to talk to me, to listen. The others are all common mouths chattering, empty heads like wooden whistles blowing common tunes." That was one of Nanny Bess' favorite sayings. "Nothing would make me think you false. Not now, not ever."

Veree's head turned back to the window again and the twin points of light were eclipsed. She spoke towards the river and the wind carried her soft words away. Elaine had to strain to hear them.

"Our steel is forged of three of the four elements—fire and water and air."

"I know that."

"But the fourth thing that makes Evian Steel, what makes it strike true, is a secret learned by Mother Morgan from a necromancer in the East where magic rides the winds and every breath is full of spirits."

"And what is the fourth thing?" whispered Elaine, though she feared she already knew.

Veree hesitated, then spoke. "Blood. The blood of a virgin girl, an unblemished child, or a childless old maid. Blood drawn from her arm where the vein runs into the heart. The left arm. Here." And the shadow held out its shadowy arm, thrusting it half out of the window.

Elaine shivered with more than the cold.

"And when the steel has been worked and pounded and beaten and shaped and heated, again and again, it is thrust into a silver vat that contains pure water from our well mixed through with the blood."

"Oh," Elaine sighed.

"And the words from the *Book of Brightness* are spoken over it by the Mothers in the Circle of Nine. The sword is pulled from its bloody bath. Then the girl, holding up the sword, with the water flooding down her arm, marches into the Tamar, into the tidal pool that sits in the shadow of the high Tor. She must go under the water with the sword, counting to nine times nine. Then thrusting the sword up and out of the water before her, she follows it into the light. Only then is the forging done."

"Perhaps taking the blood will not hurt, Veree. Or only a little. The Mothers are gentle. I burned myself the third day here, and Mother Sonda soothed it with a honey balm and not a scar to show for it."

Veree turned back to the window. "It must be done by the girl all alone at the rising of the moon. Out in the glade. Into the silver cup. And how can I, little Pie, how can I prick my own arm with a knife, I who cannot bear to see myself bleed. Not since I was a small child, could I bear it without fainting. Oh, I can kill spiders, and stomp on serpents. I am not afraid of binding up another's wounds. But my own blood . . . if I had known . . . if my father had known . . . I never would have come."

Into the silence that followed her anguished speech, came the ascending cry of another owl, which ended in a shriek as the bird found its prey. The cry seemed to agitate the two sleepers in their beds and they stirred noisily. Veree and Elaine stood frozen for the moment, and even after were tentative with their voices.

"Could you . . ." Elaine began.

"Yes?"

"Could you use an animal's blood instead?"

"Then the magic would not work and everyone would know."

Elaine let out a long breath. "Then I shall go out in your place. We shall use *my* blood and you will not have to watch." She spoke quite assuredly, though her heart beat wildly at her own suggestion.

Veree hugged her fiercely. "What *can* you think of me that you would believe I would let you offer yourself in my place, little one. But I shall love you forever just for making the suggestion."

Elaine did not quite understand why she should feel so relieved, but she smiled into the darkness. Then she yawned loudly.

"What *am* I thinking of?" Veree chastised herself. "You

should be sleeping little one, not staying up with me. But be relieved. You have comforted me. I think . . ." she hesitated for a little, then finished gaily, "I think I shall manage it all quite nicely now."

"Really?" asked Elaine.

"Really," said Veree. "Trust me."

"I do. Oh, I do," said Elaine and let herself be led back to bed where she fell asleep at once and dreamed of an angel with long dark braids in a white shift who sang, "Verily, verily," to her and drew a blood-red crux on her forehead and breast and placed her, ever smiling, in a beautiful silk-lined barge.

If there was further weeping that night, Elaine did not wake to it, nor did she speak of it in the morn.

The morn was the first day of Veree's Steel and the little isle buzzed with the news. The Nine Mothers left the usual chores to the lesser women and the girls, marching in a solemn line to the forge where they made a great circle around the fire.

In due time Veree, dressed in a white robe with the hood obscuring her face, was escorted by two guides, mothers who had been chosen by lot. They walked along the *Path of Steel*, the winding walkway to the smithy that was lined with water-smoothed stones.

As she walked, Veree was unaware of the cacophony of birds that greeted her from the budding apple boughs. She never noticed a flock of finches that rose up before her in a cloud of yellow wings. Instead her head was full of the chant of the sword.

> *Water to cool it,*
> *Forge to heat it,*
> *Anvil to form it,*
> *Hammer to beat it.*

She thought carefully of the points of the sword: holt and blade, forte and foible, pommel and edge, quillon and grip. She rehearsed her actions. She thought of everything but the blood.

Then the door in front of her opened, and she disappeared inside. The girls who had watched like little birds behind the trees sighed as one.

"It will be your turn next full moon," whispered Marta to Gale. Gale smiled crookedly. The five girls from the other sleeping room added their silent opinions with fingers working small fantasies into the air. Long after the other girls slipped back to their housely duties, Elaine remained, rooted in place. She watched the forge and could only guess at the smoky signals that emerged from the chimney on the roof.

> *Water to cool it,*
> *Forge to heat it,*
> *Anvil to form it,*
> *Hammer to beat it.*

The Mothers chanted in perfect unity, their hands clasped precisely over the aprons of their robes. When the chant was done, Mother Argente stepped forward and gently pushed Veree's hood back.

Released from its binding, Veree's hair sprang forward like tiny black arrows from many bowstrings, the dark points haloing her face.

She really is a magnificent child, Argente thought to herself, but aloud spoke coldly. "My daughter," she said, "the metal thanks us for its beating by becoming stronger. So by our own tempering we become women of steel. Will you become one of us?"

"Mother," came Veree's soft answer, "I will."

"Then you must forge well. You must pour your sweat and your blood into this sword that all who see it and any who use it shall know it is of excellent caliber, that it is of Evian Steel."

"Mother, I will."

The Mothers stood back then and only Hesta came forward. She helped Veree remove her robe and the girl stood stiffly in her new forging suit of tunic and trews. Hesta bound her hair back into a single braid, tying it with a golden twine so tightly that it brought tears to the girl's eyes. She blinked them back, making no sound.

"Name your tools," commanded Hesta.

Veree began. Pointing out each where it hung on its hook on the wall, she droned: "Top swage, bottom swage, flatter, cross peen, top fuller, bottom fuller, hot chisel, mandrel . . ." The catalogue went on and only half her mind was occupied with the rota. This first day of the Steel was child's play, things she had memorized her first weeks on Ynis Evelonia and never forgot. They were testing the knowledge of her head. The second day they would test her hands. But the third day . . . she hesitated a moment, looked up, saw that Hesta's eyes on her were glittering. For the first time she understood that the old forge-mistress was hoping that she would falter, fail. That startled her. It had never occurred to her that someone she had so little considered could wish her ill.

She smiled a false smile at Hesta, took up the list, and finished it flawlessly.

The Circle of Nine nodded.

"Sing us now the color of the steel," said Sonda.

Veree took a breath and began. "When the steel is red as blood, the surface is at all points good; and when the steel is rosy red, the top will scale, the sword is dead; and when the steel is golden bright, the time for forging is just right; and when the steel is white as snow, the time for welding you will know."

The plain song accompaniment had helped many young girls remember the colors, but Veree sang it only to please the Mothers and pass their test. She had no trouble remembering when to forge and when to weld, and the rest was just for show.

"The first day went splendidly," remarked Sonda at the table.

"No one ever questioned *that* one's head knowledge," groused Hesta, using her own head as a pointer towards the table where the girls sat.

Mother Argente clicked her tongue against the roof of her mouth, a sound she made when annoyed. The others responded to it immediately with silence, except for Mother Morgan who was so deep in conversation with a server she did not hear.

"We will discuss this later. At the Hearth," Argente said.

The conversation turned at once to safer topics: the price of corn, how to raise the milling fee, the prospect of another visitor from the East, the buyer of Veree's sword.

Morgan looked over. "It shall be the Arch-Mage," she said. "He will come for the sword himself."

Hesta shook her head. "How do you know. How do you *always* know?"

Morgan smiled, the corners of her thin upper lip curling. There was a gap between her two front teeth, carnal, inviting. "I know."

Sonda reached out and stroked the back of Hesta's hand. "You know she would have you think it's magic. But it is the calendar, Hesta. I have explained all that."

Hesta mumbled, pushing the lentils around in her bowl. Her own calendar was internal and had to do with forging, when the Steel was ready for the next step. But if Morgan went by any calendar, it was too deep and devious for the forgemistress' understanding. Or for any of them. Morgan always seemed to *know* things. Under the table, Hesta crossed her fingers, holding them against her belly as protection.

"It *shall* be the Arch-Mage," Morgan said, still smiling her gapped smile. "The stars have said it. The moon has said it. The winds have said it."

"And now you have said it, too." Argente's voice ended the conversation, though she wondered how many other women were sitting with their fingers crossed surreptitiously under the table. She did not encourage them in their superstitions, but the ones who came from the outer tribes or the lower classes never really rid themselves of such beliefs. "Of course it shall be a druid. Someone comes once a year at this time to look over our handiwork. They rarely buy. Druids are as close with their gold as a dragon on its hoard."

"It shall be the Arch-Mage himself," intoned Morgan. "I know."

Hesta shivered.

"Yes," Argente smiled, almost sighing. When Morgan became stubborn it was always safest to cozen her. Her pharmacopoeia was not to be trusted entirely. "But gloating over such arcane knowledge does not become you, a daughter of a queen. I am sure you have more important matters to attend to. Come, Mothers, I have decided that tonight's reading shall be about humility. And you, Mother Morgan, will do us all the honor of reading it." Irony, Argente had found, was her only weapon against Morgan who seemed entirely oblivious to it. Feeling relieved of her anger by such petty means always made Argente full of nervous energy. She stood. The others stood with her and followed her out the door.

Elaine watched as Veree marched up to the smithy, this time with an escort of four guides. Veree was without the white robe, her forge suit still unmarked by fire or smoke, her hair bound back with the golden string but not as tightly as when Hesta plaited it. Elaine had done the service for her soon after rising, gently braiding the hair and twine together so that they held but did not pull. Veree had rewarded her with a kiss on the brow.

"This day I dedicate to thee," Veree had whispered to her in the courtly language they had both grown up with.

Elaine could still feel the glow of that kiss on her brow. She knew that she would love Veree forever, the sister of her heart. She was glad now, as she had never been before, that she had had only brothers and no sisters in Escalot. That way Veree could be the only one.

The carved wooden door of the smithy closed behind Veree. The girls, giggling, went back to their chores. Only Elaine stayed, straining to hear something of the rites that would begin the second day of Veree's Steel.

Veree knew the way of the steel, bending the heated strips, hammering them together, recutting and rebending them repeatedly until the metal patterned. She knew the sound of the hammer on the hot blade, the smell of the glowing charcoal that made the soft metal hard. She enjoyed the hiss of the quenching, when the hot steel plunged into the water and emerged, somehow, harder still. The day's work was always difficult but satisfying in a way that other work was not. Her hands now held a knowledge that she had not had two years before when, as a pampered young daughter of a baron, she had come to Ynis Evelonia to learn "to be a man as well as a woman" as her father had said. He believed that a woman who might some day have to rule a kingdom (oh, he had such high hopes for her) needed to know both principles, male and female. A rare man, her father. She did not love him. He was too cold and distant and cerebral for that. But she admired him. She wanted him to admire her. And—except for the blood—she was not unhappy that she had come.

Except for the blood. If she thought about it, her hand faltered, the hammer slipped, the sparks flew about carelessly, and Hesta boomed out in her forge-tending voice about the recklessness of girls. So Veree very carefully did *not* think about the blood. Instead she concentrated on fire and water, on earth and air. Her hands gripped her work. She *became* the steel.

She did not stop until Hesta's hand on her shoulder cautioned her.

"It be done for the day, my daughter," Hesta said, grudging admiration in her voice. "Now you rest. Tonight you must do the last of it alone."

And then the fear really hit her. Veree began to tremble.

Hesta misread the shivering. "You be a-weary with work. You be hungry. Take some watered wine for sleep's sake. We Mothers will wake you and lead you to the glade at moonrise. Come. The sword be well worked. You have reason to be proud."

Veree's stomach began to ache, a terrible dull pain. She was certain that, for the first time in her life, she would fail and that her father would be hurt and the others would pity her. She expected she could stand the fear, and she would, as always, bear the dislike of her companions, but what could not be born was their pity. When her mother had died, in the bloody aftermath of an unnecessary birth, the entire court had wept and everyone had pitied her, poor little motherless six-year-old Gwyneth. But she had rejected their pity, turning it to white anger against her mother who had gone without a word. She had not accepted pity from any of those peasants then— she would not accept it now. Not even from little Pie, who fair worshipped her. Especially not from Pie.

The moon's cold fingers stroked Veree's face but she did not wake. Elaine, in her silent vigil, watched from her bed. She strained to listen as well.

The wind in the orchard rustled the blossoms with a soft coughing. Twice an owl had given its ascending hunting cry. The little popping hisses of breath from the sleeping girls punctuated the quiet in the room. And Elaine thought that she could also hear, as a dark counter to the other noises, the slapping of the Tamar against the shore, but perhaps it was only the beating of her own heart. She was not sure.

Then she heard the footsteps coming down the hall, hauled the light covers up to her chin, and slotted her eyes.

The Nine Mothers entered the room, their white robes lending a ghostly air to the proceedings. They wore the hoods up, which obscured their faces. The robes were belted with knotted golden twine; nine knots on each cinchon and the golden ornament shaped like a circle with one half filled in, the signet of Ynis Evelonia, hanging from the end.

The Nine surrounded Veree's bed, undid their cinchons, and laid the ropes over the girl's body as if binding her to a bier.

Mother Argente's voice floated into the room. "We bind thee to the Isle. We bind thee to the Steel. We bind thee to thy task. Blood calls to blood, like to like. Give us thine own for the work."

The Nine picked up their belts and tied up their robes once again. Veree, who had awakened some time during Argente's chant, was helped to her feet. The Mothers took off her shift and slipped a silken gown over her head. It was sleeveless and Elaine, watching, shivered for her.

Then Mother Morgan handed her a silver cup, a little grail with the sign of the halved circle on the side. Mother Sonda handed her a silken bandage. Marie bound an illumined message to her brow with a golden headband. Mothers Bronwyn and Matilde washed her feet with lilac water, while Katwyn and Lisanor tied her hair atop her head into a plaited crown. Mother Hesta handed her a silver knife, its tip already consecrated with wine from the Goddess Arbor.

Then Argente put her hands on Veree's shoulders. "May She guide your hand. May She guard your blood. May the moon rise and fall on this night of your consecration. Be you Steel tonight."

They led her to the door and pushed her out before them. She did not stumble as she left.

Veree walked into the glade as if in a trance. She had drunk none of the wine but had spilled it below her bed knowing that the wine was drugged with one of Mother Morgan's potions. Bram had warned her of it before leaving. Silly, whiny Bram who, nonetheless, had had an instinct for gossip and a passion for Veree. Such knowledge had been useful.

The moon peeped in and out of the trees, casting shadows on the path, but Veree did not fear the dark. This night the dark was her friend.

She heard a noise and turned to face it, thinking it some small night creature on the prowl. There was nothing larger than a stoat or fox on Ynis Evelonia. She feared neither. At home she had kept a reynard raised up from a kit, and had hunted with two ferrets as companions in her pocket.

Home! What images suddenly rose up to plague her, the same that had caused her no end of sleepless nights when she had first arrived. For she *had* been homesick, whatever nonsense she had told little Pie for comfort's sake. The great hearthfore at Carmelide, large enough to roast an oxen, where once she had lost the golden ring her mother had given her and her cousin Cadoc had grabbed up a bucket of water, dousing the fire and getting himself all black with coal and grease to recover it for her. And the great apple tree outside her bedroom window up which young Jemmy, the ostler's son, had climbed to sing of his love for her even though he knew he would be soundly beaten for it. And the mews behind the main house where Master Thom had kept the hawks and let her sneak in to practice holding the little merlin that she had wanted for her own. But it had died tangled in its jesses the day before she'd been sent off to the isle, and one part of her had been glad that no one else would hunt the merlin now.

She heard the noise again, louder this time, too loud for a fox or a squirrel or a stoat. Loud enough for a human. She spoke out, "Who is it?" and held out the knife before her, trembling with the cold. Only the cold, she promised herself.

"It is I," came a small voice.

"Pie!" Her own voice took back its authority. "You are not supposed to be here."

"I saw it all, Veree. The dressing and undressing. The ropes and the knife. And I *did* promise to help." The childish form slipped out from behind the tree, white linen shift reflecting the moon's light.

"I told you all would be well, child. You did not need to come."

"But I *promised.*" If that voice held pity, it was self-pity. The child was clearly a worshipper begging not to be dismissed.

Veree smiled and held out the hand with the cup. "Come, then. Thou shalt be my page."

Elaine put her hand to Veree's gown and held on as if she would never let go and, so bound, the two entered into the Goddess Glade.

The Arch-Mage came in the morning just as Morgan had foretold. He was not at all what Elaine had expected, being short and balding, with a beard as long and as thin as an exclamation mark. But that he was a man of power no one could doubt.

The little coracle, rowed by the same ferret-faced woman who had deposited Elaine on the isle, fair skimmed the surface of the waves and plowed onto the shore, leaving a furrow in which an oak could have been comfortably set.

The Arch-Mage stood up in the boat and greeted Mother Argente familiarly. "*Salve, Mater. Visne somnia vendere?*"

She answered him back with great dignity. "*Si volo, Merline, caveat emptor.*"

Then they both laughed as if this exchange were a great and long-standing joke between them. If it was a joke, they were certainly the only ones to understand it.

"Come, Arch-Mage," Mother Argente said, "and take wine with us in the guesthouse. We will talk of the purpose of your visit in comfort there."

He nodded and, with a quick twist of his wrist, produced a coin from behind the boat woman's right ear. With a flourish he presented it to her, then stepped from the coracle. The woman dropped the coin solemnly into the leather bag she wore at her waist.

Elaine gasped and three other girls giggled.

"The girls are, as always, amused by your tricks, Merlin," said Mother Argente, her mouth pursed in a wry smile.

"I like to keep in practice," he said. "*And* to amuse the young ones. Besides, as one gets older the joints stiffen."

"That I know, that I know," Argente agreed. They walked side by side like old friends, moving slowly up the little hill. The rest of the women and girls fell in behind them and so it was, in a modest processional, that they came to the guest-house.

At the door of the wattle pavilion, which was shaded by a lean of willows, Mother Argente turned. "Sonda, Hesta, Morgan, Lisanor, enter and treat with our guest. Veree, ready yourself for noon. The rest of you, you know your duties." Then she opened the door and let Merlin precede them into the house.

The long table was already set with platters of cheese and fruit. Delicate goblets of Roman glass marked off six places. As soon as they were all seated, with Argente at the head and Merlin at the table's foot, Mother A poured her own wine and passed the silver ewer. Morgan, seated at Argente's right hand, was the last to fill her glass. When she set the ewer down, she raised her glass.

"I am Wind on Sea," Morgan chanted.

> *I am Wind on Sea,*
> *I am Ocean-wave,*
> *I am Roar of Sea,*
> *I am Bull of Seven Fights,*
> *I am Vulture on Cliff,*
> *I am Dewdrop,*
> *I am Fairest of Flowers,*
> *I am Boar for Boldness,*
> *I am Salmon in Pool,*
> *I am Lake on Plain,*
> *I am a Word of Skill,*
> *I am the Point of a Weapon . . .*

"*Morgan,*" warned Argente.

"Do not stop her," commanded Merlin. "She is *vates,* afire with the word of the gods. My god or your god, they are the same. They speak with tongues of fire and they sometimes pick a warped reed through which to blow a particular tune."

Argente bowed her head once to him but Morgan was already finished. She looked across the table at Hesta, her eyes preternaturally bright. "I know things," she said.

"It is clear that I have come at a moment of great power," said Merlin. "*I am the point of a Weapon* say the gods to us. And my dreams these past months have been of sword point, but swords that are neither *gladius* nor *spatha* nor the far tribes' *ensis.* A new creation. And where does one come for a sword of power, but here. Here to Ynis Evelonia."

Mother Argente smiled. "We have many swords ready, Arch-Mage."

"I need but one." He did not return her smile, staring instead into his cup of wine.

"How will we know this sword of power?" Argente asked, leaning forward.

"We will know," intoned Morgan.

Sonda, taking a sip of her wine, put her head to one side like a little bird considering a tasty worm. "And what payment, Arch-Mage?"

"Ah, Mother Sonda, that is always the question they leave to you. What payment indeed." Merlin picked up his own glass and suddenly drained it. He set the glass down gently, contemplating the rim. Then he stroked his long beard. "If I dream true—and I have never been known to have false dreams—then you shall *give* me this particular sword and its maker."

"*Give* you? What a notion, Merlin." Mother Argente laughed, but there was little amusement in it. "The swords made of Evian Steel are never given away. We have too many buyers vying for them. If you will not pay for it, there will be others who will."

There was a sudden timid knock upon the door. Sonda rose quietly and went to it, spoke to the Mother who had interrupted them, then turned.

"It is nearing noon, Mother. The sun rides high. It is time." Sonda's voice was smooth, giving away no more than necessary.

Mother Argente rose and with her the others rose, too.

"Stay, Arch-Mage, there is food and wine enough. When we have done with our . . . obsequies . . . we shall return to finish our business with you."

The five Mothers left and so did not hear the man murmur into his empty cup, "This business will be finished beforetimes."

The entire company of women gathered at the river's edge to watch. The silver vat, really an overlarge bowl, was held by Mother Morgan. The blood-tinted water reflected only sky.

Veree, in the white silken shift stood with her toes curling under into the mud. Elaine could see the raised goose bumps along her arms, though it was really quite warm in the spring sun.

Mother Hesta held a sword on the palms of her upturned hands. It was a long-bladed double-edge-sword, the quillon cleverly worked. The sword seemed afire with the sun, the shallow hollow down its center aflame.

Veree took the sword from Hesta and held it flat against her breast while Mother Argente annointed her forehead with the basin's water. With her finger she drew three circles and three crosses on Veree's brow.

"Blood to blood, steel to steel, thee to me," said Mother Argente.

Veree repeated the chant. "Blood to blood, steel to steel, I to thee." Then she took the sword and set it into the basin.

As the sword point and then the blade touched the water, the basin erupted in steam. Great gouts of fire burst from the sword and Mother Argente screamed.

Veree grabbed up the sword by the handle and ran down into the tidal pool. She plunged in with it and immediately the flames were quenched, but she stayed under the water and Elaine, fearful for her life, began to cry out, running down to the water's edge.

She was pushed aside roughly by a strong hand and when she caught her breath, she saw it was the Arch-Mage himself, standing knee deep in water, his hands raised, palms down, speaking words she did not quite understand.

> *I take ye here*
> *Till Bedevere*
> *Cast ye back.*

Bedevere? Did he mean Veree? Elaine wondered, and then had time to wonder no further for the waters parted before the Arch-Mage and the sword pierced up into the air before him.

He grasped the pommel in his left hand and with a mighty heave pulled the sword from the pool. Veree's hand, like some dumb, blind thing, felt around in the air, searching.

Elaine waded in, dived under, and wrapping her arms around Veree's waist, pushed her out of the pool. They stood there, trembling, looking like two drowned ferrets, unable to speak or weep or wonder.

"This is the sword I shall have," Merlin said to Mother Argente, his back to the two half-drowned girls.

"I do not understand . . ." began Mother Argente. "But I *will* know."

"I *know* things," said Morgan triumphantly.

Mother Argente turned and spoke through clenched teeth, "Will someone shut her up."

Hesta smiled broadly. "Yes, Mother. Your will is my deed." Her large right hand clamped down on Morgan's neck and she picked her up and shook her like a terrier with a rat, then set her down. Morgan did not speak again but her eyes grew slotted and cold.

Marta began to sob quietly until nudged by Gale, but the other girls were stunned into silence.

"Now, now," murmured Sonda to no one in particular. "Now, now."

Mother Argente walked over to Veree who straightened up and held her chin high. "Explain this, child."

Veree said nothing.

"What blood was used to quench the sword?"

"Mother, it was my own."

Elaine interrupted. "It was, I saw it."

Mother Argente turned on her. "You *saw* it? Then it was your watching that corrupted the steel."

Merlin moved between them. "*Mater.* Think. Such power does not emanate from this child." He swung his head so that he was staring at Veree. "And where did the blood come from?"

Under his stare Veree lowered her eyes. She spoke to the ground. "It is a woman's secret. I cannot talk of it."

The Arch-Mage smiled. "I am man and woman, neither and both. The secrets of the body are known to me. Nothing is hidden from me."

"I have nothing to tell you if you know it already."

"Then I will tell it to thee," said Merlin. He shifted the sword to his left hand, turned to her, and put his right hand under her chin. "Look at me, Gwyneth, called here Vireo, and deny this if you can. Last night for the first time you became a woman. The moon called out your blood. And it was this flux that you used, the blood that flows from the untested womb, not the body's blood flowing to the heart. Is it so?"

She whispered, "It is so."

Argente put a hand to her breast. "That is foul. Unclean."

"It is the more powerful thereby," Merlin answered.

"Take the sword, Arch-Mage. And the girl. And go."

"No!" Elaine dropped to her knees by Veree's side and clasped her legs. "Do not go. Or take me with you. I could not bear to be here without you. I would die for you."

Merlin looked down at the little girl and shook his head. "You shall not die yet, little Elaine. Not so soon. But you shall give your life for her—that I promise you." He tucked the sword in a scabbard he suddenly produced from inside his cloak. "Come Gwyneth." He held out his hand.

She took his hand and smiled at him. "There is nothing here to pity," she said.

"I shall never give you pity," he said. "Not now or ever. You choose and you are chosen. I see that you know what it is you do."

Mother Argente smoothed her skirts down, a gesture which seemed to return them all to some semblance of normality. "I myself will row you across. The sooner she is gone from here, the better."

"But my clothes, Mother."

"They shall be sent to you."

The Arch-Mage swung the cape off his shoulders and enfolded the girl in it. The cape touched the ground, sending up little puffs of dirt.

"You shall never be allowed on this Isle again," said Mother Argente. "You shall be denied the company of women. Your name shall be crossed off the book of the Goddess."

Veree still smiled.

"You shall be barren," came a voice from behind them. "Your womb's blood was given to cradle a sword. It shall not cradle a child. I *know* things."

"Get into the boat," instructed Merlin. "Do not look back, it only encourages her." He spoke softly to Mother Argente, "I am glad, *Mater* that *that* one is *your* burden."

"I give you no thanks for her," said Mother Argente as she pushed the boat off into the tide. She settled onto the seat, took up the oars, feathered them once, and began to pull.

The coracle slipped quickly across the river.

Veree stared out across the grey waters that gave scarcely any reflection. Through the mist she could just begin to see the far shore where the tops of thatched cottages and the smoky tracings of cookfires were taking shape.

"Shapwick-across-the-flood," mused Merlin. "And from there we shall ride by horse to Camlann. It will be a long and arduous journey, child. Your bones will ache."

"Pitying me already?"

"Pitying *you*? My bones are the older and will ache the more. No, I will not pity you. But we will all be pitied when this story is told years hence, for it will be a tale cunningly wrought of earth, air, fire—and blood."

The boat lodged itself clumsily against the Shapwick shore. The magician stood and climbed over the side. He gathered the girl up and carried her to the sand, huffing mightily. Then he turned and waved to the old woman who huddled in the coracle.

"*Ave, Mater.*"

"*Ave, Magister,*" she called back. "Until we must meet again."

Ynis Evelonia, the Isle of Women, lies within the marshy tidal river Tamar that is itself but a ribbon stretched between the Mendip and the Quantock hills. The isle is scarcely remarked from the shore. It is as if Manannan MacLir himself had shaken his cloak between.

On most days there is an unsettling mist obscuring the irregular coast of the isle; and only in the full sun, when the light just rising illuminates a channel, can any passage across the glass-colored waters be seen. And so it is that women alone, who have been schooled in the hidden causeways across the fen, mother to daughter down through the years, can traverse the river in coracles that slip easily through the brackish flood.

By ones and twos they come and go in their light skin boats to commerce with the Daughters of Eve who stay in holy sistership on the isle, living out their chaste lives and

*making with their magicks the finest blades mankind has
ever known.*

*The isle is dotted with trees, not the great Druidic oaks
that line the roadways into Godney and Meare and tower
over the mazed pathways up to the high Tor, but small
womanish trees: alder and apple, willow and ash, leafy
havens for the migratory birds. And the little isle fair
rings with birdsong and the clanging of hammer on anvil
and steel.*

*But men who come to buy swords at Ynis Evelonia are
never allowed further inland than the wattle guesthouse
with its oratory of wicker wands winded and twisted
together under a rush roof. Only one man has ever slept
there and is—in fact—sleeping there still. But that is the
end of this story—which shall not be told—and the
beginning of yet another.*

STRANGER BLOOD

by
P.C.
HODGELL

HE MASTER of Knorth, High Lord of the Kencyrath, a proud man was he. Power he had, and knowledge deeper than the Sea of Stars. But he feared death. A bargain he made with Perimal Darkling, ancient enemy. His people he betrayed to win life unending. A house he built under eaves of darkness, and shadows crawled therein . . .

Damn. The ink had begun to clot again. Arie poked at it with his quill pen and upset the bottle. Oh, what was the use? It was too cold up here in the northwest turret of the High Keep to write anyway, especially about so dark a subject.

Arie glanced northward between mountain peaks to where the Barrier loomed up as far as the eye could see like a wall of mist. On the other side lay Perimal Darkling. Nearly thirty millennia ago, the darkness had first breeched the greatest barrier of all between the outer void and the series of linked dimensions known as the Chain of Creation. At that time, the enigmatic Three-Faced God had bonded together the three people of the Kencyrath—Highborn, Kendar, and catlike Arrin-ken—

to stop the shadows' spread. Then, apparently, the god had left his chosen people on their own. Their contest with Perimal Darkling had become a long, bitter retreat from threshold world to world down the Chain. Arie knew the old songs about every fleeting victory, every final defeat. They made a grim record, but the ones that hurt the most told of the Master's treachery. For the first time, a Kencyr had turned on his own kind and, moreover, caused nearly two-thirds of the Kencyr Host to fall with him. The remnant—Arie's ancestors among them—had fled here to Rathillien, the next threshold world, and raised the Barriers not only against the shadows but against their own fallen kinsmen as well. More than three thousand years had passed since then, but the shame and anger remained, especially at a border outpost like the High Keep. Other Kencyrs snug in the Riverland to the south could perhaps afford to forget, but not those left to guard the Barriers. Here the past still lived. Rangers even claimed that a man could walk right through the mist into the fallen world, into Perimal Darkling. Certainly, poor, warped creatures sometimes made their way out of the shadows to this side. The head of one was nailed to the northern battlement now, surrounded by gorging crows. At least this time it was clearly an animal. Just after Mid-Winter, the last patrol before storm season had brought back something that looked almost human.

Those same rangers were in the lower ward now, at maneuvers on a field of melting snow. They were mostly hoary veterans and boys Arie's age—the old and the young, all with the grim, pinched faces of those sworn to maintain the millennia-old watch of the High Keep Kencyrath down through the white years, though blood should freeze and hearts crack.

Arie knew he should have been one of them, riding, turning, fearing . . . fearing . . . the sweat of the colt, the wild force between his knees, rising, rising . . . Kethra was shouting at him . . . up, over, down . . . crushing pain, darkness . . . .

The quill pen snapped in his shaking hand.

Fit for nothing, said Kethra's voice in his mind. For nothing, for nothing, Arie whispered back.

In the distance, a guard's horn sounded. The boy started. Was it an attack? Twisted figures crawling down from the north, from Perimal Darkling . . . The horn sound again, closer, from the south.

Arie heaved himself up and hopped on one foot to the window. Below, Waning Valley plunged down from New Moon Pass, bending southeastward toward the Riverland, home on Rathillien of all the major Kencyr houses. It was nearly two hundred leagues from the High Keep to Gothregor, the High Lord's citadel. Scarcely anyone had come north to this desolate outpost since the downfall of Ganth High Lord nearly forty years ago. Lord Min-drear of the High Keep had stood by Ganth in that last terrible battle among the White Hills and afterward had ridden slowly home, a broken man carrying the ashes of his five sons in a silver box.

Now horsemen rode into the outer ward from the south behind a gray cloaked figure on a mare the color of fresh cream. The rangers' shaggy mountain ponies snorted and bowed their heads as the mare passed. She was a Whinno-hir, a Highborn's mount. Arie let his breath out slowly. So. The moment everyone had dreaded since Mid-Winter was at last at hand. From the south came riding the end of everything the High Keep Kendar had fought millennia to preserve.

Arie leaned his head against cold stone. Below lay the inner courtyard with Kendar, alerted by the horn, hurrying across it to their various posts. A week, a month, a year from now, what would he see if he again looked down from this perch? These familiar faces, or only those of usurping strangers? He willed himself to see, willed it until the blood hummed in his ears and his sight blurred, but nothing came. Of course not, he thought bitterly: His visions chose their own time and then they never showed him anything real.

Below, the sun-shadows had moved and a thin, keen wind

sprung up. No keep Kendar were in sight now. Instead, just within the gate stood two strangers. One, clearly a Highborn, seemed to smolder against the dark stones in his rich coat of crimson. He was pulling off gold-studded riding gloves. Beside him stood a second visitor, painfully thin, clad in dusty black, whose rank was harder to guess. Both were staring across the courtyard. Following their eyes, Arie saw the stranger in the gray cloak, already half way to the great hall's door.

Near the door was a ramp leading down into the keep's subterranean chambers. From the depths came a sudden hollow clang and an answering howl. The figure in gray stopped abruptly. Arie caught his breath. It was the mid-hour of the afternoon, he remembered. Every day at this time the war hounds were loosed to hunt their food in a yammering pack through the dark mountain forests. No one in his right mind would stand in their way, but no one had apparently warned the visitors, and the huntsmaster in his subterranean kennel didn't know they were there—or, worse, perhaps he did.

The gray bitch leader burst into pale sunlight from the mouth of the ramp, the rest of the pack baying behind her. They were all of the Molocar breed, four-feet high at the shoulder and strong enough to bring down a charging war horse. The stranger stood directly in their path. In a moment, he was surrounded. The hounds surged about him, baffled by his stillness, goaded by their hunger. In their midst, he and the gray bitch faced each other as though carved from stone. Now the stranger was moving. Very, very slowly, he peeled off his right glove and held out his hand. The bitch leaned forward as though to sniff. Then, with a sudden sideways lunge, she snapped her jaws shut on it. Arie thought he heard bones crunch. He saw the shoulders of the figure jerk.

Too late, Kethra's voice roared across the courtyard. A hound yelped. A moment later the pack was in full flight from the only person who could make them shiver at a word. The Warder of High Keep stood in the hall doorway, her expression nearly as black as the randon scarf knotted around her strong throat. What she saw made her scowl deepen even more.

The pack had fled, but not the gray bitch. She stood as if frozen, the stranger's hand still gripped in her jaws. Drops of bright blood splashed on the flagstones between them. A cold breath of wind swept through the court, stirring gray cloth, ruffling gray fur. Then the hound released her grip and, with a sigh, sat down at the stranger's feet.

Kethra stepped back into the hall without a word, leaving the door open behind her. The stranger followed with the hound trotting at his side. At the gate, the crimson-coated Highborn at last angrily shrugged off the hand with which the other had held him back when the pack first erupted into the courtyard. As he and the thin man crossed to the door, Arie saw that the latter cast no shadow. All disappeared into the hall.

Arie grabbed his crutch and hopped as rapidly as he could down the stairs, across the courtyard, through the door. Inside, he slipped to the right into shadows. The hall was thick with them. It was a high vaulted room, built for feasts and laughter. Some forty years ago, it had heard its last war song, raised in honor of its lord and his five bright-faced sons. Now the sons watched the hall blank-eyed from their memorial tapestries, woven of threads taken from the clothing in which each one had died. Similar death banners lined the upper reaches of the hall, pair after pair of the distinctive Min-drear hands held open-palmed in frozen, possibly futile benediction. Lady Shian, Lord Min-drear's consort, was there. Only Min-drear himself and his aging sister Nessa were absent.

Kethra stood before the fire, her body hard-edged and un-yielding against the fitful flames. Old Tarin, steward of the hall, had put the customary flask on the table before her before slipping back into the wall niche that was his post. The bottle was uncorked but still full. The Warder had offered the visitors no welcome cup.

"I tell you again," she said to the gray-cloaked stranger who faced her across the table, "Lord Min-drear sees no one. Tell me your business and I will inform him of it if I can."

"What, without seeing him?"

The stranger's voice surprised Arie. It had such a curious huskiness that he couldn't tell if a man or woman spoke—not that any Highborn lady would come among them like this. The visitor still wore cape and hood. His hands were clasped behind him, hidden in the folds of the gray cloak.

"Kendar, remember your place!" snapped the crimson-coated man.

"Hush, Kracarn. This *is* her place and we are guests. Warder, tell your lord that I have come to summon him to council at Gothregor a month hence."

Kethra gave a harsh laugh. "A summons from Gothregor! After all these years! The last time we answered, Highborn, how many of us ever returned? The White Hills are thick with the ashes of our dead and our hall is empty except for those." She gestured toward the tapestries. "Who would you have us send this time? Who is left? Old men and women, children, cripples . . ."

Involuntarily, her glance flickered past the visitors to Arie standing in the shadows by the door. He flinched, and so did she. Rage at her slip made the Warder turn all the more fiercely on the strangers.

"Five Highborn and a hundred Kendar gone from this hall," she said savagely, taking such an abrupt stride toward the intervening table that the gray bitch sprang up with a snarl. "We have paid our debt in blood to Ganth of Knorth's house. Leave us in peace!"

"Gently," murmured the visitor, dropping a hand, the left, to soothe the hound. "Others have loved Ganth as little as you. He erred badly in the White Hills. He had just come from Gothregor where he found his family slaughtered and rotting in the sun. He was not sane when he led your people against his massed foes. He was not sane later when, in exile, he drove the daughter of his second wife across the Barrier into Perimal Darkling. He was neither sane nor forgiven. He died with blood in his throat.

"But now Torisen, Ganth's son by that second wife, occupies the High Lord's seat. This council summons comes from him, although he never thought it would travel so far. I will speak plainly with you, Warder. My lord Torisen would do as his father did: gather the Kencyr Host and march against our foes here on Rathillien. He forgets, as his father did, that the true enemy is Perimal Darkling and that only border posts such as this keep the Barriers strong. Perhaps your lord can remind him of that. Otherwise, soon, the war summons may come again, and you will have to answer or be foresworn."

Kethra shook her head as if to clear it. That husky, purring voice had slid like velvet between her thoughts, half deadening them. "Torisen, Torisen . . . he was born in the Haunted Lands during his father's exile, returned to claim Ganth's power, wielded it as High Lord in a great battle at the Cataracts . . . . So a wandering singer told us."

This time, she shook all over like a bear rousing itself. A look almost of fear came into her eyes.

"He had a sister. Some say that her father cursed her as a hell-spawn and cast her out. She fell into the Master's hands, but not even he could manage her and she escaped from his house back into Rathillien. They say that she can blood-bind, and that she has spoken to the Master Runes so often and so recklessly that some of their power has bled into her voice. They call her the Darkling. Now in Trinity's name, *who are you*?"

Then, abruptly, there was someone else in the hall. High-born and Kendar both pivoted to face the thin, white-gowned figure bearing rapidly down on them.

"Lady Nessa." Kethra gave Min-drear's sister a shaky salute.

"Have you found my brother yet?" The white figure fluttered anxiously about them like some ghostly moth. Only her anxious, red-rimmed eyes showed through the slits of her veil-mask. "Oh, I've looked everywhere, everywhere!"

"Even on the foundation level, lady?" the Warder asked with a note of desperation.

"Clever Kethra! No, but I'll search there immediately. Oh!" She stopped short, noticing the strangers for the first time. "Who are you?"

All three visitors bowed. "That is Kracarn of Tagmeth; that, Bender," said the Highborn, shaking back the gray hood. Underneath was a thin face marked by silver-gray eyes and high cheekbones, one of them with the faint white line of an old scar cutting across it. She gave Kethra a lopsided, almost rueful smile. "And I am Jamethiel Priests'-bane, the Lordan of Ivory . . . the Darkling."

"I am honored to meet you," said Nessa in a preoccupied way. "Now excuse me. I must find my brother." With that, she darted away, followed at a tactful distance by a Kendar attendant.

"Have you misplaced Lord Min-drear?" Jamethiel asked Kethra politely.

The Warder made an inarticulate sound. She suddenly stepped around the table, grabbed the other's arm, and wrenched her right hand into the light. Arie felt his stomach turn.

"You said only scratches," Kethra said fiercely. "By God, Ganth's daughter or not, you will carry no infection forth from this house!"

With that, she swept the flask off the table and emptied its fiery contents over the mangled hand. The Highborn shuddered violently but made no sound. Nor did she try to withdraw from Kethra's grasp any more than she had from the hound's jaws earlier. For a long minute, Highborn and Kendar locked eyes as liquor dripped unnoticed into a black pool on the floor between them. Then Kethra dropped the hand with an oath, hurled the bottle into the fireplace, and stormed out of the hall without a backward glance.

"Border hospitality," said Jamethiel. "I have on occasion been made to feel more welcome."

Kracarn came forward quickly, wrenching a white scarf from his neck. "Damn these people anyway, Highborn and low," he said angrily, wrapping the scarf around her hand. "I think they must all be mad! Why did you let them treat you that way— you, the High Lord's sister!"

She flexed her hand carefully, painfully. "There. More mess than damage, I think. That Warder is so upset she hardly knows what she's doing. But why? Something is very wrong here, Kracarn. When I know what it is, I'll know how to react, won't I?"

Tarin emerged from his recess, expressionless, and gestured to the woman to follow him. As she left the hall with the gray dog still at her side and the thin, silent man at her heels, Arie saw that she was absentmindedly licking the last traces of liquor and blood from the tips of her long, white fingers.

In her wake, the hall seemed very empty and silent. Silent? No. There was a throbbing, a deep pulse. Arie felt as if his head was swelling with it. He desperately willed it to stop, willed himself not to see, but already the hall before him was fading. In its place was a much larger, grander hall, its high roof supported by black marble columns, its floor paved with green-veined stone. Thousands of death banners lined its walls. Tapestry faces grimaced. Threadbare hands clutched at rotting fabric. All was dead fiber, and yet the walls beneath were stained with blood.

Arie backed away. "No," he said out loud. "No, it isn't there. It isn't *real*."

He tripped on steps, then turned and scrambled blindly up and up, past the second level gallery, into the close turnings of the highest tower. The wind came whistling down to meet him.

At its summit, the tower opened out on all four sides. Arie sank down beside the sheer drop, trembling. Then he began to cry. It wasn't fair. He hadn't asked to be so weak, or crippled, or—or cursed with these visions. No one here understood what that was like. Kethra certainly didn't. He hadn't even dared to tell her when he had begun to see things. She would think he was feeble-witted on top of everything else or, perhaps, going mad.

Arie rested his cheek against the cold stones and closed his eyes. The wind rushed about him, slowly stripping away his fears. He began to sing to himself, very softly, first songs that the wandering singer had brought to the keep more than a year ago and then songs of his own. The wind deafened him to his own words but seemed to make them ring all the more clearly in his mind. He worked them this way and that, changing, polishing them, and for a while was content.

It was nearly sunset when he opened his eyes again. Light streamed between the two opposite peaks to the west and shadows slowly rose in the Pass below. To the north, a premature darkness clouded the Barrier. Its surface moved restlessly in patterns that must have been miles across, and lightning flickered inside. There almost seemed to be something solid within the mists. Each flash half defined shifting outlines as of roofs and chimneys and gables as if at any minute the haze would roll back and there would stand the Master's House, looming over the mountains, the High Keep, over all Rathillien. It was a mirage which often appeared before one of those terrible spring storms from the north, from Perimal Darkling, that shook the keep down to its very roots. Arie picked up his crutch, shivering. It was more than time that he went below.

As he stepped out of the stairwell onto the second level, he heard his name called. Here the western wall opened into a long, rib-vaulted gallery lined with windows through which light poured. Someone sat under the center arch in the heart of the blaze.

"You sing well," said the High Lord's sister.

"Y-you heard me, lady?"

"I have a good ear for a wind-borne voice. Sing again."

Arie surprised himself by obeying, and even more by using the words he had been trying to write down earlier that day. Since then, the song had grown. As he sang it, he strained to make out the figure against the white flame of the sun. The gray cloak was thrown back now, revealing cream-colored riding leathers, a short byrnie of rathorn ivory, and high buff boots, all travel stained. Arie had never seen any Highborn lady but Nessa, and very little of her. This woman seemed impossibly slim compared to the powerfully built Kendar among whom he had grown up, and infinitely more graceful, with a hint of underlying tension. Even in repose, she seemed poised for sudden movement.

"Very good," she said when he had finished. "You have the true singer's voice—and sight. How did you know that the Master's hall is paved with green-veined stones?"

Arie gaped at her. "I—I didn't know. I just saw . . ."

Then stammering, he told her about his visions—the corridor extending into infinity, the window opening on such a landscape as Rathillien had never known, the black marble staircase ascending to a doorway barred with red ribbons as if it led to a lord's bridal chamber.

"I remember those stairs," said Jamethiel in a low voice, as if to herself. "Someone was waiting beyond those ribbons, and perhaps still is. When did you see these things?"

Arie told her.

"So," she said thoughtfully. "It all began when the patrol brought back that wretched 'almost human' creature from near the Barrier soon after Mid-Winter. Yes. That makes sense . . . but what a half-witted thing to have done!"

"Lady?"

"Nothing—I hope. Arie, how long has it been since the High Keep had a direct clash with the Master's folk?"

"Centuries, I think. Lady, it's been so long since the Master's fall. Is he really still there beyond the Barrier, still waiting?"

"Oh, yes. Listen to your own song. The man bargained for immortality and got it, he and his people both, after a fashion. Then, too, time passes more slowly in Perimal Darkling than here. The Master can and will wait until we forget him, as my brother has, until we lower our guard. But your leg hurts, doesn't it? What did you do to it?"

"Kethra put me on a half-broken colt when I was a child. I—it reared and fell on me."

"I see. Come to the window."

Arie hesitated, then limped shyly forward, only to stop again abruptly. The darkness at the Highborn's feet had risen. It was the gray bitch.

"Give her your hand," said Jamethiel.

Arie would rather have bolted. Instead, he found himself holding out a shaking hand, bracing himself for the pain which he felt sure would come. The dog sniffed it. Then, incredibly, his fingertips were wet from her tongue.

"Good," said the Highborn. "Now, after me, you are her master. Sit down . . . please."

Arie sat on the window ledge. He could see the visitor's face clearly now in the failing light. It looked very young and tired.

"Does your hand hurt much?" he blurted out.

The thin lips lifted in a wry smile. "Considering the things that have happened to me and that I've done to myself—yes, including that idiotic recklessness with the Master Runes that left me croaking like this—these wounds hardly count." She raised her bandaged hand and looked at it. Her smile slipped away. "In fact, compared to the binding of a creature's body and soul, these scratches are beneath contempt, and I have forced this hound to sell its freedom for a few drops of blood!"

Her long fingers curled stiffly into a fist.

"Lady!" Arie cried, and caught her injured hand in both of his as if to prevent it from striking out at the nearest stone. Its warmth and the feel of fine bones just under the skin startled him. Somehow, he hadn't quite believed before that this strange woman was mere flesh and blood, however much of the latter he had already seen.

"Sorry," she said with a crooked smile, withdrawing her hand. "But this keep, it's so old, so . . . fragile. Like an egg-shell. I can feel darkness tapping on the outside, tapping at my self-control, too. How easy it would be to fall in a place like this. Arie, listen: to protect yourself, you have to know what's going on. Somehow, the will of this keep's defenders has been badly undermined, so much so that Perimal Darkling lies just beneath the surface here. Patrolling the Barrier is hardly enough when that sort of rot sets in. And each time the rangers bring back a darkling, things get worse because every creature out of the shadows brings some of them with it. That 'almost human' thing certainly did. So far, no one but you has seen these visions, but soon everyone will if this goes on. This entire keep is in danger of becoming no more than a shadow of that greater fortress in Perimal Darkling, the Master's House."

Arie wrestled with this. "Then, when I saw the room with the green-veined floor . . ."

"It was because Bender and I had just been in your hall, the counterpart of the Master's," said Jamethiel bitterly. She glanced at the gallery wall. Arie, also looking, started violently. The rapidly fading daylight cast both their shadows on the stones, but the Highborn's was darker and had a human face. There stood Bender, as he must have all this time.

"That is an unfallen darkling," said Jamethiel. "I am another one. We both were inmates in the Master's House. Neither of us consented to his evil, but we were both changed nonethe-less. Bender is . . . as you see him. And I?" She shivered sud-denly, and drew her cloak around her as if for warmth. "I have darkness in my veins now. Enough to blood-bind this poor brute to me body and soul. Enough to cast the very shadows I fight."

Thunder rumbled nearer, louder, and a cold northern wind breathed down the gallery. It was nearly dark now. To the north, verdigris lightning played across the Barrier as through the heart of a black opal.

Then from below came a booming sound. It echoed up the stairwell like some great shout of warning from no human throat and the gallery rang with it.

Jamethiel sprang up. "What in God's name is that?"

"The alarm, lady." Arie lurched to his feet. "Someone has sounded the Keepguard Horn in the lower hall. We must be under attack."

Below, the large room was rapidly filling as the keep Kendar poured into it in answer to the alarm, hurriedly buckling on armor as they came. Kethra stood by the extinct fire, silent and grim. Before her on the table lay something long and pale. It was Nessa's body.

The crowd parted for Jamethiel. She bent over the still form.

"Dead," said Kethra thickly.

"Yes, and already beginning to stiffen." She reached for the mask which, out of respect, no one else had touched.

"But where is her gown?" asked Arie in a thin voice from the foot of the table.

Kethra looked at him, then at the corpse. What she had taken for the familiar garment in the stress of the moment was in fact only the first of many under-tunics.

"I'm afraid that isn't the only thing missing," said Jamethiel, and turned back the veil. Shock rippled through the hall. Under the silk was a grinning, bestial face whose eyes long since had gone to feed the crows. "I suggest you look on the northern battlement for the head of this poor lady," the Highborn said soberly. "Now. Before dawn brings back the birds."

Kethra turned on her, shock and rage at war in her face, but before she could speak, a Kendar burst through the crowd and threw himself gasping at her feet.

"Warder! In the lowest corridor by the western foundation . . . Tucor, Erlik, and I on guard duty . . . we found Lady Nessa's servant all broken and then . . . w-we saw her in the shadows, beckoning. Erlik and Tucor went to her. I-I saw her put her arms around them and then . . . she began . . . to squeeze. Warder! She crushed them, she crushed them both. I-I ran. Forgive me, but I couldn't fight *her*."

"Who?" roared Kethra.

"I-I think it was the High Lord's sister, but she wore Lady Nessa's gown . . . ."

The rustle of cloth as Jamethiel swung her gray cloak over the body caused the guard to look up. His jaw dropped when he saw them both.

"One thing at least is certain," said Jamethiel grimly. "The dress was hers."

Kethra turned on her again, seething. "Battlements, cellars, exchanged heads—how much of this do you understand, Highborn?"

"Sweet Trinity, less than you should," said the other in exasperation. "Warder, do you know what a changer is?"

Kethra gave her a startled look and then almost by reflex began to recite the ancient lesson: "'In the Master's House there were those who embraced his evil. To them also life unending was given, but they purchased it with the corruption of body and soul until they could take on the mockery of any form but hold none that was true. So were the changers born.'" She gave a harsh laugh. "Are you saying that's what our guest in the cellar is, Darkling? After all these centuries and on a night when you just happen to be our guest, too?"

Kracarn put a hand on his lady's arm almost pleadingly. "Jamethiel, it's beneath your dignity even to talk to this madwoman. Kendar!" He raised his voice. "One of you go summon your lord. God's claws, his sister has just been murdered!"

No one moved.

"Kracarn, please. Warder, if I'm right, this keep last saw a changer not centuries but only months ago when your patrol brought back the head of that 'almost human' thing to grace your battlements. Yes, that's what I think it was."

Kethra snorted. "D'you think we wouldn't know a changer if we saw one?"

"I don't think you would recognize one if it threw you down the stairs. Remember, these creatures can counterfeit any appearance. But they were also once like us and still are in some respects. What would *you* do if someone fed your kinsman or friend or lover to the crows like a common piece of carrion without benefit of death rites or pyre?"

"Do?" The Warder stiffened at the very thought of such an abomination. "*Do?* Why, I would tear down the bastard's house stone by stone and stake him out among the rubble. I would give him his own blood to drink . . . ." She stopped short. "Sweet Trinity. Is that what we did?"

"I think so. And now with the same spring thaw that brought me comes that poor creature's avenger to breach *your* walls and spill *your* blood—although, being a changer, he goes about it rather more obliquely than you would."

Throughout the hall, Kendar shifted uneasily. More than one made the Dawkwyr sign both against this avenger out of the shadows and against the evil which they themselves might unwittingly have committed. But Kethra looked at the still figure on the table and her expression hardened.

"Whatever we may or may not have done, this poor lady was innocent. Now her blood is a stain on our honor until we avenge her death." She turned to the uneasy crowd and raised her voice. "Hear me! We may have a different kind of quarry tonight, but it is still quarry and we are still hunters and warriors. This creature will die with blood in its throat, so I swear! Re-Kencyr . . . ."

"Warder!" Jamethiel's voice cut across the ancient battle cry. "You have no idea how different a hunt this will be. I do. Leave it to me."

Kethra gave her a scornful look. "I'd as soon send this boy. Crippled as he is, he's at least as strong as a poor stick like you."

"Ancestors preserve us," said the Highborn, exasperated. "What has strength got to do with it? You'll never slay this creature by force anyway. God's claws and toenails, what do you think will happen if the lot of you go charging down into those cellars? Think of the confusion. Think of this creature's powers. It may even be one of the breed who can snatch the very thoughts from your mind. Down there in the dark, how long will you be sure that the person coming up behind you is really your brother, your sister, your friend? Then the killing will start. I tell you, the changer has set a trap for you all and that," she pointed at Nessa's corpse, "is the bait."

"Bait?" Kethra started forward, big hands flexing. "*Bait?* The last of the Min-drears . . ."

An abrupt silence fell on the hall. No one even seemed to breathe.

"You had better tell me," said Jamethiel. "Whatever it is, you can't hide it forever."

The Warder had turned away, shoulders bowed. "Lord Min-drear is dead," she said in a choked voice. "His poor sister couldn't accept it, but it's true. We gave him to the pyre on Mid-Winter Day."

"And kept it a secret all this time?" Kracarn was outraged. "The news should have gone to Gothregor months ago! Lord Torisen will have to assign this keep to another Highborn family and they, of course, will bring in their own Kendar. You should all have made arrangements to leave by now!"

A low growl rose from the assembled Kendar. They closed ranks around the two Highborn. Arie began to shiver. He saw something in those familiar faces that he had never seen there before, and it terrified him.

"Kracarn . . ." said Jamethiel. "Shut up." She looked with amazement at the wall of hostile faces ringing her in. "My God, what are you people thinking of? D'you really believe that killing us will keep the news from Gothregor forever? And when my brother hears, what then? I give you fair warning: he annoys easily. But I still don't entirely understand. The last of the Min-drears? This boy . . ." she looked at Arie. "He has the build of a Highborn and the Min-drear hands. Isn't he the old lord's son?"

"Yes," said Kethra, as if the word hurt. "But not his consort's. Enough! For the moment, this is still our home and we will defend it as we see fit, without the help of one who once ate the Master's bread and might, for all we know, still earn it."

"Warder!"

Kethra spun around, aware that she had really overstepped herself this time and prepared to bluster. Instead, her eyes met those of the visitor, and she fell back a step.

"Threatening my life is one thing," said that husky, purring voice. "Questioning my honor is another. At the very least, to do so is . . . unwise. Shall I remind you of your manners, Warder? Yes, I believe I will. Three times within one day you have ignored the cup rites. Once for my arrival. You will forgive me if I fail to count the bottle which you so graciously emptied over my hand. Once for your slain lady. Her parting cup should have been drunk before she grew cold. Once for the hunt. Vengeance must be sworn and sanctified in proper form."

"Lady, now is not the time," protested Kethra, thrown on the defensive and more than a bit shaken.

"I say it is. Moreover, all must take part and each rite must last its full hour. Let everyone in the keep assemble here. Steward, bring all the ale you can find. Bender will help you. The rest of you, prepare the hall."

There was a moment's startled hesitation. Arie felt as if someone had kicked the feet out from under him and suspected that others felt the same. It was a long time since the full, innate power of a Kencyr Highborn had been exercised within these walls. Kethra opened her mouth, shut it, opened it again. If Jamethiel's demands had gone any further, she would have rebelled, but the customs invoked had weight with her, and so did the other's manner.

"I think one of us really has gone mad," she said. "All right. Do as she orders. The changer can work no mischief down there by itself. Our hunt and our vengeance are only delayed."

In short order, the hall was made ready. A hundred men and women sat on the benches, each with an ale mug in one hand and a naked sword in the other. All turned grim faces toward the head table where the Warder and Arie sat with the visitors. Nessa's body lay in state on a trestle between the high table and the benches. A thick candle marked with hour bands burned at her head, now retrieved from the battlements.

Kethra rose and growled the code of welcome. The response was muttered sullenly through the hall and the drinking began.

Bender put a small cask on the table in front of the Warder.

"A guest-gift," said Jamethiel. "My cask of wine for your flask of liquor. I occasionally remember my own manners, such as they are. You may have a taste," she added to Kracarn, "but then you must drink the common ale. There is little enough of this."

They poured and drank. Arie knew that he had never tasted better wine.

There was silence in the hall at first, broken only by the splash of ale. Outside, the storm rumbled closer. Fitful gusts of wind breathed through the hall's small upper windows, stirring the banners. Candles flickered and a pool of molten wax began to form beside Nessa's head. Arie drank more wine.

The first hour passed at last. Kethra stood and gave the call to mourning.

The voices in the hall were louder now, raised as though to compete with the approaching storm. The stones of the keep shivered as the thunder spoke again. In the lulls, Arie became aware of Jamethiel's quiet, slightly husky voice reciting the ancient stories of betrayal and flight and Rathillien, the new world, of striving and suffering, joy and triumph. Kethra relaxed and listened as the noises in the hall mounted unnoticed. Arie drank more wine.

The second hour passed more quickly. The summons to vengeance was greeted by a low, hoarse roar and the raising of many cups.

Kethra sank back in her chair. That husky voice had caught her now, all the more so because this time it told a story she had heard before only in fragments. Arie also listened, rapt. As the Highborn described it, he seemed to see that great mass of people known as the Horde slowly circling, circling in the Southern Wastes as they had for centuries past. But then, abruptly, the circle broke and the Horde began to move northward, three million strong, toward the Riverland. The Kencyr Host led by Torisen High Lord marched south to meet it. Host and Horde came together at the Cataracts. Battle followed on the narrow stair beside the falls, and confusion, and carnage.

As Jamethiel spoke, Arie almost thought he heard other, nearer sounds: shouts, oaths, a bench crashing over. Out of the corner of his eye he caught movement, as though many figures were weaving about in confusion. Shadows leaped and, crying, fell.

But the voice went on, quiet, husky, arresting. It spoke of a girl escaped from darkness who came in search of her brother and found him in the chaos of battle at the Cataracts. It described their reunion, her doomed attempt to live as the Kencyrath said a Highborn woman should. Then followed flight, friendship among the scrollsmen, random training, and much else besides in a life as breathless as a midnight race along the edge of a precipice.

"Except," said Jamethiel with a sudden smile, "when I occasionally fall on my head and so manage to get a little rest."

"A Highborn woman, uncloistered, unmasked." Even with the evidence before her, Kethra still found that hard to believe. "Has the Kencyrath changed so much since your brother became High Lord?"

"No," said the other, a bit sadly now. "Not really. But there are new possibilities. As for me, my brother hasn't exactly been pleased with my path, but he hasn't done all he could to stop me either."

"I should think," said Kethra wryly, "that it would take a great deal to do that."

Just then, Kracarn slid out of his chair and under the table, still clutching an ale mug. Arie started to laugh. Then, for the first time in hours, he looked past the Highborn to the hall beyond and his mouth dropped open. Half of the High Keep Kendar were sprawling on the floor and the rest slumped over the low tables.

"Oh, yes," said Jamethiel quietly, sipping her wine. "Very little stops me. That, however, might." She lowered her cup and regarded the sword point which Kethra had leveled at her throat.

"No more stories," grated the Warder. "No more honeyed voice. What have you done to my people?"

"Gently, gently. They only sleep, like my companion here, thanks to the phial which Bender poured into their ale. My congratulations on their hardheadedness, by the way. I demanded the full rites, but never really thought it would take all three hours for the potion to work. You have a choice now, Warder: strike, or finish your wine and come with me." She gave a sudden wry grin. "You might at least give me the benefit of the doubt. For once, I know what I'm doing—I hope."

For a moment, Kethra stood glaring. Then she drained her cup with a gulp. The two rose and crossed the body-strewn floor to the stairs leading downward. Bender and the gray bitch followed them.

Arie was left at the table, staring blankly at Lady Nessa's body. The third hour passed in a slow stream of hot wax running down the thick candle at her head. Then the rising storm slammed into the keep with a shout of thunder. The hall doors burst open. Wind came questing into the hall, licked back

Nessa's veil. For a moment her pale face, oddly tranquil, caught the light. Then the candle blew out.

Arie grabbed his crutch with something almost like a sob and stumbled after the others toward the stair. The murk of the subterranean levels received him soundlessly.

The first basement was occupied by the winter stables and the kennels. As he went, half falling, down the stairway, Arie heard the uneasy movements of horses and a dog whimpering somewhere in the dim maze of wooden partitions.

He caught up with the others halfway down into the second basement where the fire timbers towered fifty-feet from brick floor to ceiling. Impossible to ignite by accident, these huge logs had only been made to burn after a year of dropping hot coals into their hollowed-out trunks. It had taken the largest of them many generations to burn through to the bark. Their dusky orange glow lit the hall, but Arie could feel little of their warmth. Someone had left open the trap door in the southwest corner which led down to the foundation level. Chill air rose from the black hole, heavy with the smell of earth. The stairway went straight down into it.

A moment later, they were all standing on the dirt floor of the keep's lowest level with the torchlit passage stretching out before them along the western foundation wall.

Kethra and Jamethiel went first. The Warder still carried her sword naked in her hand and used it to cut tangled webs from their path. The Highborn, unarmed, kept her left hand locked in the gray dog's fur. Arie limped after them, still rather wine-befuddled, wondering if any of this was actually happening. The torches bracketed at intervals in the outer stone wall had begun to burn with a bluish tinge. High above the hall, the death banners must be flying over the drugged Kendar, but only a dull vibration in the stones and a groaning from the inner wall of ironwood—like that from the timbers of a ship at sea—marked the presence of the storm. Not even the voice of the thunder could reach them in this grave of narrow passageways.

They found Nessa's attendant at the mouth of the third corridor leading off under the main body of the keep. As the guard had said, she was horribly broken, as if someone had taken great pains to snap every bone. Beyond lay Erlik and Tucor. They had been crushed together face to face, tooth uprooting tooth, shattered rib bursting through flesh and armor to lock with rib in a horrible parody of a lover's embrace. The ground all about them gleamed darkly in the torchlight.

Kethra swore out loud.

The gray bitch suddenly strained forward under Jamethiel's hand, growling. The next moment she broke free and disappeared down the side corridor.

"After her!" cried Jamethiel.

They ran, the Highborn and the Warder racing on ahead. Arie stumbled. Bender's thin hand closed on his elbow and drew him on. Surely they were going down hill now, but he had never heard that these passages sloped. The ceiling and walls also seemed wrong, as though the former were rising and the latter opening out between the islands of torch-cast light into shadowy depths. He caught glimpses of high vaulted chambers, arcades, and halls where there could be nothing but ironwood and ashlar walls.

These are shadows of the Master's House, he thought dizzily. But in the presence of three darklings, they were rapidly becoming more than that.

Then from ahead came a scream of canine agony.

Kethra sprang forward with a hoarse shout, brandishing her sword. Jamethiel tripped her. When the Warder tried to rise, a slim arm snaked around her throat, deft fingers barely touching the pressure points. Kethra gasped.

"You fool, not with the sword!" hissed Jamethiel's voice in her ear. "Remember, this creature's blood is utterly corrupt. It *burns.*"

Kethra shook off the Highborn and rose, seething. "One more trick like that, Darkling . . ."

"And you'll feed me to the chickens. Just as you wish, but later. Here it comes."

The two swung about to face down the passageway. Arie peered around them. He could no longer trace the phantom outlines of the openings, but the sense of open space remained. They stood under a torch between solid walls. Beyond, however, the brands were nothing but blurs in midair, bobbing in the cold wind that slid past where no wind had a right to be.

From ahead in the gloom came a faint rustling sound, moving closer, closer. Something pale entered the farthest circle of light. Arie gulped. That was Nessa's gown, but what in all the names of God was wearing it? The advancing form looked like that of a woman, but even as he watched it thickened, the curve of breast and hip becoming less distinct. Seams ripped. The dim blur of a face swam closer in the murky light. The Warder drew in her breath sharply.

"Kethraaaa . . ." came a low, hissing and yet horribly familiar voice from the shadows. "Keeeethraaa . . ."

"Min-drear?" the Warder whispered. "No. *No!*"

She lunged forward, steel flashing. Her sword bit deeply into the shoulder of the advancing changer. A few drops of blood spattered on the ground, on her hand, and ate hungrily into both. The awful wound closed around steel, burnt it away. Kethra found herself clutching only a sword hilt. The creature grinned down at her with a face rapidly becoming more and more like that of her dead lord.

"Keeethraa . . . have you missed me? Cooome, an embrace for old love's sake . . . ."

It had caught hold of her arms and now began to squeeze. Her coat split down the back. Bones creaked. Arie started toward her with a cry, but Bender held him fast.

"Warder!" The Highborn's voice cracked off the stone walls. "It takes its form from your memories. Think of something else!"

The creature faltered, its face beginning to lose definition. With a snarl, it thrust Kethra aside.

"Soooo . . . the Master's toy. What do *you* remember, changeling?"

Arie saw its features begin to alter again as it shambled forward, cheekbones becoming more pronounced, silver-gray eyes widening. Jamethiel went back a step.

"I deny you," she said hoarsely. "I damn you."

Her hands jerked up, bandaged fingers separating stiffly. With horror, Arie saw her start to make the Darkwyr sign in reverse.

Bender caught her arm and sent her spinning backward. She collided with Arie, knocking him into the wall. The stones against his back felt strange—sheet ice over deep water, about to crack. He pushed both Jamethiel and himself away from them.

Bender completed the mirror sign. The wind stopped. Cold grew. In the uncertain light, it looked as if what little flesh the man still had was melting away as from someone years dead, but his hands held the sign without a tremor.

The changer had halted uncertainly in front of him. Now it reached out as if to grab the man and its own fingertips shriveled at the touch. It turned, snarling, thwarted. Behind it lay Kethra. She had fallen against the wall at the edge of the light. Arie could see her left arm and the lower part of her body clearly, but the rest was indistinct. Instead of stones behind her, there seemed to be pavement, stretching back out of sight, marked with strange patterns. Kethra was straining to pull herself out of the darkness. She would not succeed before the changer reached her.

Without thinking, the boy released Jamethiel's arm and slipped past Bender. The face and form of the changer were in motion again even as he threw himself between it and the Warder.

"Cripple," it said, almost in Kethra's voice. "Worthless little cripple." Then it burst into long peals of jeering laughter.

"Shut up, mother!" he screamed at it. "Shut up, shut up!" He swung his crutch.

The pain of splinters ripping into his palms as the shaft was wrenched out of them brought him to his senses with a gasp. It was towering over him, chuckling now with a sound like bubbles rising through quicksand. He stared up at it, too appalled to move.

Behind him, Kethra staggered to her feet.

"Now!" cried Jamethiel. "Hellbender, bring it down!"

The man dropped his hands. Kethra swept Arie aside. The changer had half turned at the sound of the Highborn's voice. Now it swayed and toppled as both Bender and the Warder hit it simultaneously. Each pinned down an arm. Arie, to his amazement, found himself trying to control one of its legs. The limb slowly writhed in his grasp. He felt a terrible strength gathering in it.

Jamethiel dropped to her knees beside the misshapen head. She tore the white scarf off her hand, hooked her fingernails in the half closed wounds, and ripped them open. Blood spiraled down her wrist. Bender forced the changer's mouth open and she held her hand over it. Blood streamed off the heel of her palm down into the working throat.

The changer gagged, and then it convulsed. A knee smashed into Arie, knocking him two paces down the corridor. Caught by a whiplash arm across the face, Jamethiel staggered back into the wall under the torch. Her head struck the stones sharply. Bender drew her clear.

Convulsion followed convulsion. Nessa's gown was ripped apart in seconds. Beneath it, the pale flesh twisted and writhed, as if each sinew was a separate thing. There was a dull crack as a bone snapped in the midst of a muscular contraction, then another and another. Still, it wasn't until the shattered end of a femur tore its way out through the side of one leg that the thing began to scream. There were words mixed in that rush of agony and dark blood. The changer was begging for death, begging despite its torment in the correct ritual terms. Only a Highborn would use that formula. Only a Highborn had the authority to grant what was asked.

Jamethiel stood over it, her bruised face very still. "Bring me fire," she said in a low voice. "Hurry."

Bender took the torch out of its socket and put it in her hand. She extended it to the distorted thing on the floor. Its hand shot up and gripped the burning wood. Flames leaped down the ruined sleeve of the gown. In an instant, fire clothed the entire form. Flames spread, covering walls, floor, ceiling, and yet none of them burned. It was as if the shadows themselves were being consumed. The heat and stench of the pyre drove Arie and the others back to the western foundation. It was there, when at last the flames and the unnatural wind died together, that they realized Jamethiel was not with them.

They found her sitting on the stairs, hands clenched together with no regard for the torn flesh. Orange light from the fire-timber hall spilled down the steps around her, casting her shadow black on the floor. Bender stood in it. *Of course,* thought Arie with a kind of light-headed omniscience, *that's because he has no shadow of his own.* Kethra regarded the Highborn belligerently, fists jammed on hips.

"Well?" she demanded.

"That all depends," said Jamethiel bitterly. "As you may have noticed, I nearly got you killed. That damned sign. I always was too quick with my hands. This time, at the very least it would have cost me my soul or Bender his—if he still had one. Instead, I've killed a Highborn, one of my own blood, with my blood. Set one to catch one, eh? Perhaps, after all, there isn't that much to choose between two shades of darkness."

Kethra regarded her soberly for a minute more. Then she unknotted the black scarf of office around her neck.

"I make my choice," she said and, taking Jamethiel's injured hand, carefully wrapped the cloth around it.

Arie woke the next morning in a corner of the lower hall, groggy with wine and dreams. He remembered finding Jamethiel on the steps and the long climb upward. He remembered his mother and the Highborn sitting at the head table drinking the last of the wine, talking through the last long hours of the night while the storm slowly spent itself outside. He *thought* he remembered scraps of their conversation:

"A keep is more than its Highborn. My brother and I still agree on that, if on little else."

"The boy is weak. Brave, yes, but weak."

"So am I—physically. Strength isn't everything. Then, too, he sees things, true things. A singer with the sight can be very powerful, very . . . dangerous."

"To you?"

"Perhaps. Someday he may see more in me than I care to know about myself, but no one can stop a true song or, I hope, a new idea."

"Still, a half-Kendar lord . . ."

That last bit must be a dream. Arie had fallen asleep to the sound of their voices. His last clear memory was of a fur robe dropping over his shoulders.

At last he opened his eyes, and found that not all the warmth of his makeshift bed came from the robe. The gray bitch lay curled up beside him. Her right paw was bandaged and there was a lump on her head. Something in the protective curve of her great body told him that the hound had been assigned a new master. Timidly, he reached out and stroked her gray flank.

It was still very early morning, barely past daybreak. Most of the Kendar still sprawled snoring on the floor and Nessa kept her solitary state, but a voice spoke in the courtyard. It was Kethra, pledging the rider's cup. Arie threw off the robe. He and the hound limped to the door together.

Jamethiel sat her Whinno-hir in the courtyard, one hand still wrapped in the Warder's black scarf resting on the mare's neck. Bender and Kracarn waited nearby, one as inscrutable as ever, the other clearly feeling very ill-used. Kethra was offering them the cup.

Jamethiel saw Arie and smiled. "Mind you," she said to the

Warder, "no promises. All I can offer is a new possibility, and hope."

"Hope." Kethra put her hand rather awkwardly on Arie's shoulder. "Yes, we can live on that—as long as necessary. In the meantime, a month from now I and my son will come south to your brother's council. Then, if Arie wishes it, he will stay with you for a while. There are things you can teach him that I can't."

"Do you wish it?" Jamethiel asked.

Arie could only nod.

"Very good. Your songs will help us all push back the darkness. In a month, then!" She raised her bandaged hand in farewell, turned the mare, and in another minute had disappeared through the main gate.

"A month," said Kethra. "Not much time. Still we will make it count. You will sing for us often, I hope. The shadows have been too long in these halls."

They went back into the keep together, the Warder, the lame boy, and the gray hound.

THE
CURSE OF
IGAMOR

by

MICHAEL
DE LARRABEITI

NE FINE summer morning many hundreds of years ago the Lord of Aigues Mortes, a town thought by many to be the most beautiful in Provence, rose from his bed and, in his loudest voice, summoned the two most important of his numerous servants, the Constable and the High Chancellor.

His lordship came straight to the point. "I need more money," he said. "The people of this town do not pay enough for the protection that I and my soldiers give them. I shall increase the taxes." He pointed to the Constable. "You," he continued, "will go into the city square and make an announcement."

The Constable shifted on his feet and stared at the priceless Persian carpet on which he stood. "We have tried to increase the taxes before," he said, "but the people of this town make excuses and say they'll not part with another penny."

"Yes," added the Chancellor, "we've done everything, but the people murmur under their breath and curse us as we pass."

The Lord of Aigues Mortes turned on his heel and squeezed his hands together behind his back until the knuckles bulged white. He looked through his tower window and stared at the landscape that was spread out below and beyond the city walls. A strange landscape it was, too, a trackless wilderness of marshland and salt lakes, stretching away for miles to the very edge of the glittering Mediterranean, and in those vast swamps lived thousands of white horses, wild and strong and free. They could run like the wind, those horses, and no one could catch them, and often they swam deep into the rolling waves, swimming until their tangled manes were covered by milky foam and they looked for all the world like giant sea creatures. The people who lived in Provence said the horses had been left there by the Saracens when they had sailed away to Africa in ancient times. Some even thought that the horses were bewitched. "Keep away from the marshes," they would warn, "especially at night."

But the Lord of Aigues Mortes never thought of such things. He was not troubled by the superstitions of the lowly. All he cared about was how much money he could collect, how many soldiers he could maintain and how much power he could wield over others. He turned at last from the window, his face dark with thought and red with anger. He banged his desk with his fist.

"Well," he shouted, "we'll see about that. I know how to deal with these peasants of mine. I'll threaten them with such a fate they'll be only too pleased to pay their taxes, however much I ask for," and he stormed out of his palace and hurried across his private courtyard and into the main square where he knew he would find most of his subjects setting up market stalls and opening their small shops. The Chancellor and the Constable, with his staff of office under his arm, followed their lord step for step, one behind the other.

"Stop," cried the Constable as soon as the three men arrived on the square. "Stop and listen, cease all noise and bustle," and he gave a twirl of his staff.

All noise stopped on the instant and the townspeople stood as statues, facing their liege lord. When the silence was complete the Lord of Aigues Mortes raised an arm and pointed to the sky.

"You will pay your taxes," he began, "or I'll know the reason."

"But we do, my lord," said a citizen standing nearby, "we do. Regularly and in full."

"But you do not pay enough," said the Chancellor.

"But," said another citizen, "if we pay more we shall not have enough to feed ourselves, or our children who often go hungry as it is. And if our children should die then there will be no one to pay taxes in the future, my lord. Not for your son or your son's son."

"Your children," retorted the mighty lord. "What do I care about your children. I have soldiers to keep, this city to defend against my enemies. I have walls and battlements to repair, my courtiers to feed. Children! I tell you what . . . if you do not pay twice what you are paying now, why then, I shall take your children from you . . . I shall send for Igamor."

At this the citizens caught their breath and went quiet and pale. The Lord of Aigues Mortes could not have said a more terrifying thing. According to an ancient legend of that city, Igamor was a huge and terrible horse of the marshes, only black, as black as the blackest night, with eyes of crimson flame and teeth like sabers that clattered and clashed as he galloped. Igamor had a long long back that could stretch and stretch so that he could carry many more riders than an ordinary horse. Igamor had hooves of iron and a coat of wire which clung to human flesh like burrs of steel and never let go. Once you sat astride or touched him with a hand then you were bound to him forever. Once he had you in his power Igamor bore you off across the marshes at a headlong pace, rushing with you to his cavern under the waves and you were never seen again. For generations the simple inhabitants of the town had believed in the legend; from age to age parents had warned their children against falling foul of Igamor for, once taken, there was no coming back. But now they shuddered and the marrow of their bones shriveled. Never had the Lord of Aigues Mortes threatened them with such a fate. The citizens hung their heads and were silent.

The Chancellor and the Constable laughed out loud to see their lord's subjects so subdued before him and their laughter echoed round the city walls.

His lordship spoke again. "Listen," he said, "Igamor is known to me and does my least bidding . . . unless you do exactly as I say I shall send for him and order him to come for each of your children in turn, even into your very houses and his back will stretch and stretch until all the children of this town are mounted upon him and then Igamor will carry them away across the marshes and down to the sea. And let no one dare breathe a word of what I have said to anyone who comes from outside this city . . . the first one to disobey me will be the first to see his child take a ride on Igamor's back. Now cross yourselves, all of you, or I will rip the hearts from your bodies."

The townspeople knelt at their lord's command and made the sign of the cross upon their breasts and their lord sneered. "The tax collectors will begin their work tomorrow." And with that he stamped away followed as always by his Chancellor and his Constable.

As soon as the three men had returned to the private apartments they burst into huge gusts of laughter.

"There," said the Lord of Aigues Mortes, "there will be no more trouble now, they'll pay up like lambs."

"It's amazing," said the Constable. "Igamor is not even true, it's just an old legend about a black horse that carries children away."

"That's all right," said the Lord of Aigues Mortes, "it's just an old superstition but the people of this town have always believed it and as long as they believe it . . . why then, it's real, at least for them. As long as they obey me I do not care how, or why."

The very next day every citizen was required to pay the extra tax and they did. Day followed day and the people of the town grew hungrier and lost their energy and their gaiety. From that time on they went about their business with a mournful air. The town became silent, like a place stricken by the plague. No one laughed, no one sang and the children no longer played in the streets or ran along the battlements. The black curse of Igamor hung over the whole town. Only the Lord of Aigues Mortes and the Chancellor and the Constable, the soldiers and the courtiers were happy. That was how they wanted the town to be: subdued and obedient. The townspeople became sadder and sadder; it looked like the end . . . luckily it wasn't.

At the beginning of every summer a One Man Band came to town and made a living, for a day or two, by playing music in the streets. He was the best One Man Band the townsfolk had ever seen and he carried a drum on his back which he played by means of a cord tied to his left toe. In front of his face, supported by a metal bracket that stood out from his shoulders, were three instruments: a clarinet, a trumpet, and a mouth organ. On the inside of each knee was strapped a brass cymbal and they clashed together as he walked, making a great deal of noise. In his hands he held a concertina, and on his head he wore a jester's cap of many colors and sewn all over it were silver bells, each one producing a different sound. His music was wonderful and made everyone who heard it glad to be alive.

The name of the One Man Band was Jeeno and on his shoulder sat a tiny pale brown monkey. This monkey had a long curling tail and her name was Heloise. When Jeeno marched and played, Heloise would jump up and down and strike the silver bells in time to her master's music. Heloise was as intelligent as a human being and it was said that she could even speak.

That year Jeeno landed, as he did every year, from a ship

that had moored in the small harbor that lay near the town. Once on shore he wasted no time, but strode out along the narrow causeway that led across the marshes toward the city walls, walking quickly because he was anxious to see the people of Aigues Mortes and play his music to them.

About a mile from the town Jeeno began to beat his drum and Heloise began to strike the silver bells. As he approached the South Gate the One Man Band smiled to himself. At any second, he thought, children would come running along the road to greet him with shouting and singing.

He was disappointed. Nearer and nearer he came to the gateway but not one person appeared, nor did anyone wave from the battlements. It was most unusual but Jeeno was not dismayed and, now playing all his instruments as loudly as he could, he marched right into the main square.

The Lord of Aigues Mortes went berserk. The last thing in the world he wanted was for his subjects to be made happy. He liked things the way he had got them, with every man, woman, and child in the town subdued and spiritless. There was to be no singing and dancing for them, and he ordered his Constable to suppress this plebeian noise.

The Constable rushed from the palace apartments and seized Jeeno by the arm. "Ho," he said, "you . . . stop that hubbub, tramp. It's illegal."

"Music illegal," said Jeeno, shocked, "since when?"

"Since I say so," said the Constable. "Now let me have no more trouble. Set about your business quietly, otherwise it will be prison for you."

"How can I make music without making a noise?" asked Jeeno.

"That's your problem," said the Constable. "My job is to enforce the law, not understand it! Now move along or I'll throw you into a dungeon, now be off."

Jeeno saw that he had no alternative but to obey. He left the Constable and climbed to the top of the fortifications to look for some of the children of the town, hoping that they, rather than their parents, would tell him what was going on.

But what a sad sight met his eyes when at last he found them. Not one was playing hopscotch or five-stones and nobody shouted or played hide-and-seek. Aigues Mortes was like a town smitten with the plague.

"What is the matter with you, my friends?" asked Jeeno. "I never saw a town so."

The children looked at the sky and fidgeted with their hands. They liked Jeeno and had always liked him. They wanted to tell of the heavy taxes and the threats that their lord had laid upon them, but no one dared. No one wanted to break the solemn oath they had sworn and so become the first child to be carried away by the fearsome horse.

"It is a secret that we may not tell," they explained, "not to you nor to any other human being."

Jeeno laughed at them and it was the first laugh they had heard for weeks. "Very well," he said, "it would never do for you to break a promise, but Heloise is not a human being is she? Tell her," and he walked away from the children and began to unstrap and unfasten the instruments from his body in order to prepare his bed, for when he came to the town he always slept high on the walls.

Heloise stayed with the children until the sun went down over the sea, and when she came to curl up with Jeeno for her night's sleep she brought with her the full story of the Lord, the Chancellor, the Constable and Igamor, the long long horse.

"So," said Jeeno when he had heard it all, "so the Lord of Aigues Mortes thinks he can take stories and frighten good people with them, does he? Scare them to death with make-believe, eh?" He picked up the monkey and looked deep into her eyes. "Well then, Heloise," he went on, "we must see what we can do about this lordling and his friends."

That night, when it was past midnight and the whole town was asleep, the pale shape of the little monkey scampered down from the city walls as softly as a whisper. Through the narrow streets she ran until she came to the great lord's apartments. There she scrambled up to the balcony and slipped into the main bedroom. His lordship was snoring, his mouth wide open and his nose pointing to the ceiling. Heloise did not hesitate but jumped onto his pillow and spoke into his ear.

"Wake, your lordship," she said, "oh hurry, you are deceived by those who call you friend. Tonight a stately ship has appeared in the harbor, without captain or crew, without sail or flag. How it came there is a mystery but its cargo is the richest ever seen. Jewels and silks there are, spices and sweetmeats and incense and wine . . . all are yours, but the Constable and the Chancellor have set out already, secretly, on foot, along the Causeway, but your servants have made a horse ready for you at the East Gate. Do but hurry and you shall overtake your rivals."

Heloise repeated her message and then left silently by the way she had come. The Lord of Aigues Mortes stirred in his sleep, moaning like someone in a dream. He woke and looked around the room and the moonlight came and went, rose and fell.

"I've been dreaming," he said to himself and he rubbed his eyes, then he remembered. "A treasure ship . . . in the harbor," and he jumped out of bed and pulled on his clothes, but although he dressed as rapidly as he could Heloise was halfway across the city before he had finished, on her way to the Chancellor's villa.

He, too, slept and snored and into his ear Heloise poured the same tale of the mysterious treasure ship, and told him that he had been betrayed by a greedy lord and an untrustworthy Constable, but that a horse waited for him at the North Gate.

The Chancellor sat up in bed and rubbed his eyes and shook his head. He looked round the room but he saw nothing, only the moonlight that came and went, rose and fell.

"I've been dreaming," he said, "or have I? The Constable, his lordship, a ship of gold. I must go to the North Gate and take horse," and he sprang from his bed and began to dress.

While the Chancellor struggled into his clothes Heloise ran to the courthouse, vaulted through an open window, and landed softly in the Constable's bedroom. There he lay fast asleep, sprawling and loose-limbed with his staff of office under his pillow.

Heloise whispered her story again, telling of the ship laden with treasure, only this time she spoke of the greed of the Chancellor and the Lord of Aigues Mortes and she told the Constable of a horse waiting for him at the West Gate.

When she had done, Heloise ran from the room and the Constable awoke and raised himself on one elbow and looked about him.

"I've been dreaming," he said. "But wait . . . my lord . . . the Chancellor . . . it would be just like them to leave me out. I must speed to the West Gate, take horse, and run them down," and he jumped from his bed and began to put on his uniform.

The Lord of Aigues Mortes came hurrying to the East Gate. The moon raced between the huge wet clouds, making the shadows of the town leap and fall, dance and disappear. The mighty lord looked hard into the gloom and, in the blackness of the gateway he saw the shape of a horse, the outline of its back, the shine of a polished saddle, and the glint of a stirrup.

"By my faith," said the lord to himself, "some good servant has indeed placed a horse here. It was no dream I had, there must be a great ship in the harbor, full of riches, and the Chancellor and the Constable have gone to it with never a word to me. So be it! I will soon catch them on this magnificent steed."

With one bound the Lord of Aigues Mortes was in the saddle and he stretched his hands forward for the reins . . . but his hands found nothing. He peered into the darkness and a cloud dropped down from the moon, pushed away by the wind, and suddenly his lordship could see and what he saw made his heart knock against his ribs. It was horrible. The horse in front of him stretched away into the night, along the circle of the city walls, to be lost in darkness. There were no reins, there was no head to the horse. The Lord of Aigues Mortes screamed long and loud, he tried to dismount but his legs were stuck solidly to the animal's sides. He screamed again and attempted to push his body free with his hands, but they had become glued to the horse's dark hide of wire. He could not move; he was helpless. Again he screamed . . . and again.

"Igamor, Igamor, who will save me from Igamor?" he cried, but although many lying in bed that night heard his cry not one person ventured into the streets. The townsfolk were too fearful and their children had been told often enough that only a fool went out when Igamor was abroad.

The Chancellor ran under the North Gate and in the gloom outside the city wall he saw a horse, waiting patiently for its rider. He looked closer and saw the saddle and the flashing steel of a stirrup.

"So," he said, "my dream was no dream, some good friend has indeed left me a horse here, there will indeed be a ship of riches in the harbor and that untrustworthy lord of mine and that sly Constable are already on their way with never a word to me. So be it! I shall ride them down on the road," and with no more hesitation than that the Chancellor leapt up and into the saddle.

He felt forward for the reins, but his hands touched a rough spiky coat and a powerful magnetism pulled his hands downward and held them there and his legs and thighs were held fast to the horse's flanks. And the moon sprang from the heart of a black cloud and the Chancellor screamed in terror. The horse before him stretched away into the night along the circle of the city walls. There were no reins; there was no head. The Chancellor screamed again, his voice was strident and the sound it made appalling. It echoed round the narrow streets and everyone in the town heard the scream: "Igamor, Igamor, will no one save me from Igamor?" But not one single person dared venture into the streets. The townsfolk shivered with fear and their children knew that only a fool went out when Igamor was abroad.

The Constable, stumbling in his haste, arrived at the West Gate. In the silver gloom of the archway he saw the fine head of a horse, the droop of the reins, and the gleam of a bright stirrup.

"Aha," he said. "I do indeed have a friend and it seems certain that in the harbor is a cargo of wealth meant for me, and while I stand here the wicked lord of this town and that self-seeking Chancellor are hastening away to steal what should be mine. So be it . . . I will follow after and ride them down, and all the treasure shall be mine," and the Constable leapt onto the horse and seized the reins.

As soon as he was in the saddle he felt a strange power weld him to the animal. His hands were held fast and his legs and thighs were sucked to the sides of the horse and held in a giant's grip. The moon thrust itself from behind a cloud and sped on to the next and the Constable saw the coarse coat of the horse, the long black mane, and the blaze of a wild and fiery eye. He twisted in the saddle, looked behind him and then screamed in terror. The long long back of the horse stretched away into the night along the black shadow of the city walls. The Constable struggled and pushed and fought against the power of Igamor but he was held fast and forever. He screamed again: "Oh save me, save me from Igamor, this cannot be, I am the Constable, save me from Igamor."

There was not one adult or child in bed that night who didn't pull his blanket over his head and tremble in the dark when they heard the Constable scream, but no one went to help him.

They had been warned only too often that nobody but a fool went out when Igamor was abroad.

Then Igamor snorted and shook his head, impatient to be running through the marshes and down to his home in the sea. His teeth clashed in the night and the long long body began to shrink and soon Igamor was the size of one huge horse only and the Lord of the town and the Chancellor and the Constable came together and saw one another and realized that they were indeed doomed. They screamed and begged for mercy and they cursed, each blaming the other two for his predicament, but it made no difference. Igamor stamped an iron hoof and galloped across the marshes toward the sea, splashing the salt water high above his shoulders until at last he disappeared beneath the waves, bearing the three men with him.

Very early the next morning, only five minutes after the sun had risen from the sea and poked its first ray over the city walls, the townsfolk were awakened by the sound of music, loud music. Jeeno, the One Man Band, was playing his instruments for all he was worth and Heloise was sitting on his shoulder, striking at the bells on his cap. Round and round the city walls they went, but the citizens and their children stayed rigid in their beds remembering the screams they had heard in the night and expecting at any moment to hear the iron tread of Igamor. But the music went on and on and became louder and louder and nothing happened to the musician or his monkey.

At last one child, braver than the rest, went to his bedroom window and threw the shutters wide and watched Jeeno making music on the city walls. Soon another shutter banged open, then another, and then another. Then the child who was braver than the rest pulled on some clothes and ran out into the street and many followed and in a little while everyone, old and young, was marching along behind Jeeno and Heloise, strutting in time to the music and singing, too.

When everyone in the town was following him Jeeno stopped playing and held up his hand. The marching and singing ceased and Jeeno stood on his big drum so that he could be seen and heard by the whole population. He told the children and their parents that their lord, and his Chancellor and Constable, were gone and gone forever, and that everyone should be happy and live as they'd lived before. Then Jeeno looked across the city walls and beyond to the wide marshes.

"I must go now," he said, "I have much work to do and much music to play. People wait for me in many towns, and I must not disappoint them." And Jeeno laughed and the townsfolk laughed, too, even though they were sad at his going. "We shall return next year, Heloise and I," he continued, "and you will run out on the road to greet us, but remember, if you allow a new lord to rule over you, why then make sure he does not lie to you, especially about Igamor. You see, Igamor would never carry off an innocent child. It is only as you grow away from childhood and become old and evil that you have to beware of the long long horse with the long long back. I know because Igamor is my friend."

Then Jeeno and Heloise came down from the walls and marched away through the East Gate playing music as they went, and they were followed for a mile or two by everyone in the town, singing and dancing. Eventually however Jeeno left the townsfolk behind, and the sound of his music became fainter and fainter until at last it could be heard no more.

TAM LIN

by

JOAN D. VINGE

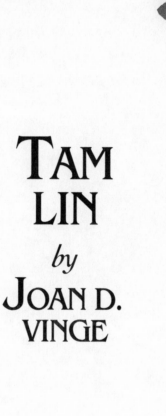

J ENNET!"

The light of a perfect Midsummer's Day poured in on Jennet like warm honey as she threw open the stained glass windows. She leaned out past the parapet of gray stone, her unbound hair spilling over and down. She waved.

"Jennet!" "Jennet!" Voices drifted up to her on the summer breeze. "Hurry!" "Are you coming?" "You'll miss everything!" Half a dozen girls gathered on the wide green lawn far below her, their festival dresses like a bouquet.

"Wait for me!" Jennet flung herself away from the window, ran back across the room to her looking glass to finish dressing. Carven hands held the glass motionless before her; a carven face watched over her from its frame. The servants in the house were all afraid of the mirror, and would never look into it, claiming that the woman's face in its frame had an evil eye. Jennet had laughed at their crossed fingers and turned backs; but sometimes, gazing up into its uncanny features, she had almost felt it gazing back . . . .

Today she only turned slowly before the glass, adjusting her clothing a last time, with pride and defiance. Her skirt was green silk, with the look of dappled leaves; the velvet bodice she had beaded herself was as dark and soft as moss. Her hands sparkled with colored rings. Her lace-heavy sleeves were dyed all the colors of a garden, and her embroidered cloak of green velvet lay spread over the horns and angles of the corner chair behind her. She had sewn her Midsummer clothing in secret through the chill, dark months of an endless Highland winter. This year she would not be denied what everyone else who had ever been young had shared.

She plaited her heavy, flaxen hair with quick fingers, leaving most of it to spill unbound down her back. She crowned it with a fragile circlet of gold, for she was the laird's daughter. But today she had bound the circlet with wild flowers and tiny golden bells on ribbons.

"Jennet—!" The voices of the others were growing shrill outside. She tucked sachets of lavender and rose frantically into her pockets, and threw on her cloak. She stole a last look at herself in the mirror as she swept past it; and her breath caught. For a moment she was certain that she saw someone else there instead . . . . But her mother was dead; she existed now only in the portrait that hung in the great hall downstairs, and in Jennet's heart.

Jennet stood still for a long moment, staring at herself. In this woodland-colored clothing her upslanting green eyes and the fragile angles of her face, which were so unlike her father's, seemed suddenly perfect and right to her. She looked up into the carven features that had gazed down from the mirror's frame at her for so long—the face she had come to think looked more like her own than any living person's. It was so like her mother's face that she sometimes almost believed her mother's presence lived magically within the mirror, holding her reflection in its arms; a small, cold comfort. The mirror was all the legacy that she had from her mother—the only thing besides Carter Hall, the estate that lay in ruins. For a moment she imagined the mirror, and herself, standing in Carter Hall. A rush of strange excitement filled her, as she felt herself transported . . . her mother would understand her yearning for today . . . . Her mother, her yearning . . .

She opened her eyes again, and a cold tremor tickled her as she found herself once again in her room. She smiled fleetingly, uncertainly, over her shoulder as she started toward the door.

She slipped out of her room into the empty upper halls of the manor house—even the servants were allowed the day off to attend the revels—and ran down the endless spiraling stairway to the Great Hall. The oak-paneled Hall was dark and still; the great stone fireplace lay hollow and cold like a ruin. It was tradition that all fires be put out on Midsummer's Eve, to be lit again from the bonfires that would burn tonight. Above the great stone hearth was the portrait of her mother, dressed in green velvet, as eternally young and beautiful as a resident of Faery. Her mother's gaze was distant and filled with longing, as if she were searching for something she had lost and would never find again. Jennet hesitated a moment too long, looking up at the painting and down at the ashes, before she started on, moving lightly as a ghost.

"Jennet!"

This time it was her father's voice that called her, echoing in the vast chamber. It caught her like a snare. She turned back stiffly, wrapping her cloak about her as if it could make her invisible. But sunlight shafting down from the high, diamond-paned windows limned her in a cloud of dazzling light.

"Jennet," Lord Ashwell said again, his voice sad and stern with disappointment.

She looked up at him, reluctantly, and then frowned. The priest, Father Brand, stood behind her father like a shadow, as he had ever since she could remember. When her mother had died, her father had turned obsessively to religion. But it had never brought him any comfort as far as she could tell. As a child she had imagined the black-robed priest was her father's grief personified.

Her father dressed in black, too, as if he were still in mourning after all these years. His thinning hair was starkly white, as it had been for as long as she could remember; his face was as lined as soft leather. Old before his time, he spent his time in prayer and meditation, or discussing the scriptures with the priest, when he was not seeing to his duties as laird. And he expected his daughter to do the same. "Where are you going, Jennet, dressed like that?"

"To the festival," she said, feeling her voice sharpen with resentment. "Like everyone else!"

Her father shook his head imploringly. "You know that I said you should not go. I asked you to pray for guidance."

"Father, I prayed to St. John all morning!" She threw back her cloak. "And I listened to everyone else laugh and sing as they left for town." She felt her mouth begin to quiver with self-pity, and pressed her lips together.

"These are heathenish practices," he said, "fit only for peasants. They're not for us."

"In church they told us that the festival is for blessed St. John the Baptist," she said stubbornly.

"Some condone heathenism by calling it something else," the priest murmured. "I do not."

Jennet lifted her head. Sunlight glittering with dust-motes haloed her in gold. "I don't care what you think."

"Jennet!" Lord Ashwell said, "Forgive her, Father. She's only a child . . . ." He glanced at the priest almost diffidently.

Jennet shook her head, making the tiny bells sing. "I'm not a child! You keep telling me I have to marry. If I'm old enough to have a husband, I'm old enough to go to the revels on my own." She gathered her rustling skirts. "And I will." She turned away.

"Aye . . ." her father murmured. "Jennet!" he called after her suddenly. "Then be home before sunset! You know the powers of the darkness. The Fair Folk—"

She turned back at the unexpected note of fear in his voice, in time to see the priest look at him, frowning. But she knew her father's obsession with the Faeries, something that even the priest had not been able to alter, with all his years of prayer and scorn.

Her heart pinched for a moment, as she met her father's eyes. She had never understood his terror of the Faeries, or his desperate fear that they would somehow harm her. Whenever she had even tried to ask him about it, he had only shaken his head and turned away from her. She took a deep breath. "Father, you push me to wed; but there's no knight or lord I've seen in the Highlands that I'd choose by light of day . . . . Maybe if I see one by firelight I'll find him fairer." His growing insistence that she accept a suitor confused and depressed her even more than his brooding superstition. She was his only child, and she had always known how much he loved her. She could not understand why he was suddenly so eager to have her claimed by a stranger. She tossed her head. "Besides, Annie says that if I don't see seven fires burning at once on Midsummer Night, I'll never marry at all."

The priest muttered his disapproval, counting the obsidian beads of his rosary like a miser counting coins.

"Then, Jennet, by the Holy Rood—" her father cried. "Do not go near Carter Hall! Not tonight."

"Why?" she asked. Carter Hall was only a ruin on land she had inherited from her mother. It had burned down a hundred years ago. For years she had heard tales that it was haunted; the tales had haunted her, until she had stolen away to see it for herself, without her father's knowledge. But as she wandered there in secret, listening for something nameless in the wind that rustled the leaves, waiting for something more . . . she had seen nothing more frightening among the vine-softened ruins than a squirrel or a lizard. She knew that her father disliked Carter Hall, but she had never realized until today that he feared it. "Why not?"

"It sits upon one of the Old Places, where . . . where the

lands of Faery touch on our own world." Her father spoke as if every word were painful on his tongue, as if he were speaking of something shameful or obscene. "On certain days of the year, gateways open between the world of Faery and our own. On those days the Fair Folk pass through . . . they are soulless, never caring what grief they bring into mortal lives!" His voice trembled, and he looked away at her mother's portrait.

"That is nothing but heathen superstition, my lord," the priest said flatly. "In truth, the devil dwells at Carter Hall—and debauches reckless maidens." He looked at Jennet, and the touch of his eyes made her flesh crawl.

Jennet felt her cheeks redden, not certain what emotion caused her to blush. Her breathing quickened.

Seeing her expression, the priest shook his head. "Mother to daughter . . . women have been man's woe since the birth of Eve." Her father made an odd motion with his head that might have been agreement, or denial.

Certain now that her own emotion was only anger, Jennet turned and stalked out of the hall.

Out on the lawn her friends still waited, and Jennet's smile opened again like a flower at the sight of their laughing faces and the bright, endless afternoon sky of Midsummer. The sweet birdsong, the perfume of the gardens and the colors of the day filled her senses, making her forget the suffocating gloom of the manor house. She giggled a little too merrily as her friends gathered her in, exclaiming at the beauty of her dress. Together they swept her away across the wide, shadow-dappled lawns toward the road to town. Today she would be giddy and carefree and gay. Today, for once, she would be like everyone else.

They walked the rutted track as quickly as their doeskin slippers would let them, scarcely feeling the stones underfoot in their excitement. Jennet listened eagerly to the delights that were waiting ahead for her, down the curving track, through the glen and the oak woods beyond, in the meadows outside the village gate.

". . . And in the evening, when the young lairds and even the village lads came asking you to dance with them around the fires—"

"Or to leave the fires and walk in the woods—!"

"Och, for shame—"

Tittering laughter flowed over and around her. Jennet curled the laces of her bodice between her fingers, her thoughts wandering in spite of her curiosity. "Annie, Meg . . . what about the Faeries?" She almost bit her tongue; she had sworn that today she would not talk about the Old Lore. But—"My father says they are real enchanted folk. That they come into our world to make mischief on Midsummer Night." In her mind she saw again the ruins of Carter Hall.

"Och, your father and the Faeries! Can't you forget about them even for one day? Faeries are nothing but the peasants' fancies," said red-haired Meg, who was the oldest among them, and proud of it.

"No, don't say that!" Annie shook her head, holding her crown of flowers in place on her raven hair. "It's bad luck to mock them. My mother says so. Their curse can ruin your life. They live forever, and they know everything."

"My brother saw one when he was a boy," someone else said. "They're as small as cats."

"No," said mousy little Winnie, "they're taller than we are, and so beautiful that to see them makes your heart stop."

"My father says they are soulless," Jennet murmured. "They think only of their own pleasure, and not of whom they hurt by it."

"It's true!" Annie nodded. "They steal babes from the cradle and leave changelings behind. They carry off fair youths and maids to be their lovers."

"Rot," said Meg, who had been away to school. The others giggled.

"Well, what about Lady Rowan?" Mary asked. "They say . . ."

"Mary!" Meg said sharply.

"What about my mother?" Jennet asked, feeling cold in the pit of her stomach.

"They say in the village . . . that she danced with the Faeries . . ." Mary said meekly, "and was never seen again."

Jennet heard small gasps from two or three girls around her. "That's a lie." She frowned, pressing her lips together. "My mother died of a fever when I was a baby." And yet, and yet . . . her father's priest had hinted too often of some shameful secret, calling her mother wicked and unnatural; until she knew that her father had not told her all of the truth . . . .

"Of course it is. A silly rumor." Meg put an arm around Jennet's shoulder. But there was something in her eyes as she glanced away again; an unease that Jennet sensed in all their glances sometimes, when they looked at her and away again too quickly. "Don't gossip, Mary."

"Look, up ahead—" Annie said, bravely changing the subject. "There's Jamie Farquhar on his gray. He's such a bonnie lad! I hope he'll dance with me. I won't come back until dawn if he does!" More giggles.

"I've never met a man who could tell one foot from the other in the dance," Jennet said sullenly, her merry mood vanished.

"Well, your father hardly gives you a chance," Annie said. "The suitors he pushes on you are a lot of old men." It was always at the priest's urging. "Tonight you'll have your pick of lads. You look like the Faery Queen, all aglow."

Jennet blushed, prickling with an emotion that was not precisely pleasure.

"Then she'd best stay away from Carter Hall!" Mary rolled her eyes, rubbing a stone bruise from her foot.

Jennet started. "Why?" she whispered.

"Tam Lin!" Mary breathed.

"Tam Lin!" "Tam Lin—" The others echoed her, shivering with awe and dread.

"You've never heard of Tam Lin?" Annie asked eagerly. "Someone will surely sing about him today—"

"Stuff and nonsense," Meg said firmly.

But Jennet shook her head. "My father told me not to go near Carter Hall tonight. He said it's a gate to Faery. The priest says the devil lives there, and preys on young women."

"The devil, aye!" Mary snickered. "The fairest devil in all Christendom haunts Carter Hall. They say he is a Faery knight, who knows no chivalry—"

"They say that any maiden who sees him, he forces to give him her valuables as payment . . ." Annie's voice dropped to a whisper. ". . . or, if it pleases him, her maidenhead!"

Jennet looked down at her soft-shod feet treading precariously over the stones, and said nothing.

"For shame," Meg interrupted. "You sound like a pack of wantons." But her mouth twitched with a smile.

"Well, it is Midsummer Day," Mary insisted. "I mean, St. John's Day . . . . My nurse said to pray for all the John's-sons and Jack's-sons that will be born to poor village girls come spring—"

"Hush, enough!" Meg cried.

They walked on in thoughtful silence among the rustling trees. At last the village came into view, and the meadow filled with bright tents and brighter revelers. Jennet was swept up into a merry whirl of dancers and pipers, sweet berry ices and honey cakes, balladeers and foot races. It seemed to her dazzled mind that everyone on earth must have come to this place today. She saw the tartans of the many clan lairds who had come to the festivities—although her father, who should have been here to oversee them all, was not—and many of their sons buzzed around her like bees after honey. She knew most of them too well already. Politely but insistently, she refused every invitation to dance.

One by one Annie and the others kilted up their skirts and deserted her for handsome lads; until even Meg danced away, with her betrothed, to the piper's tune. At last, left alone, Jennet accepted the entreaty of a smiling young man in a feathered cap of green, and let him lead her into the sway of dancers. She followed him gamely through the leaps and circles of the lively dance. But he moved as all the dancers seemed to move, lacking some elusive grace; until her own quick, fluid movements seemed to be out of place and wrong, instead of everyone else's. The young man was handsome and merry and looked at her with eyes that pleaded for her to return his shining infatuation. But his face was handsome in so ordinary a way, his merriness so common, his laughter so expected . . . .

She broke free at last, as the dance ended, and left him standing morose and alone. She wandered on among the stalls and jugglers, more solitary than ever; and all that she heard and tasted and saw seemed to fade, turn flat and disappointing at her touch. She moved distractedly through the crowd of strangers, searching, searching . . . yet somehow knowing that she would never find what she sought. The young men who circled past her seemed to have no reality. They were only objects; she felt their stares weighing her in the same way, like a measure of gold. Her father would force her to marry, the way he would breed a heifer, whether she wanted to or not.

She drifted like a wraith through the crowds while the shadow of evening fell swiftly down the mountain wall to the west, bringing twilight to the village meadow, the way a shadow had darkened her mood. As night fell, a strange anticipation began to fill her; a sense of something waiting to be named. Her wandering feet led her through the torchlight among tents that billowed gently in the evening breeze. On every side laughing couples carried bits of wood and branch to the kindling of the Midsummer Fire in the center of the field.

Jennet stood watching as the fire was kindled in an ancient, almost-forgotten way; the kindling ceremony had the feel of a religious ritual. Many of the peasants still held the beliefs of their ancestors in their private hearts. Cheers and shrieks greeted the sudden blaze of fire in the darkness, the symbol of the sun, a paean to constancy in their lives. Eager youths caught up brands from the fire, carrying them off into the falling night to start other fires on the peaks of all the nearer hills, and in the cold hearths of homes everywhere. Children whirled flaming sun-wheels up into the night. There would be more dancing now—more drinking of wine and beer, more celebration until the fires slowly died away, when couples would pledge an ancient troth to one another, leaping over the embers hand in hand. But in the morning most of those pledges would be forgotten, as ephemeral as the dew; and the spell of ancient days would fade again with the dawn.

Jennet circled restlessly through the shadows beyond the fire's ring of light, slipping deeper and deeper into the waiting darkness. At last she kilted up her skirts and ran away into the night.

Her heart beat fast with anticipation, and her feet led her swiftly and surely through the night-silvered glens. The moon was just past full, and high tonight, giving her all the light she needed; giving her glimpses of startled foxes and hares and mice turned to silver like herself.

A long rise was before her now. She began to climb, pushing aside the twigs and branches that caught at her clothing like clutching hands, trying to keep her from her destination. At last she won free into an open space, a clearing cut long ago from the ancient, vine-heavy forest, a place that was slowly being reclaimed by nature.

From here she could see way down the steep, rocky slope of the hill's far side. A glittering necklace of light below was the place where two rivers met and flowed together, like lifesblood, down a black, steep-walled valley into the distant loch. She could see the moon's perfect face reflected in the far-off surface of the water.

She turned further, drawing her green cloak about her, shivering slightly although the breeze was barely cool against her flushed skin. Before her now she saw the fallen stones of Carter Hall. The sight of them stopped her breath, although she had known what she would find. She moved slowly through the long grasses toward the ruins, watching, listening. She heard only the murmuring of crickets, suddenly hushed by her passing. She walked softly among the rubble, looking up at the black-boned arches that opened a way through walls long-fallen. She found her way into a stone-studded courtyard she remembered, where there was a well that still held sweet water, waiting patiently for hands that never came to draw it.

She leaned against the well's edge, feeling dry moss crumble beneath her hands. Roses grew wild up the face of the time-eaten wall beside her. Roses, the country folk said, were the favorite of the Faeries. An elixir of love could be distilled from their blossoms. She reached out, drawing down a silver-white flower, breathing in its sweet, spiced fragrance, like the rich scent of mulled wine. The bent stem seemed almost to struggle against her hold; she snapped it in two, and kept the flower in her hand. She reached up, plucking another rose heedlessly; cried out as its thorns tore her skin. The rose fell into her lap among her rustling skirts; a dark drop of blood welled on her finger. She put the finger to her lips, tasting the salty sweetness of it.

"Lady," a voice said, "pull no more roses."

Jennet looked up with a gasp. A young man stood before her, where only a moment ago there had been no one. His fair hair seemed to her to be spun from silver thread, his skin to be as pale and translucent as moonglow. She could not see the color of his eyes, but their gaze burned her flesh.

"Why do you steal my roses, Jennet?" he said. "Why do you break their stems? Why do you trespass here, without my invitation?" His voice was as light and lilting as a harp's, but arrogance and anger and regret were in it.

Jennet met his burning gaze, felt terror stir inside her. This was no mortal man, clad in the gray of shadows and the green of woods. This was the Faery Knight, whom she had sought without seeking, and found. The dark pools of his eyes were endlessly deep, and nowhere inside them could she see a soul. But their beauty melted her terror; her fear became something new and nameless, making her breathing quicken, starting a fire deep inside her.

"Carter Hall is mine," she said, finding her voice. "I'll come and go here as I please, without your leave. Who are you, to tell me what I may not do?"

"I am Tam Lin, Lady." He moved toward her, catching her wrist. "This place is claimed by the realm of Faery, and the Queen herself gave it to me. I see you've heard of me . . . and the price I demand of trespassers?"

Jennet pressed back against the wall, feeling thorns catch in her clothing, drowning in the fragrance of roses.

"That is a fair Midsummer cloak you wear. It would make a fitting gift for my Queen—as soft as a maiden's cheek, as green as the new life of summer." His hand caressed her shoulder, slid down her arm along the velvet cloth, and seized the cloak with his hand. "I'll have it as payment for your trespass."

"No." Jennet lifted her own hands, pulling the cloak closer about her. She met his stare boldly, but her body trembled under his touch.

His eyes flickered, dark and fathomless. He caught her wrists in his hands. His were slender and long-fingered, but painfully strong. "Then I will have your gemstone rings. Will you give them to me?" His voice demanded acquiescence and mocked her with the knowledge of his power over her. But his eyes suddenly seemed to her not to soullessly demand, but to plead that she agree.

Jennet tightened her hands into fists. "No," she whispered. "I will not."

"Then you have but one thing more in your possession that I desire. A most precious thing, which you can never replace." He moved closer still, until his body pressed hard along the length of her own, holding her prisoner against the wall of roses. "Are you ready to give me that?" he whispered, almost sadly. His eyes devoured her now, and one slim hand brushed her breast.

She shrank back against the wall; suddenly, burningly aware that she had chosen a path with no return, and that she had already taken too many steps along it. But she had taken it of her own choice . . . She gazed up into his face, the fairest she had ever seen. Her body pressed against his own; a tingling anticipation started and spread, deep inside her. "Oh, yes," she murmured.

His hands unclasped her cloak and this time she did not resist him. He threw the cloak aside onto the damp grass, caught her in his arms and laid her down upon it with a swiftness that made her gasp. His mouth found hers hungrily, and his lips were as sweet and hot as mead. His hands seemed to work magic on the clothing that kept them from her flesh, and her dress fell away from their knowing assault. His silver fingers flowed like warm water over her naked body, finding all the secret and hidden places that had always been forbidden to any man's touch. She let her own hands explore him, learning a man's secrets that had also been forbidden to her, making him gasp and sigh. And now at last she realized why they were forbidden, while astonishment and pleasure made her plead for more. His lips quenched her cry and his own, as man's mystery touched woman's most secret place, and entered. And she knew at last that he was a man of flesh and blood, and not a phantom out of Faery. The sharp, electric pain of their meeting did not last, and instead, as they moved together, her pleasure began to grow again. It grew and grew as a timeless, swirling tide rose beneath the moon and crested, filling her with wave upon wave of ecstasy.

They lay together afterward, tangled silver limbs shining among the shadows, while he kissed away her silent tears. They rested peacefully for a long space, and through it all he never spoke. She was silent, too, drinking in his beauty; afraid now to speak, afraid to break the enchanted spell that bound them here.

After a time he roused, his lips seeking her lips again, and her throat, and her breast. She felt his body against her and realized, with new knowledge, that they would love again. She answered him eagerly. The second time was even a greater joy, and the third, like a dream. At last, wrapped in her cloak, utterly spent, they slept.

Jennet woke as she felt Tam Lin stir in her arms. She opened her eyes, blinking sleep away. He raised his head, looking past her; she realized that she could see faint color in his face, in the forest crown behind him. Dawn was breaking. He gave a small exclamation of dismay, pushing himself up.

"Tam Lin—" she whispered, knowing that he would leave her.

He looked down at her, almost in surprise. But then he smiled, first with pleasure, and then with sorrow. He leaned down to kiss her once, lingeringly, on the mouth. And then he was up and away, fading like a shadow into the deeper shadows of the wood.

"Tam Lin!" Her cry was as plaintive and as meaningless as the cry of doves awakening in the trees. Nothing answered her but the rustling of leaves, as if an invisible host were passing by. She huddled inside her cloak until the breeze died away. Then, in the silence that followed, she silently pulled on her clothing. She made her way out of the ruins and down the hill, drifted like a sleepwalker back through the brightening day to her father's house.

Her father said nothing when she returned, but in his eyes she saw resignation, and a profound relief. Had he believed she had been carried off into Faery? Was it true of her mother? Seeing his face, she could not ask him. But somehow now she no longer needed to. Somehow it seemed as if she had always known. Last night had only crystallized her knowledge. The priest had always said that she was her mother's child . . . At last, perhaps inexorably, she had discovered her heritage.

The days passed. Her friends came calling, and over chess and tennis told the stories of their Midsummer evenings. When they asked her of hers, she said only, "I fell asleep, and had a dream." Sometimes she felt that it truly had been a dream, it seemed so uncanny to her now. And yet now, day after day she lived half in a dream of longing for the lover she would never know again. Her father's mournful demands that she choose a suitor and her friends' giggling inanity seemed equally distant and ever more insignificant as her own thoughts turned inward. Often she wandered by Carter Hall, plucking roses; but there was never a hand to stop her, or caress her.

The weeks passed. Summer ripened, and with it the fruits and the fields. And her body slowly ripened, too, with changes she at first did not comprehend. Her breasts grew as round as apples. She tired easily, like a small child, and although sometimes she could barely stand to look at food, her waist swelled, too, until her dresses strained.

At last, in the smoke-filled days of early fall, the morning came when she stood before the silent gaze of her long mirror and realized that a child was growing inside her. Her Midsummer's secret dream was no longer only a dream, and soon it would no longer be a secret. The reality flowering inside her filled her with a fierce joy and possessiveness. Tam Lin had taken away a part of her self that she would never have again. But he had given her a part of him to cherish, a focus for her love and longing. Soon all the world would know, but she was only glad.

The russet and gold of autumn burst over the land and faded, the nights grew even longer. The apple-crisp days of October fell away like the dying leaves. And on All Hallows' Eve, the last of October, her father called her before him in his study. His priest was with him, standing like a carrion crow at his shoulder. "Jennet," Lord Ashwell said, almost meekly, "even I can no longer fail to see what Father Brand says is being whispered through all the halls. You are with child. Tell me who is to blame, and I will see that he marries you at once."

She felt herself flush, even though she had been expecting this. She shook her head, almost absently.

"My lord, if I may say a few words," Father Brand murmured in her father's ear. "Jennet," the priest said to her, in a tone that was a mockery of sweet reasonableness. "Listen to your father. You must remove this great sin from your heart . . . ." His cold eyes impaled her as she met his gaze with silence. "I still recall when you were a sweet, fair, obedient child who believed in the word of God. I tried to teach you to have faith, to put yourself into the Lord's hands willingly"—he held out his own large, moist hands to her—"and save your soul from the sins of your mother. It is still not too late for you to come to Him through me . . . ." He hesitated, went on brusquely. "Tell your father who shares the blame for your sin."

"There is no one to blame but myself," Jennet said, looking toward her father instead. The priest pulled in his hand as if he had been singed. "There is no lord in all this land," she went on, more boldly, "who can give my baby a name."

"Jennet," her father said pleadingly. "Stop this foolish play. Where is the baby's father?"

"He is nowhere on this earth," Jennet said, keeping her voice as steady as she could. "My love is Tam Lin, the Faery Knight, not a mortal man." She saw his image in her mind's eye, still as clearly as though she had seen him only yesterday, and her heart constricted. "And even if he were, I would not give him up for any lord you have."

The priest's breath hissed softly. "The devil's child," he muttered, more to himself than aloud. He clutched the crucifix he wore, his eyes averted, and Jennet did not know whether he was warding off her unborn child, or herself.

She turned to her father, who had fallen back a step; he clung to the carven edge of a highboy for support. "No," he murmured, "no . . ."

"Tainted blood," the priest intoned, pushing forward again. He faced her father. "I warned you, my lord. Tainted blood will tell. From mother to daughter, back to the time of Eve. Eve is the root of Evil."

"Stop it!" Jennet cried, her hands balling into fists. For too many years she had borne the humiliations of his crawling innuendos in her mother's place, for her mother's sake. "You evil man," she said shrilly, "you have no right to talk about me or my mother—"

"She was a witch!" The priest spat the words like venom. "The devil carried her away to hell. You must be exorcised of this demon, this hellspawn growing inside you—" He reached out for her, his eyes hot and hungry.

Jennet jerked back in disgust and fright.

Jennet's father straightened and moved swiftly forward, striking the priest's hand away. Jennet and the priest turned to gape at him together. Her father's soft, yielding manner had disappeared, like the scales that fell from the eyes of Paul; he stood straight as a rod, every inch a lord. His arm drew her to him and circled her, shielding her against his side.

"I warned you," the priest said, rubbing his wrist; his control melting, running down him like wax. "You should have forced her to wed, so that her wickedness would be controlled—"

"Be silent!" Jennet saw her father's face redden with genuine emotion, genuine rage, for the first time since she could remember. Clear-eyed, a man awakened at last from a suffocating dream, he said to the priest, "You are an unnatural man, and you make profane the world you do not understand. Leave my house at once, and do not come onto my lands again." Jennet stared at her father, feeling as if she were dreaming instead.

"You will all rot in hell!" Father Brand lifted his hand as if to strike them; turned abruptly and strode away across the hall, his words echoing about him.

Jennet buried her face against her father's shoulder, felt his arms around her. His hand stroked her hair, comforting her, as it had not done in years.

"What really happened to my mother?" she asked, at last. "She wasn't a witch—"

"No," her father said softly, sadly. "But she had Faery blood."

Jennet looked up at him without surprise, her eyes shining. "Yes . . ." she whispered.

Her father nodded and lowered his eyes. "She said it had brought ruin to her family, because blood called to blood . . . . On Midsummer's Eve, just after you were born, she found a doorway into the Other World, and passed through it."

"How do you know?" Jennet lifted her head. "How do you know that's really what happened to her?"

"I saw her go."

Jennet stiffened.

"I followed her that night. I saw what no man should ever see. My courage failed me . . . I let her go. All these years I have tried to deny it. . . ." He shook his head. "They say the Fair Folk take what they will, and give nothing back. But she gave me you. You are all I have, and I've tried to protect you from . . . from . . . Don't leave me, too, Jenny!" His voice quavered again like an old man's.

Jennet shook her own head, holding him tightly. She drew a long, shuddering breath as the clouded darkness of long years began to break around her. "I am my mother's daughter . . ." she murmured. But at last she could be sure that she was not her mother—

She drew away again. "I must find Tam Lin, Father. He is flesh and blood, at least in this world. My baby wants a father, too. Tonight is All Hallows' Eve, when they say spirit people pass through the world again. I must go to him." Her brows tightened. "This time I'll make them give something to me."

Her father nodded. His face was lined with sorrow, but it still seemed to Jennet that he stood taller and more freely, as if a weight had been lifted from him. "Then go with my blessing . . . though I fear that I cannot protect you either, child."

Jennet hurried from the hall.

Jennet strode alone through the autumn twilight in the unfamiliar comfort of leather boots along the road, past the town, up through the skeletal woods toward Carter Hall. She saw no one as she passed, for most of the villagers stayed inside on Hallowe'en, when they whispered that the spirits of the dead roamed abroad. Even if anyone she knew had seen her, they would not have known her, for she had dressed herself in a heavy doublet and hose, bound up her hair beneath her hooded cloak, as if she were a man. The cold wind tugged at the green velvet cloak, whipping it ahead of her, pushing her onward. The brittle husks of dead and dying leaves whirled past her like spirits, crunched beneath her feet like fragile bones. The world was dying around her, with the year. But new life grew inside her, giving her hope and courage.

At last she reached the ruin, made her way among the fallen stones to the courtyard of the well. There in the sheltered space white roses still bloomed, untouched by frost, though all around them leaves and vines had shriveled and died.

But the courtyard lay empty and silent. The only sound was the scuttling of leaf-feet across the weedy paving stones. "Tam Lin?" she whispered. "Tam Lin!" she called. Only the wind answered her, moaning through the trees. She leaned against the well's rim, exhausted by her long climb. The last embers of sunset faded from the western sky.

As the ruins faded into the night around her, Jennet slowly crossed the courtyard to the roses once again. In the darkness they seemed suffused by an unearthly light that drew her like a moth. Their sweet fragrance hung heavily in the air as she came near. She caught the stem of a blossom with cold-numbed fingers, and snapped it from the vine. Holding her breath, she pulled another.

"Lady," a man's voice said, "pull no more."

She turned with a gasp. Tam Lin stood before her, clad in shadows, alight with the same uncanny glow.

"So, Jennet," he said softly, almost with surprise. "Why have you come here again, and dressed for battle, when all the world is dying? Have you come to me to be rid of the bonnie babe that we have made together?"

Jennet flushed. "No!" Shaken again by his prescience, she laid her hands on her gently swelling stomach. "I came to seek its father, and—and bring him home with me."

"Still a willful maid." He laughed; his laughter was hollow with mockery. "How would you bring home a ghost? I live in the Hidden World; I would melt away from you in the light of day."

"You are flesh and blood enough to make me no maid!" she snapped, stung. "You don't deny you are my baby's father."

He shook his head, and the fathomless eyes fell away from hers. "You have more than a little of the Fair Ones' manner about you," he murmured to the stones, almost ruefully. He looked up again. "You had your reasons to come here once. You ensnared me more than I you. . . . But this time you will not get what you seek. I cannot stay with you. You should not have come here again. Leave me alone with my sins."

She dared to move closer, no longer afraid that he would disappear. She touched his cheek hesitantly; felt cool, solid flesh. His lips brushed her fingers, and she felt her heartbeat quicken. "Who are you, Tam Lin?" she asked. "Why do you dwell in this place? Were you once a mortal man?"

He nodded slowly, at last. His gaze came back to her, haunted. "Once I was Thomas Lynn, the grandson of Lord Roxburgh. He took me to live with him. But one Hallowe'en night, as I came back late from the hunt, I passed by a Faery place as the Fair Folk rode out. My horse shied and threw me. The Queen of Faery caught me. She called me the fairest knight in any earthly land, and carried me off to her realm. I've lived there like a prince these long years, as her consort." He closed his eyes. "What wonders I've seen there, Jennet! Anything I've desired—my every wish—has been granted. I have sipped nectar of pearls from the horn of a unicorn. I have worn the jeweled scales of dragons, and slept on clouds, and swum like a merman in the depths of an azure sea. I have been shown pleasures . . ." He took a deep breath, and opened his eyes. "There are pleasures there that I cannot even name. I would never have left Faery, even if I had been able—"

Jennet struggled with her despair. "Then why do you wait here for a human maid? Who do you not ride with *her* when she passes through our world?"

"Because I long for what I've lost." He shook his head, as if his own perversity confused him. "I'm not of Faery, Jennet, I'm a human man, and I long for my own kind. This place lies in your world, but its past is twined with that of Faery, like these roses with the briars." His hand caressed the roses almost thoughtlessly. "The Queen does not love me; I am hers to cast away . . . ." His voice faded into the darkness of his hidden thoughts. He looked up at Jennet again, for a long moment, as if he were truly seeing her for the first time. And then, to her astonishment, he sank to his knees before her. "My life is cursed, Jennet! I am a helpless captive. In the land of Faery, the Queen is like a goddess, and I am only her plaything. She cares nothing for me." He clutched Jennet's skirts. "She keeps a human lover for seven of her years, which are seven times seven of ours. And then, while he is still young and fair, she sacrifices him to renew her people's power. Once they killed one of their own, but now it is always a human . . . . Even now she seeks another boy to replace me. And tonight, before they leave this world at cockcrow, I will die, and her people will feed on my life—"

"No!" Jennet shuddered. Her hands caught his shoulders, feeling them strong and alive beneath her grasp. "But you're here now, and she is not. Come away with me quickly, and—"

He slid from her hold, rose fluidly to his feet. "I cannot. She holds my soul captive with her spells. I am a shadow-man, I would fade away with the dawn and disappear. I can't save myself . . . ." He took her hands in his with a grip that hurt her. "But you can save me, Jennet! You came again because you love me . . . ." A strange expression passed over his face, and was gone. "Your love is the only thing that can bring me back. It can give you the strength to face the Queen, and claim me back. It can give you the strength to face the Queen and claim me for your own." He pulled her to him, pressing his lips to hers; kissing her wantonly, with his whole being, until her bones seemed to melt with the heat of her yearning. "I am your own true love, Jennet." He let her go again, moving away from her like a will-o'-the-wisp.

"How? How can I save you? I will do anything—" she whispered, hugging herself because he had let her go.

"I will do anything . . ." he echoed her distantly, a gleaming shadow of light. "To save me . . . To save me you must go now to Milescross beyond the town, and wait there. It is a place where the forces of this world and the Hidden one commingle. At midnight, when the old day yields to the new, the Queen's host will ride by; it is a part of their ritual to pay homage there. But it will give you power, too. If you would win me, it must be there."

"But I've never even seen the Fair Folk. How will I know you, among so many . . . ?" The thought of truly gazing on the Faeries filled her with dread and desire. "Will I even know what I see?"

"The Queen will lead them three times around the stone cross that stands where the roads meet. Look for a milk-white stallion, for I ride the only one. Let all the others pass by. I will ride on the outside, nearest the town—that is my chosen place, because I was once of this world. When you see the white, run to him and pull me down. And then—listen to me well, Jennet—"

She nodded, her heart drumming.

"You must hold me tight! The Fair Folk will try to take me back. They cannot touch you while you stand at Milescross. Instead they will change me into strange and terrible things. But once you have me, never let me go, or I am lost forever." He took her in his arms again. "Hold me close, Jennet, until you hold in your arms a naked man . . . and do not fear me. I am your baby's father. Love me as you love your child, and I will not harm you. As long as you believe in yourself, believe in our love, the Queen cannot stop you."

"I will," Jennet murmured. "You are mine, and I will never let you go."

"My love," he said softly, "my life is yours," as he slipped from her arms again. "I must go now; the Queen must not suspect. But wait for me at Milescross—I will be there at midnight, I swear upon my lost soul!"

Jennet watched him disappear among the trees in the wan moonlight. The barely-formed new moon slipped behind scudding clouds, and cast her into sudden darkness. She turned, for one last glimpse of the shining roses. But behind her now there lay only more gloom, withered vines and blasted leaves.

She turned away again, shivering as sudden doubt laid chill hands on her. But she started resolutely down the hill, going as slowly as an old woman, stumbling over roots, stung by branches, her clothing caught and torn on brambles.

The moon sailed its errant course among the clouds, sometimes lighting her way with an eerie radiance, and sometimes abandoning her to struggle on through the sighing blackness alone. At last she reached Milescross, where two ancient tracks met, a mile beyond the town. Looking back across the flat, sere fields, she could barely see the handful of lights still burning late in the village church. Even as she watched, another light winked out. Tonight all the folk of the Highlands stayed snug

and shuttered inside their cottages, hiding beneath the bed-
clothes from the creeping chill of autumn, and from the restless spirits of the night.

She stood trembling with exhaustion and cold, alone in the
empty meeting place of the roads below the crude cross that
had been carved from a far older marker stone. She could not
guess how much time had passed, but she felt that she must
have been lost in the darkness, finding her way to this place,
for hours. Surely it could not be long until midnight . . . .

She found a hiding place among the bushes beside the road,
crouched down among the bare, rattling twigs, hunched inside
her green cloak and the unfamiliar shapings of a man's
clothes. The smell of dank earth, mold, and decay filled her
nostrils with every breath. She waited, growing wearier and
stiffer and more wretched with every creeping minute, more
afraid with every moan of the wind or rustle of restless leaves.
But as she waited, it seemed to her that she felt a faint, fluttering kick within her, like the beating of butterfly wings. She
was not sure whether it was her child, or only her hope for it,
that stirred inside her; but it drew her thoughts back under her
control, and warmed her with fresh resolve.

And at last, as the moon broke from the clouds once more,
she heard, like distant music, the jingle of many bridle-rings
and the soft thud of hooves in the dust. Jennet rose to her
knees, peering out through the tangle of branches and withered leaves. No night had ever seemed longer, no sound had
ever seemed sweeter, than this one. She almost laughed with
joy.

Suddenly, out of nowhere, a troop of riders was approaching
on the road . . . and she knew at a glance that they were not of
her world. Their shimmering forms kindled the night with
ghostlight, brighter than the moon. She began to hear laughter
and bits of song; voices speaking, but too muted for her to hear
clearly. She crouched down again, watching breathlessly as
they drew closer and closer, until at last the host of riders be-

gan to fill the crossroads, circling the marker stone. She still could not understand what they said, for they spoke an unknown language. Their voices were as lilting as music, weaving harmonies on an otherworldly melody; but strangely dim, as if they were speaking in another room, or in a dream.

As they began to pass her hiding place she peered out again, and forgot even to listen, held captive now by their beauty. Theirs was more than a simple, earthly perfection of form—it was a shining, ethereal transcendence. Her heart constricted. This was the way she had dreamed of angels shining . . . . This was what she had always sought without knowing, and never found, in any mortal face. And yet there was something about these fair, ageless beings with their porcelain features, their upslanting eyes of shifting jade, that seemed almost familiar; an echo that the corner of her own eye had sometimes caught, shimmering about her own face . . . .

Their clothing was gossamer-fine, as if they had wrapped themselves in mist, alight with jewels and beads and fluttering silken ribbons. Their pale forms were as sensually revealed as if they wore nothing at all, and yet more richly arrayed than any earthly royalty might dream of. Cloaks that seemed to be made of liquid—so fluid and limpidly pure were their colors— clung to their slender bodies or floated on a breeze that was not the cold wind of autumn. She breathed in the warm, sweet vanilla scent of an endless summer as they rode past her once, paying homage to this place of power, and began to circle the stone a second time. Even the steeds they rode were more graceful than any creatures she had ever seen, as delicate of form as fawns and as beautifully bedecked in jewels and gold as their unearthly riders.

She watched them begin to pass a third time, so lost in wonder and longing that she could think of nothing else. She remembered her mother, who had abandoned this world for theirs, and knew now why she had gone to them. But her mother had left her only child behind, in this dreary world of cold and loneliness . . . .

A milk-white horse filled Jennet's vision, like the full moon emerging from a field of clouds. She looked up at its rider; his face was almost lost in the glowing light which enshrouded him. But she knew that face . . . she knew the look of despair its rider wore, as he gazed not ahead, but outward, longingly, toward the town.

Tam Lin—her heart cried out his name. She rose to her feet, whispering a prayer to she didn't know whom. She darted out into the road, and caught the white steed's rider by the arm, dragging him down with all her weight. The stallion half reared and shied away; his rider clung to the saddle, staring in horror. But then his eyes knew her, and he let himself fall. "Tam Lin," she cried, throwing her arms around him, "I have you!"

The Faery mob milled and shouted on every side, surrounding her; vanilla and musk, warmth and cold, light and darkness dazzled her senses. She shut her eyes against the sight of trampling hooves and the din of voices, not lilting now but strident with shock and anger. She felt Tam Lin's body, warm and solid against her own.

"Jennet . . ." Tam Lin moaned, writhing in her arms. She opened her eyes—and screamed, as she saw not her lover's face, but the vast, gaping jaws of an enormous black bear. She felt its hot breath and spittle in her face, felt its brutal, heavy arms embrace her to crush her life away.

Almost, she let go her hold and flung herself away. Instead she shut her eyes again, blinding herself to the sight of it—and felt only a human body clinging desperately to her own. "No! Tam Lin!" she gasped.

She opened her eyes again, and a roaring lion filled her arms. Its claws sank into her back, its dripping fangs lunged for her throat. She screamed again, falling backwards with the force of its attack—shutting her eyes. "Tam Lin, Tam Lin!" she cried. And felt only a man's strong hands knotted in a death-grip on her clothing; felt his lips cover her throat and jaw with kisses.

She opened her eyes once more, by an effort of will, and in her arms was a red-hot bar of iron. Its pulsing surface seared her hands, its weight dragged it from her grasp. "Tam Lin! Tam Lin! Tam Lin!" she screamed wildly, shutting her eyes. And in her arms she felt the unexpected touch of bare flesh, and the burning wetness of tears.

She opened her eyes a last time, and in her arms lay the man she had come to claim, naked and spent and real. She pulled off her cloak and flung it over him, hiding him from the view of the watching Faery troop.

They sat silent and motionless on their steeds now, ringing her round, gazing down at her with dark and strangely vacant eyes, while she stared back at them defiantly. And then their ranks opened, and before her was their Queen, sitting astride a golden mare with cloven hooves, whose heavy mane fell like a silver cascade, dripping diamonds.

Jennet shrank down and flung up a hand, struck blind by the glamour of the woman who gazed back at her. The Queen of Faery had not one face but infinite faces, changing and changing again, and every face more beautiful than all the rest. Heartbreaking, breathtaking, soulless and pitiless in her mystery, she was all things to all men . . . and all women. Jennet covered her own face, as drab and lusterless and coarse as earth; tears of shame and humiliation welled in her eyes as she faced the unbearable perfection of the Faery Queen.

But then Tam Lin stirred in her arms, looking up at the Queen and back at her with a stunned and wondering expression. "He is mine!" Jennet said, daring to lift her eyes again. Her voice was strong and clear, not the harsh croak she had half expected. She had won him—*she* had won him—from this creature of unearthly beauty and power; pulled him back into his own world from the land of Faery. She had stolen him from his fate; she had forced Faery to give up something of value, in return for all it had stolen away . . . . And for all her magic, the Queen was powerless to stop it. Suddenly the beauty of the watchers about her seemed to dim, their fragile faces seemed not quite so young or fair. The Queen herself was no longer too brilliant to look upon; and although her beauty still took Jennet's breath away, it was only beauty, and Jennet no longer felt lessened by it.

The Queen's eyes, like fire seen through cut gems, sought Tam Lin. "Had I known what you would do tonight, Tam Lin," she said, and her voice was like crystal shattering, "I would have ripped out your own fair eyes of gray and given you eyes of wood—that you would never have seen the secrets of my realm, and lived to speak of them to these cattle!"

Tam Lin did not answer, still running his hands over his body as if he could not believe his own reality. Jennet saw terror and yearning both in his eyes as he gazed up at his Queen, and listened to her words.

Then the Queen looked once again at Jennet, studied the fragile traces of Faery in her face that her own eyes had glimpsed in secret moments. The Queen's hand pointed, and Jennet felt herself washed in tingling glare. "Shame be on your ill-fared face, for this betrayal! An ill death may you die—" The Queen flung up her arms, her golden steed leaped up and out, and soared over their huddled figures. In a whirlwind of dry leaves and dust, the troop followed her, sweeping away into the night.

Jennet and Tam Lin sat side by side on the road in the cold moonlight, staring into the empty night. At last Tam Lin stirred and got uncertainly to his feet, wrapping himself in her cloak. Leaning down, he took her hand. "Come, Jennet, you're trembling with cold. I am yours—take me home."

But Jennet sat unmoving. "She cursed me," she said. Her own voice was faint and far away. She looked up at him, pale and uncertain.

Tam Lin let her go, to look away once more into the distance. Somewhere in the night an owl hooted, and another answered. He took her arm again, pulling her to her feet, still looking down the empty road. "It means nothing. You won me from her, didn't you? You got your wish; and you saved my life."

"But . . ." Jennet whispered. Had he known this would happen—? She searched his face.

"All deaths are ill deaths, Jennet," he said wearily, but he did not meet her eyes. His face was as fair as she remembered, and yet a light had gone out of it; faint lines furrowed between his brows. In the cold blue moonlight she could not tell if he looked any more human. "Come. Think of our child—" He folded her into the cloak, with his cold, pale arms around her.

Jennet straightened her shoulders, standing freely on her own beside him. She had won him back from Faery; she had evened the scales. She had freed his soul, and her own. If there was no longer magic in his touch, it was no more than she should have expected. With every choice, something was lost forever . . . . She saw now, with aching certainty, that it must have been as true for her mother as it was for her.

She looked up at Tam Lin again. Gently she caressed her stomach, the child within it. She *had* gained from this choice, as well. When she looked into her mirror, she would never see someone else there again. She had chosen her own path, like Tam Lin . . . like her mother before her. If it did not lead her, or any of them, to the ending they had dreamed of, at least the choosing had been her own. She took Tam Lin's waiting hand, and they began to walk together down the road.

THE
STONE
FEY

by

ROBIN
McKINLEY

HE WAS OUT near twilight one evening, looking for a strayed lamb and muttering under her breath about the stupidity of sheep; truly they were the stupidest creatures ever created. It was a great misfortune that wool was so useful an item, and mutton so nourishing. Her dog, terribly embarrassed that he had not noticed the lamb's absence earlier, slunk along at her heels. "Anyone would think you went in fear of a beating," she said to him, and he flattened his ears humbly. She sighed. Aerlich was an admirable sheepdog, but he took himself very seriously.

It would soon be too dark to see anything, but a succulent young lamb would not survive the night in the wild rocky scree beyond the farm; if a folstza didn't get him, a yerig would. Damn. And she needed all her lambs; there had been several stillborns in her small flock this year, and none of the ewes had thrown twins; she was already short her usual market count.

Aerlich paused, raised his head and pricked his ears. He tried to growl, or thought about growling, or started to growl and then changed his mind; dropped his head again, and looked confused.

Something had appeared from the twilight, from the low scrub trees, from the rocky foothills of the Horfels where they stood; something stood on the faint deer trail they had been following, and faced them, holding a lamb—her lamb—in his arms.

He walked toward them. The lamb seemed quite content where it lay cuddled next to his breast. Aerlich growled again, stopped again, sighed, and sat tightly down by her feet. She could feel how tense he was, for what came to them, cuddling their sleepy lamb, was not human. If he had turned away, tried to run; if the lamb had bleated or struggled, Aerlich would have been on him at once. Aerlich, who was afraid of almost everything, was fearless as a sheepdog. He had once almost gotten them both killed trying to take on a whole pack of yerig by himself, and she, with as little foresight as her dog, had gone to help him. They both still wore the scars, but the yerig hadn't been hungry enough to take the victory they could have had, and she and Aerlich had been permitted to save their sheep.

What walked toward them now walked silently, on bare feet; she stood her ground, but she found her knees were trembling. Aerlich pressed against her nearer knee as the walker drew close to them. He stopped only when he was an arm's-length away, so that he could hold the lamb out to her; and she, bemused, accepted it into her own arms. It gave a little grunt of annoyance at being so disturbed, but settled again straight away, its head on her shoulder, its stupid, gentle eye glazed with drowsy contentment.

He was just her height; she looked into black eyes, the iris as black as the pupil.

"Thank you," she said; her voice sounded so unnatural that Aerlich stirred, and growled again, audibly this time, but the half man before them never glanced at the dog. He looked into her eyes for a long moment, and her heart beat in her throat; and then he smiled, or only seemed to smile as the night shadows moved across his face; and then he turned away, and disappeared again into the fast-lowering twilight.

It was deep dark by the time she got back to the farm. Partly from weariness, partly from the dark, partly from bewilderment at the strange meeting with the creature that had given her back her lamb, she stumbled several times. The successive jerks in their progress eventually woke her prodigal. It noticed perhaps that it had missed its dinner, and grew irritable. Aerlich, trotting at her side, looked up at her anxiously as it began to kick and baa aggrievedly. "If you don't be good, I'll make you walk," she said to it, and tripped over another rough spot in the ground.

The bereaved mother had made herself hysterical over her loss, and having gotten so far into her hysteria it took a while before she could be convinced that she was no longer bereaved. The animals were all restless with her fretting, and by the time the barn was quiet and the doors shut for the night, she and Aerlich were both exhausted. She leaned against the barn door and looked at the sky; it was vaster here, she believed, than anywhere else on earth, and she had never had any desire to discover empirically if this were true or not. The stars were coming out, white and shining, over the crowns of the Horfels; there were the merest wisps of clouds drifting, high and far away, across the midnight blue: fair weather again tomorrow. It was a windless night, and almost silent. Her shepherd's ear—and Aerlich's relaxed body sprawled beside her—told her that none of the small rustlings she heard were dangerous to sheep.

A breath of cooking smell crept to her from the farmhouse; dear Ifgold, she'd told him she might be out late after her lost lamb, though he'd only scowled. It was almost worth the aggravation—at least since she'd found it, or it had been found for her—not to cook dinner an extra night, and Ifgold was never mean about return favors.

She sighed, and Aerlich raised his head from the ground and looked up at her, and stirred his plumy tail when she smiled at him, but it was only a very little stir, because, after all, he had not found the lamb himself. Aerlich's mother had been one of the merriest beings she had ever known; how could such a charming mother have given birth to so solemn a son? But he had inherited her sheep sense, which was the important thing.

The food smells tickled her and her stomach rumbled, but she wasn't ready to go inside yet. She slid down the barn door and sat on the ground next to her dog, who looked at her earnestly a moment, and then, tentatively, put his chin on her knee. His mother would have jumped onto her lap at once, and then scrabbled up to put her forepaws on her mistress' shoulders. On a whim she leaned over and picked Aerlich up as she would a lamb, and set him on her lap. He started to scramble off again in alarm—whether it was his dignity or hers that he felt had been outraged she couldn't begin to guess—and paused with his hindquarters still across her thighs. He bent his head around and looked seriously into her face, and visibly changed his mind. He didn't fit in her lap any more than his mother had, but he scooted around again, slid down her outstretched legs, let his forepaws trail over her hips, and rested his head on her stomach. He half shut his eyes and sighed profoundly.

She looked up at the sky again, her fingers trailing through Aerlich's silky hair. She had lived in this farmhouse all her life. When her mother, Thassie, had married Tim, she had brought him here to the farm, where she and her mother before her had lived all their lives. Tim had contentedly built a short wing off the kitchen for his jewelry-making, and took his pieces to town occasionally when his wife or his eldest daughter went on market-day. But the outside world didn't impinge too much on Tim; she was surprised he'd bestirred himself enough even to marry her bustling mother. And while Thassie was Mother, Tim had always been Tim, even to the littlest of them.

He was good with babies—better than Mother, really—and was happy to nurse the very young ones while Mother tended her vegetables; but as soon as they were old enough to start learning their letters and doing useful chores, he lost interest. Ifgold had said to her once, sadly, that he thought Tim had to remember his name every time he looked at him, his only son.

"He's that way with all of us, you know," she said, offering what comfort she could.

"I know," Ifgold said slowly. "I don't know why it still bothers me . . . . At least you have market-day; he has to recognize you then."

She smiled faintly. "Not true. He looks surprised when I come to his stall and tell him it's time to go home. It takes him a minute to realize I have the right to say it."

If anyone was to see strange things in their Hills, it should be Tim, dreamy Tim, who made such necklaces that one was even bought by a sola to give his lady in the great City of the king. His daughter was only a shepherd.

She knew what it was that she had seen; she remembered her grandmother's tales, for her grandmother was a little less matter-of-fact than her mother. Perhaps there was a little more of Tim in her than she realized, for she remembered those tales far more vividly than a shepherd need, of the wild things that lived in their Hills; there was even supposed to be a wizard who had lived for thousands of years somewhere to the south of them. But she had spent too much time alone with her dog, wandering the low wild foothills, not to know that there were creatures that lived there that she could not call by name; things besides the yerig and the folstza, the small shy orobog, the sweet-singing britti; things that were not birds or beasts, or lizards or fish or spiders.

Things like what had brought her back her lamb. She recognized him from one of her grandmother's stories: he was a stone fey. They were shorter and burlier than the other feys, with broad shoulders and heavy bones; in her childhood she had imagined them as shambling and clumsy, but she knew now it was not so. It was his skin that had told her for sure, for his skin was grey, the grey of rocks, and yet it was obvious—as her grandmother's story had told her it was obvious—that it was not the color of ill-health, and there was a rose-quartz flush across his cheekbones.

The smell of dinner would not let her sit any longer. She patted Aerlich and said, "We must go." He skittered off her lap at once and grovelled, certain that he wasn't supposed to have been there in the first place, and she laughed. "You are impossible," she told him. "Come along; you must be hungry too."

Ifgold looked up from his work at once when he heard the door; Tim, staring dreamily into the fire, didn't look up at all. Thassie didn't raise her eyes from the piecework on her lap, but she got that listening look on her face that all her children knew well. Berry sat frowning over a book at the end of the long kitchen table; she looked up briefly with a smile for her big sister as sweet and vague as Tim's, and then went back to her book. The littlest ones were already in bed.

"I found the lamb," she said.

"Good," said Ifgold.

Thassie smiled. Her tidy fingers seemed to spin the thread through the neat hems and corners; between her quilts and her vegetables the farm needed no extra income. Her daughter's sheep were her own idea. The farm had had sheep in her grandmother's day, but Thassie was an only child, and it had taken her brood to begin to push the farm's productivity back up to what it had been. But Thassie was firm about where her children's profits went: Ifgold and Berry needed more schooling than the small village school could give them, and everything that could be spared from seed and fenceposts and shingles and sheepdip went into the small but plump linen bag in the bottom of the wardrobe in Thassie and Tim's bedroom. Kitchet complained regularly that she had picked enough vegetables and dug enough holes and pulled enough weeds to have earned three ponies and she only wanted one, but no one stood up long to Thassie. Or almost no one. Her eldest daughter smiled a little wryly.

Ifgold would be going to a school in the south soon, and she would miss him, not only for the dinners he cooked out of turn, but because he was the only one of them all she could talk to. Mother was inimically businesslike, dispensing sympathy as neatly as she added up columns of figures; and Berry was as impossible to talk to as Tim was, or nearly; and the others were too young.

She bent to kiss her mother and then Tim. "Lamb?" he said. "I did tell him," Thassie said.

She shrugged. "Lamb. One strayed. I was lucky to find it."

Tim, who barely recognized his daughter from the rest of the people on market-day, heard something in her voice, and looked up at her almost sharply; but Ifgold said innocently, "Luck indeed. But you could use a little." Ifgold knew—unlike Tim—that ewes should have twins sometimes, and that none of hers had this season. Thassie murmured something in agreement, and Ifgold got up from his books—Berry took the opportunity to reach across the table and grab whatever it was he had been reading—and dipped up some of his stew on a plate. She sat down gratefully and let him serve her.

He put a bowl on the floor as well for Aerlich. "Everyone else has eaten." Looking across the table he said in sudden outrage, "You're supposed to be doing your schoolwork!" He glowered, but Berry ignored him, absorbed in the stolen book.

Curious, she reached out and delicately raised the book in Berry's hands till she could read the spine: *Tales of the Feys*. She dropped it as if it burnt her fingers, and Berry, startled, said, "I have done my schoolwork."

Embarrassed, she muttered, "I'm sorry. I didn't mean to disturb you."

From the fireside, Thassie said, "Finish the chapter, Berry, and off to bed with you."

Berry left, grumbling, and Ifgold reclaimed his book. He turned it over to look at the back, and then looked measuringly at his older sister; but she refused to meet his eyes, concentrating on her food. "I can at least do the washing-up," she said.

"I was hoping you'd say that," Ifgold said.

Tim drifted over to dry the dishes for her, but she had to put them away if they were to go anywhere that anyone could find them again. It was not usual for him to do any of the homely chores unless they involved a hammer or saw, and she had not liked the sudden intent look he'd given her when she'd come in.

"The lamb," he said, as she hung the dishrag over the edge of the sink and prepared to blow out the lamp that hung beside it. "It was all right when you found it?"

"Yes," she said. "I—" She wanted to tell him about the stone fey; Tim might even understand. But something stopped her words. She stood staring into the sink a moment, but she did not see the sink or the rag or her white-knuckled hands; she saw a grey-skinned face framed in black hair, and the intense black eyes that had looked into her own. When she looked up, Tim was still watching her with the same sharpness so unlike him. "I think I'm just tired," she said.

She climbed the stairs to her bedroom. She had fought and won the right to have a private bedroom; she was the eldest, and earned the most money—after Thassie—and she had to keep strange hours during lambing season. In exchange her room was the smallest, no more than a closet with a crack of window, but she didn't mind; it had a door on it that closed her in and the rest of the world out. Except Aerlich, who slept on the narrow bit of rug between her bed and the wall.

She hung her clothes on their peg, and leaned her elbows a moment on the windowsill—which was just about two elbows wide—and looked up again at her Hills. Even on cloudy nights she could look out her window and see in her mind's eye what the weather obscured; but tonight it wasn't necessary. Even the last faint shreds of cloud had left, and the sky was ablaze with stars. She wondered where the stone fey was, if he looked at the sky before he slept; if he slept out-of-doors or in some secret, stony cavern; if he slept. Perhaps at night he walked far over the Hills on his bare, silent feet; perhaps he had been walking far this evening, when he found her lamb, and would never come this way again. She shook her head.

When she had trouble sleeping, she counted over in her mind the little pile of coins that was going to buy her own farm some day soon, the farm for herself and Donal; a little pile that when she had first wrested the right to it from her mother was small enough to fit under her thin mattress without discomfort. But it had grown bigger, slowly, and it lived now in another linen bag, smaller than the one in her parents' wardrobe, in a spare boot under her bed. With Donal's little pile they would soon be able to buy what they needed to settle on the bit of land they had chosen—that she had found one day, wandering far afield with her sheep—not too far from here, not so far that the Hills and the sky would look different from their new windows.

Donal had hired himself out this year as a logger, far away in the western mountains, near the mines; he had been gone only three months, and she would not see him again for another nine. She missed him bitterly, for while their parents' farms were far enough apart that they did not see each other daily nor at busy times even weekly, they had grown up together, had been good friends since she was eleven and he was ten and a half, when she'd met him at a market-day, trying to steal one of her first sheep. He hadn't realized it was one of hers— he said—and by the time they had it sorted out (involving several bruises and one black eye—his) they were well on their way to becoming excellent friends. But as friendship had turned to love and thoughts of a life together and a farm of their own, they had discussed their chances, over and over again. She had finally, reluctantly, agreed to his plan to go away; his salary for a year was worth three times what she could earn by her flock—and probably more than that, this year.

She might not have had the strength of will, finally, to push it to the end with her mother, had she not had Donal to help her. Donal, youngest of six as she was eldest, was as determined as she, for perhaps precisely the opposite reasons, to have a life independent of his family—and he had had little choice, for the fourth and fifth children had already been afterthoughts, and there was little left for the sixth but kindness. Donal was the last person to be willing to plunge himself into another overflowing family, another family where he would always feel slightly superfluous . . . . She had wondered more than once if that had not been part of his initial attraction for her: someone to remind her when she wavered of how splendid it would be to be making their own fresh, new, individual mark on a piece of land unaccustomed to human feet and hands, and ploughs and scythes.

The only time she had ever seen her mother upset to the point of complete physical stillness was when she told her that she and Donal wanted their own farm. The eldest daughter had always brought her husband here; for generations it had been that way, back almost to Aerin's day, so her grandmother had said. She didn't know why it meant so much to her that she should leave, that her land should be new land, land that had not been farmed for generations of her own blood; perhaps she hadn't known till she met Donal. But that wasn't true, for she hadn't known Donal when Berry was born, and she was glad even then that there was another daughter, that even if it wouldn't be the eldest daughter, there would be another girl to grow up and take Thassie's place on the farm.

It wouldn't be Berry, though. Berry would be a scholar, or perhaps a teacher; she could hardly weed. Sometimes the little ones were a nuisance, but at least they provided three more girls, and Lonnie already was a passionate farmer.

But tonight she was too tired to think, and there seemed to be a cloud over her mind that was more than just tiredness; and the knowledge of the contents of a spare boot under the bed did not cheer her, nor the consciousness that every night was one day sooner that she would see Donal again give her any pleasure. She went to bed and fell asleep at once.

She saw the stone fey again only a sennight later. Since she had a smaller flock this year, she had taken the opportunity to range a little further than she usually did—which was how she almost lost a lamb—looking for new pasture. Their country was stony, and all the local farmers with livestock were perennially occupied with keeping them fed. Her and Donal's farm would be little different; nowhere near the Hills was there rich land, but the Hills were the Hills. In the south, it was said, the trees were so lush they covered the sky in some places, and they could even grow oranges; but the Hills were her flesh and bone.

Her mother's farm was the furthest out. In Dockono, on market-day, she was the only one who came from the east. There was one other farmer whose land lay in as inhospitable a spot, to the north of her, and several from the south, but most of the farms lay west. It was a joke among those who met on the market-day streets that her farm and Nerra's must be blessed by the mountain wizard, for there was no other reason for there to be farms there at all.

Her and Donal's valley lay even further away from the market at Dockono than her mother's farm, but it would be worth it for her, living in the Hills instead of only in their shadow; and by its individual geography its land was a little more arable than much of what lay near it, which pleased Donal. It had been in a year of drought that she'd found it; she'd had a small flock that year, too, even smaller than this year, and even so she had had to range far, often gone from home for several nights together, to find enough fodder for her growing lambs.

But she had no drought as excuse this year. After she lost the lamb she should perhaps have gone back to her usual ways. But she didn't. She told herself that she would be extra watchful; she knew that Aerlich, still smarting in shame, was being extra watchful; and she told herself further that there was indeed no reason that her mother's farm did thrive—had thrived for several hundred years—and that if she could find new pasturage she should. For Lonnie's sake, perhaps, or Kitchet's. Kitchet liked animals better than vegetables too, and might want to have sheep. She did not think of the stone fey. So she told herself.

But she was not surprised when she saw him. She looked up, one afternoon, and he was sitting on a rock; near her, but not too near. She had no idea if he had been there all along, or if he had only just arrived, stepping so softly that even Aerlich—intent, at present, in facing down one of the oldest ewes, who felt she was beyond having to pay attention to a young whippersnapper of a sheepdog—had not noticed him; or if he had materialized out of air, or out of the rock he sat on.

He turned his head slowly to meet her gaze. He did not look surprised; he did not look anything at all. He merely looked back at her as she looked at him. The angles of his face cast queer, inhuman shadows over his stone-grey features, and his black eyes gave her no clue of what he might be thinking.

She dropped her eyes first; then, remembering herself, glanced over to see if Aerlich needed any help with his ewe. He did not. She did not want to look up at the fey again—they were on a hill, and he sat a little above her—but her eyes were drawn to him in spite of herself. How often did a mortal see a fey, after all, particularly a stone fey, who were supposed to be the shyest of all the feys? Why should she not look?

He was still looking down at her, and she felt an unaccustomed flush rising to her face. Should she say something? Could she just get up and leave? Aerlich would justifiably feel put-upon if, just as he got the herd settled for the day, she decided to move. She found, suddenly, that she was sitting uncomfortably, and had to rearrange herself. But the stone she was on obstinately remained uncomfortable, and at last she got up and found another rock, higher on the hillside. When she glanced at the fey again he was still there and still watching her, but she was now even with him. No closer, but she did not have to look up anymore.

"What is your name?"

The sound of his voice startled her, as if a stone had spoken; yet her grandmother's tales had informed her that feys did speak when they chose to. She blinked at him while her surprise subsided; it was the choosing that startled her, not the speaking, although his voice was not, somehow, what she would have expected. A stone fey should have a deep, harsh voice, a rumbling, stony voice; his voice was none of these things.

"Maddy," she said.

Silence fell. She stared out over her herd. They were grazing across a little plateau, and the Hill fell away below them as it rose at her back. When she looked for the fey again, he was gone.

Two days later she found an "M" in a beautiful mosaic of shimmering greys, nestled at the threshold of her sheep barn. No one ever came to the barn but herself and Aerlich; she cleaned it herself, and even replaced fallen shingles herself. She would far rather shovel sheep dung than ever come near a seed or a plough; her mother's other children could help her there. Hating vegetable duty was how she got started on sheep.

She saw the stones gleaming from the ground even as the sheep pattered over them and disappeared into the twilight inside, milling and protesting as they felt obliged to do each evening. Aerlich got them neatly into their pen and waited for her to close the gate and bestow upon him the words of praise he deserved. He looked around, astonished at her absence. She was standing by the outer door, staring down. He whined, a tiny, questioning whine, and her head snapped up. She came inside, and closed the gate, and told Aerlich he was the finest sheepdog in Damar. He looked up into her face worriedly, however, even as his tail dutifully wagged, for her voice lacked conviction.

She went back outside, Aerlich at her heels, and looked at the shimmering grey stones again. They were both subtle and conspicuous; the gleam of the grey looked as if it were only a trick of the light, as if at just a slightly different time of day they would not show at all. They looked, most particularly, like things of twilight, like the uneasy ghosts one was supposed to be able to see only during that greyest of daylight; as if, when the sun set, they would fall back into being pebbles of no particular heritage and in no particular order. They were set so perfectly into the low stone-flagged ramp at the door of the barn that they looked as if they had been there always, though she knew they had not. They had not been there even so recently as that morning—and yet the barn was in clear sight of the house and most of the fields around it. How—?

Staring at the silver "M" was making her head ache. It lay just where she had sat, Aerlich in her lap, the evening she had lost the lamb, and had it found for her.

There was nothing to do; nothing to say. She went indoors to start dinner.

She saw him again the next day. He seemed to be waiting for her; and yet she had not known, till she arrived at the little half valley on a knee of one of the foothills, that it would look good to her, and she would decide to stay.

Aerlich happily began to dispose of the sheep as suited him, and she flopped onto the ground. It was a good thing she raised her sheep primarily for their fleece; they were doing far too much walking, lately, to make them at all appetizing as mutton. Even the lambs must be getting thin and stringy. She watched while several of them at once sprang straight into the air, as young sheep will do, coming down again in a series of more or less graceful arcs, all now facing in different directions. They then pelted off, whichever way they were headed, apparently for no more reason than the pleasure of doing something dumb so often gives sheep of any age. Even a year ago such behavior still occasionally made Aerlich slightly hysterical, when he wasn't yet entirely accustomed to being the only sheepdog, and was first learning to do without his mother's somewhat overbearing direction. Maddy had had to help him sometimes, setting an example of placid resignation to the whimsies of their charges. Aerlich knew all about this sort of thing now, and was proud that he was in charge alone. The look of weary acquiescence on his face now as he trotted off to head the wanderers back toward the flock again was a precise canine version of Maddy's own expression under similar circumstances.

She started to laugh, and from nowhere, in this wild place, she had the feeling she was being watched. She swallowed her laughter and looked around, and there he was, sitting on a rock near her as he had sat on another rock in another stretch of rough Hill-grass a few days before. Perhaps he spends all his days sitting on rocks in the foothills, she thought lightheadedly; and picked herself up from her sprawl on the ground, and tried to sit with dignity. But she wasn't used to having to do anything with reference to dignity (except Aerlich's) when she was out with her sheep, and she scowled and fidgeted, and eventually got to her feet and went toward her unexpected visitor—except, she thought, I suppose I'm his unexpected visitor. I really have no reason at all to be coming so far . . . .

She paused a few steps from his rock, first startled by her own presumption and then held by the thought that he might run away from her, like a stzik or deer or any wild thing; or turn into a rock, or vanish, or whatever the feys did. She looked into his face, timidly, and his eyes looked back at her, as inscrutable as any deer's. She did not receive the impression that her arrival was unexpected; rather, and for no good reason, except for the patient, quiet grace of his sitting and the slow way he turned his head to follow her with his eyes, that he had been expecting her for quite some time, and that she was late. Her stomach felt funny, and she decided to sit down where she was.

She wasn't prepared for him to get up from his rock and come so near to her that the little breeze of his motion brushed her face. He sat down beside her, and she tried to look at the ground around her feet, at the small rocks, spotted or plain, rough or smooth, at the grasses, short and sharp and yet a hundred different shades of green; but she saw nothing, for while her eyes looked her mind was wholly taken up with the sound of his breathing.

He smelled of green things, of the sorts of green things that grow in still, shady places, of mosses and ferns, with a background sharpness like a stream-washed rock, or herbs trodden underfoot. It was a cool sort of smell, and she wanted to reach out for him, to see if his skin was cool to the touch; and then she wanted merely to touch him, for any reason whatsoever, and she clasped her hands tightly together, and stared miserably at her lap. He turned toward her and breathed something that might have been her name, and she raised her shoulders as if against a blow; and then felt his fingers, their touch only a little cooler than her own, on the nape of her neck, stroke up to her hairline, run along the curve of her jaw, and turn her face toward his.

Going home that night, she had little idea of where she was or where she was going; the sun was still in her eyes, the feeling of his black hair and smooth grey skin under her fingers, the taste of his mouth in hers. She even thought she might jump straight into the air for no reason, and dash off in whatever direction she found herself in when she came down again, only for the pleasure of doing something dumb. When Aerlich had safely brought his mistress and his sheep safely home, she blinked up at the barn for a minute as if she didn't recognize it; and then she had to think for another minute to remember how to lift the bar down and open the doors.

There were more "M"s wound around the stones of the little hard-packed yard in front of the sheep barn over the next few weeks. They twined together like vines, like the tiny stitches of her mother's quilting; they seemed to make a larger pattern she could never quite grasp. And they seemed to say her name aloud to her when she stepped over them, echo her name under the small sheep hoofs, murmur her name after her as she walked away. In the evenings, the sheep safely penned for the night, she wanted to pause at the edge of the ramp, to listen to the whispering she might or might not be imagining; but Aerlich no longer enjoyed lingering anywhere in the barn's vicinity, and he would trot determinedly toward the farmhouse, his white tail-tip gleaming in the gathering twilight. He'd pause about halfway and turn, his white chest shining at her, though she could not see the reproachful look in his eyes; and she would pull herself away with a sigh, and follow him.

She tried to tease him about being over-anxious for his supper, but he only looked at her sidelong, and she realized, for the first time in the four years of his life, that he did have a sense of humor; that he had teased her with his earnestness as she teased him for it—and she missed it now, because he would no longer play. He worried about her as he worried about his sheep, harried her as best he could for her own good—and, she thought, no longer credited her with much intelligence. She started to get angry with him one evening for this, and then realized how idiotic it was, to yell at your sheep-dog for disapproving of your private life; perhaps she didn't entirely know what she was doing.

And yet she had always known exactly what she was doing;

as the eldest of six children it was a central fact of her sanity, if not her survival. She always knew what she was doing, and she made her choices clearheadedly.

She grew vague with her family, more like Tim or Berry than Ifgold or Thassie. She was asked, finally, if she were ill— after several conversations had stopped when she entered the room. She smiled, a smile they seemed not to like, and said that she was not. But Ifgold and her mother each asked her again, separately, drawing her aside, as if she might admit to something if she were alone. But she shook off their hands and their prying questions; she was not sick, and nothing else was any of their business. Even Tim asked her, one evening when she had come in particularly late and had had no reason to tell for it.

This at last made her angry, and she said sharply, "I am not ill. Do I look ill?" Aerlich crept away from her and disappeared behind Tim's chair. Tim was staring at her, a wrinkle between his brows that she couldn't remember ever having seen there before, and his eyes seemed darker than usual as he watched her, and she had the unpleasant feeling that since he looked at any of his children so rarely, perhaps when he did look at them he could see more. She turned abruptly away, and her mother was just at her shoulder, and laid a hand across her forehead. She started to jerk away, and then sighed and stood still.

"No," Thassie said. "You don't look ill, and I don't believe you have any fever. But you don't look like Maddy either."

"She looks haunted," Berry said. "Maybe she has a—"

"Hush," their mother said, fiercely for her. "Hush."

"It's what Grandmother would have said," Berry persisted. "You remember, her story about cousin whatever, third cousin forty times removed or something, Regh her name was? She went too far into the Hills to gather herbs, and—"

"Berry," said Tim, and Berry stopped in shock. She looked at her father with an expression suitable to one who has just heard a piece of furniture speak and give orders.

"I don't care what your grandmother would have said," Thassie said, and the tone of voice was so odd that Maddy was almost drawn back from wherever she'd wandered, these last weeks, to ask her mother if she were telling the truth. But she didn't.

"All I care is that she stop burning dinner," said Igard, one of the little ones. "You used to be able to trust Maddy. But she's as bad as Berry now."

"I don't burn dinner," Berry said irritably. "Hardly ever."

"Only about once a week," Igard said doggedly. "And you only have to cook once a week."

"That's enough," Thassie said.

"Yes, but—"

"Enough."

Silence fell, and Maddy permitted herself to wonder if she had changed so much. There was the way Aerlich watched her, even as her family did, unhappily; and the sheep began to shy away from her hands, which had never happened before. She did most of her own doctoring; she had to. The nearest healer who knew as much about sheep as she did lived on the other side of Dockono and by the time he got to the farm, or she got to him, it was often too late. She had an assortment of nasty little bottles and jars for most common ailments, and she knew how to pin a sheep in almost any position to get at whatever portion of its anatomy she needed to get at (with occasional help from Ifgold); but lately they seemed to flinch away from her in a way that had little to do with ordinary sheeply brainlessness.

That night when she went to bed she sat down on the floor and put her arms around Aerlich. He pulled his head free to lick her face—sadly, she thought, almost as if he were saying good-bye. "Is it truly so terrible?" she said. "It doesn't mean anything—I'm still Maddy. I *am* still Maddy. And it will all be over soon. I know it will be over soon." She shivered as she said that and put her face down on Aerlich's shoulder, and he sat very still, pressed up against her.

She asked her fey what his name was and he told her, Fel. She asked him if he had parents, brothers, and sisters; he said he did, but he preferred solitude and saw them seldom; he did not volunteer any more. She wondered if all stone feys were solitary, or if he was unusual, but she did not ask him. She did not know what she might ask him, and feared to anger him; it was too important, too desperately important, that she be permitted to go on seeing him.

He never smiled when he saw her; her heart always paused, just for the moment when their eyes first met, in the hope that he would; and then, disappointed but obedient, took up its patient work again. She remembered that he never smiled only so long as it took him to come to her and put his arms around her; and then it no longer mattered, and till the afternoon, when she had to take her sheep home, it did not matter, till the next day.

He told her the fey names of different rocks and herbs; stone feys did not care much for trees or large animals, but they had names for each stage in a fern's life, and for the individual flavors of different waters, dependent on what minerals were dissolved in them and what plants might trail their leaves through them. Through him she saw her Hills as she had never seen them, and loved them as she had never loved them; but this new love had an ache in it. He smiled sometimes, briefly, over his rocks and ferns, but his eyes were always calm. He showed her how to walk quietly in the woods, for there were woods higher up on the sides of the Hills, and as the season progressed she found herself drawn higher and higher; and he taught her to move secretly even through the lower lands where there was little but rock and scree.

Or at least he taught her as much as he could; she was aware that she was not a very good pupil, however hard she tried. He did not scold her, any more than he praised her, or than he smiled at her. But she did not quite dare ask him about this either—even to ask him why he taught her. It was perhaps simply that what she offered him was enough—or so she told herself. What her sheep offered her was enough, too, because she knew they were sheep.

She left the sheep-tending to Aerlich, who was perfectly competent to do it; and fortunately they did not run into any more yerigs. But when, occasionally, during the days, she checked to see that Aerlich was still in command, she often caught him looking back at her with a puzzled, lonesome gaze that irritated her; what was a sheepdog for but to take care of sheep? He and Fel ignored each other; politely but implacably.

They never arranged to meet, but when she set out in the morning she seemed to know which way to go; and once they'd climbed well away from the farm she began to look eagerly around each bend in the path and over each boulder for him to appear. Occasionally it was a long time before she saw him, and she would go on, faster and a little faster, and a little faster yet, her breath coming a little too quickly for the climb, and the sheep beginning to protest the hurrying, till he did appear. And occasionally she did not get back home till after dark, which was foolish of her, for it was tricky enough to keep the sheep together and aimed in the right direction in daylight; and she dared not lose even one this year, for the sake of her farm. Her and Donal's farm. Her mind shied away from thoughts of Donal, though she preserved memory of him carefully, like an heirloom quilt in an old wooden chest, dried flowers tucked in its folds; something she wanted kept near her, something she might want to take out and shake free, and use, some time in the future; just not right now.

And Ifgold was no longer there to cook for her when she was late. She had forgotten that he was to leave so soon; or perhaps more time had passed than she realized. Ifgold had tried the hardest to talk to her in the first weeks of her meetings with

Fel, but she had told him that she had nothing to say, and smiled her new, dreamy smile; and then, when he persisted, she grew short with him, and began to avoid him. And then it was too late, for he was leaving.

"Will you write to me?" he said, a little desperately.

"Of course," she said, but they both knew she lied.

Ifgold shook his head. "I don't know what to do," he said, and his voice cracked; but he was still at an age when boys' voices do sometimes crack, and his eldest sister patted him on the shoulder and told him not to worry. His face crumpled like a much younger child's, and he turned away from her. Thassie was taking him to Dockono in the wagon, since he was lugging a box of his precious books with him, where he would meet with one other southbound scholar, that they might travel together. Ifgold turned once, when he was seated in the wagon; Maddy raised her hand in a final farewell, and he, reluctantly, raised his hand in response.

She almost ran up the Hills that day, for waiting to see her brother off had made her late getting started; and a few days later, when she took the early lambs to market, she failed to get as good a price for them as she should have, because she could not concentrate on her bargaining.

One of the nights that she should have made dinner she got back very late to be greeted by a furious Berry, who'd been impressed into duty in her absence—and who had contrived that there should not be enough dinner left for the latecomer. Maddy had to do with bread and apples, which wasn't nearly enough. As she bit slowly into her third apple, it occurred to her suddenly that she missed Ifgold. She had been thinking that she might justly complain to Thassie about Berry's behavior; she always paid back a dinner out of turn, and after a long day following sheep, she needed a hot supper, especially since her noon meal was always cold. It used to be that she took a tinderbox with her occasionally, and something that wanted cooking; Aerlich particularly liked those days. But Fel shied away from fires and hot food, and so she had not done so for a long time.

She took a second bite of the apple. But it probably wasn't worth complaining about; very little seemed to be worth much lately, except counting the hours till she saw Fel again. Funny about missing Ifgold; he was only her brother.

That night she dreamed, terribly, of Donal. She dreamed that he was caught under a falling tree, and he held his hands out to her, and called her, weeping, to help him; but Fel was waiting for her, if not around this bend in the path, then around just this next one . . . . She woke up, but the tears on her face were her own. It was still deep night. She crept to her windowsill, but there was no space to lean her elbows anymore, for she put the pebbles and small stones that she found in Fel's company there, to remind her of him during those long hours they were parted; and she drew back now as if they might burn her.

"We will not go high into the Hills today," she told Aerlich in the morning; and the silver stones under their feet as they left the barn lay silent. When the sheep were rounded up and moving, she set out in a direction that was not the direction she wished to go. They grazed that day across ground she had once often used, and it had grown almost lush—as lush as sheep-nibbled Hill-turf can ever grow—for its rest. Aerlich was as dutiful as ever, but he did look often over his shoulder as if to check that she was still there; and when he felt he had a minute free he would rush over to her, to press his jaw up against her legs, and gaze adoringly into her face—and then dash off again, back to his flock. She couldn't eat her noon meal, and her hands shook, and she found herself irrationally annoyed that Aerlich no longer expected her to have anything to do with herding sheep.

The second day was the same, except that the call to climb into the Hills was stronger; and on the third day she answered it. Aerlich understood at once as she chose the path that led them away from their once-familiar trails, and his head and tail drooped, though he kept the sheep no less snugly together for it.

Fel was sitting on a rock, waiting, as he had waited so many other days. He did not ask her where she had been; he gave her no words of reproach, but looking into his smooth, undisturbed face, she knew he had none to give. Their day together was shadowed, for her, by this knowledge, and before they parted that evening she took his face between her hands and stared long at him, at the strong straight nose, the curl of the black eyelashes. "The gods save me," she said hopelessly. "I love you." Fel did not reply, and she turned away, to follow her sheep.

She did not go into the Hills again. After the first few days she found it difficult to sleep, for she heard that call—whatever it was—even at night, and she trembled, and thrashed under her blanket, and her head ached, and in the morning her eyes were heavy. The call became something that she oriented herself by; it told her where not to go; it reminded her why she felt so awful all the time; it gave her suddenly empty life meaning by its existence. She dreamed no more of Donal, and she managed to be interested when the family received Ifgold's first letter. His journey had been uneventful; he was finding his feet with his peers, a few of whom were from even as vast a sweep of nowhere as himself; the masters were kind but the work was appalling. "Appalling" was his word, but it was obvious that he was delighted with it.

She held the letter in her hands to read it over to herself, after Thassie had read it aloud to everyone, and the memory of Ifgold and their friendship was very strong; he wrote just the way he talked, and she could hear him, and she missed him. She was free of the Hill call, for a moment, as she remembered her brother.

She wrote back. He answered almost at once, a letter just for her, although Igard and Lonnie nagged her into reading it aloud to everyone; and Ifgold must have guessed they would, for he said nothing that she need disguise. At the same time the relief in him was written larger than any of the words on the page, even as he spoke of harmless things, the work he was set, a boy he grew to be friends with. She read the letter several times. Her hands did not shake so much as they had.

She still could not sleep a night through; she still heard the call to come into the Hills, to leave her foolish sheep and her humorless dog and her dull family, and come to the Hills. She thought the call said *forever*. She thought: if he truly wanted me, he would come for me, and she squeezed her eyes shut.

He did not come, and the silver stones by the barn grew grey with use.

It came easier as the weeks passed, and the seasons turned again; and she no longer burnt the food she cooked, and she was very rarely home late, and then only for a very good reason. The rest of the lambs were sold, and as everyone's flocks this year were short, she got a good price for them, and did not lose so much as she had feared; and this time she bargained hard. The sheep lost their skittishness around her, except insofar as sheep are always skittish, and occasionally she took tinder and flint with her, and food to cook, and had a hot meal in the lee of a boulder, and shared it with Aerlich, who began occasionally to let her make decisions about the sheep again. When she thought of Fel she thought only to wonder why what had happened had happened at all; and if the call still came from the Hills, she ignored it, as she learned to ignore a certain place beneath her breastbone, which had once not been empty, and now was.

A full year came round, and Donal came home. He came to her first even before his family. They'd written few letters in the past year; that had been part of their agreement, that neither would feel slighted while each was buried in work, in earning the money for their life together. She had found it only too easy to write rarely, and then in haste, and briefly, about sheep and weather; and she could not have said, beyond the very first ones, what Donal's letters to her had contained. But he had written that he was coming; and, almost against her will, she felt a rising excitement as the last few days of their long separation passed. She woke up in the mornings almost happy, and she recognized the sense of expectancy before she remembered why she felt it; and in the resultant storm of conflicting emotions she finally tried only to put all of it out of her mind. But it wouldn't leave her; and Donal was coming home.

She heard unfamiliar hoofbeats in the yard early one evening, and knew who it must be; and her mind had no part in the decision, for her feet picked her up and flung her out the door. Donal hugged her hard and then lifted her and swung her around.

"You're thinner," he said, just as she breathlessly said, "You're stronger." They were both right. Donal had never been burly, but a year's hard labor had filled him out, neck, chest, shoulders, and thighs; it was as if the old Donal had a new shadow. She looked at him a little fearfully, for he suddenly reminded her of someone else, someone who no longer existed for her; and she grabbed at his newly broad upper arms to steady herself, and stared into his face; he was very little taller than she. He looked back at her, puzzled and then hurt by her expression. "Aren't you happy to see me?"

"Of course I am," she said, and threw her arms around his neck and kissed him, and his arms closed eagerly around her. When he let her go she looked into his face again, and cupped her hands around it; his hair was brown, and his eyes brown, too, warm against the black iris, and his skin was a warm ruddy brown from the sun. She felt her face relax, and more easily she slipped back into his arms, and kissed him again, and his mouth smiled against hers.

When they turned, the rest of the family had come out, and

Thassie had Lonnie's shoulder in a firm grip and gave her a shake as she was inclined to snigger. Kitchet had already gone to pet Donal's horse; they were having a low snuffly conversation off to one side. Maddy's eye met her mother's, and a little hard look went between them; and Maddy snuggled against Donal's side and put her arm around his waist, and Thassie smiled.

Donal refused to be parted from her, and so swept her off with him to visit his parents. Her family sent her with him willingly—a little too willingly, she thought, but she did not pursue it. Everyone treats me like a convalescent, she thought more than once: they welcome me back as if from the gates of death, after an illness they had despaired of. The thought was bitter, and mixed of several bitternesses. And Donal, she saw, watched her anxiously when he thought she did not see; and she wondered if perhaps her mother had said something to him, but decided it was unlikely. Thassie was too grateful that her strayed daughter looked like coming back to the fold to risk the coming back by unnecessary words about the straying. And little does she know the truth of it, her daughter thought grimly.

But Maddy's determination to behave as she should, as if what had happened had not happened, or had not mattered, held her in good stead till she found that Donal's kindness, and obvious pleasure in her company, began truly to bring her back to what she once had been. She did not ask him what he guessed, and tried to pass it off lightly when he, too, treated her as gently as a recent invalid, and teased him that they had only been parted for a year—really, she was still Maddy. He searched her face with his eyes—and at night, when they lay together, with his lips and fingers—hoping to find the truth of her words; she did not know if he thought he had succeeded.

They were gone to his family a fortnight. Maddy had not argued when Donal insisted that she go with him, only arranged that Lonnie and Kitchet should go together with

Aerlich and the sheep; not that Aerlich needed human companions, particularly not young almost useless ones, but even Lonnie should enjoy a break from her usual farm chores, and Kitchet idolized her biggest sister, and was delighted to get to do what Maddy did.

Kitchet was full of the wonders of sheep-grazing when they got back: the views from her favorite hillsides, the cleverness of Aerlich, the personalities of sheep. "Personalities!" Maddy said, laughing. "You give them more credit than I ever have. Well! You will grow up to be our next shepherd. I'm glad. I agree, wandering alone over the Hills is like nothing else. . . ." Her voice trailed off, and the adults grew very still; but Lonnie said in her blunt way, "It's *boring*. Nothing but rocks and scrub and more rocks and scrub, and sheep are stupid and they smell, and Aerlich does everything." Everyone laughed, and the tension was blown away.

And then at last she and Donal went off to look at their farmsite. She had wheedled him into staying an extra day with her family—their chosen valley was less than a day's brisk march from her mother's farm—saying that the weather promised rain, and she didn't want to come trailing into their new home dripping wet and miserable. Donal laughed and agreed to wait. They spent one cloudy day on a little knoll close enough to her mother's farm to look down on the buildings from where they sat watching the sheep. Aerlich seemed exhausted, and let Maddy do more of the work than he had since . . . she stopped the thought abruptly. But it didn't rain, and on the next day dawn arrived with a glad blue sky, and she had no further excuses, though a sense of oppression weighed her spirit more and more.

But she put a bright face on it and after a quick breakfast she and Donal set out. At the last minute she decided to take Aerlich too. The sheep would be content in their small outdoor pen, with plenty of silage; and she awarded Kitchet the task of keeping an eye on them. She and Donal would return the next day.

Aerlich was surprised when she whistled him away from the sheep pen. He looked at her, and he looked at the sheep, nosing through their fodder, rubbing along the fence for splintery spots that might catch at their fleece so they could bolt away in terror, and running blindly into each other so that they could complain about it—and the weight on her spirit lifted long enough to let her laugh at him. "Come along, silly," she said. "It's a holiday."

He stiffened all over and turned his face away because she'd called him silly, and she smiled, and the oppression lifted a little more, because she remembered the days when he had treated her humorlessly, as a burden. She said gently, "Come, Aerlich," and he came.

But he didn't seem to know what to do with himself, and for most of the day kept close to Maddy's heels, bumping into her if she stopped suddenly. But she was almost as dumbly following Donal, who strode out confidently. He called over his shoulder sometimes about this bird, "I haven't seen one of those in a year!" or that fall of rock, "Isn't it ever going to fall down the rest of the way?" or general cheerful nothings she didn't bother to hear. For her own breath came short, and the Hills, her Hills, gave her no joy, neither the rock and turf underfoot nor the bird-speckled sky overhead; nor the rough green smell of the hardy Hill-grass and the low sturdy trees; and she knew at last some measure of her real loss, and the reason her heart beat so hollowly.

She hurried Donal on when he would have stopped for lunch, and he fell in with her haste willingly, misinterpreting it as eagerness to reach the end of their journey. But when they came down over the little rocky shoulder that heralded the gap in the Hill's side that gave into their valley, her feet slowed involuntarily, and Donal went on alone. He was out of sight around the spur when he missed her; but as he turned back to call she came round it herself and stood beside him.

There was grass in their valley, real grass, and a few real trees, for the Hill curved around it on three sides, and the entrance to it was southwest. It was sheltered from the bitter winter wind, and from the irresponsible summer wind that sometimes knocked down half-grown crops and scoured the thin topsoil away from the rock that always lay near beneath the earth of the Hills. A little stream watered it, and spread out to become a pool before it parted again into several rivulets that ran in all directions; it had been a joke in her family that this tiny lake fed the stream that ran near her mother's farm, and that she would be able to send messages, once she and Donal had made their own farm beside it, by wrapping notes around stones and dropping them in the water. Kitchet—very young then—had believed it.

She looked at her valley, at its green spring promise of the fulfillment of her and Donal's dreams, at everything they had worked for the last six years, and she burst into tears. Donal said, "My own darling, whatever is wrong?" But he saw at once that she was beyond speech, and so took her in his arms and rocked her gently, while she held onto him as she might a tree in a storm; and Aerlich sat at their feet and whined, a tiny, anxious, high-pitched whine.

She quieted at last, and they walked hand in hand to the pool where she washed her face—and gasped, for it was brutally cold—and then they sat down together, and he put an arm around her and she rested her tired head on his shoulder and gave a long shuddering sigh. The tears seemed to have washed away her ability to think; what could she say? She was not sure she could explain anything satisfactorily even to herself; so what could she say to Donal, when there was so much she could not say to him, and would not say to herself?

"I can't stay here," she said at last, dully, and there was a silence, and Aerlich put his head on her leg and looked up at her.

"I—I think I have guessed that much," Donal said. "I—perhaps I guessed it some time ago." There was something in his voice she could not identify.

"I'm sorry."

His shoulder lifted briefly under her cheek. "This valley was always more yours than mine. I only want to farm. It's you who has Hillrock for bones."

"We could go somewhere else," she said tentatively; and he caught her up at once, sharply: "*We?*"

Then she knew what she heard in his voice: fear. His *we* hung in the air between them, as cold as the mountain water, and she said, "If—if you wish to come with me," and heard fear in her own voice.

He sighed, and his breath caught in his chest halfway. "I do wish it. Perhaps I wish it as desperately as you wish not to stay here. . . . I'm sorry. I thought you loved the Hills best of all; better than me, better certainly than your sheep, which I've always believed were only an excuse to let you run free up here. I want to farm—somewhere—and I want you, and I don't—I don't want to have to choose between you."

She said, muffled by his shoulder, "My brother has written of the land around his school; he can't altogether stop being a farmer for all he's a scholar now. He says it's good land, rich, and underused." She heard her voice speaking, as if from very far away; it sounded vague and unconvincing. She remembered Ifgold's words in his letter, and wondered if he had written them just for this occasion. She remembered, from even longer ago, the tales that many of the local farmers told about the southlands; how, very far away, farther even than Ifgold's school, there were orange groves. But she had heard the tales with indifference, and remembered them little; for she had Hillrock for bones. "He says they've only begun to learn to irrigate, but . . ."

Donal laughed. "If it weren't for you I would never have thought of staying in the Hills. It's wild land here—not farmland. But I was afraid to say anything. Afraid that you'd decide I was too dull and ordinary a fellow, too tame, for you and your Hills . . . . This valley would have been fine," he went on hastily; "there is some real earth here. But south, to Illya, where your brother is—to grow something besides korf and a few vegetables! Yes, I should like it above all things. I'm sorry. If I'd known—if I'd guessed—I'd have spoken long ago."

She looked up into his face, transformed with happiness, and a new little glow began to bloom in her own heart, and she realized that he would be tender with her always about his mistake; and that since she would for long need the tenderness she would let him go on thinking the mistake was his.

"We can set out as soon as you like," he went on, eagerly. We'll not need to take much with us; it will make better sense to start fresh when we arrive."

"I'll write Ifgold, so that he can look us out a place to stay," she said slowly, and her voice sounded less hollow, and she smiled timidly at Donal. "He lives in a boarding house near the school; perhaps there's even room there, while we look around us."

After a moment she went on, "I'll sell the rest of my damn sheep; Kitchet can start her own flock if she wants to, when she's old enough."

"The sheep are your problem," Donal said firmly. "I refuse to have anything to do with anything that doesn't have roots and isn't green."

Maddy was suddenly conscious of the weight across her leg, and she looked down into a black and white face with hopeful brown eyes. "Aerlich will come with us. If we decide—if I decide—not to have sheep, I'll buy him some geese to herd."